Brothers Unholy

NASTEE

Contents

Disclaimer: v
Possible Trigger Warnings   vii

Prologue   1
Chapter 1   21
Chapter 2   31
Chapter 3   41
Chapter 4   49
Chapter 5   57
Chapter 6   69
Chapter 7   82
Chapter 8   101
Chapter 9   107
Chapter 10   123
Chapter 11   137
Chapter 12   149
Chapter 13   174
Chapter 14   189
Chapter 15   216
Chapter 16   226
Chapter 17   237
Chapter 18   256

It's Time to Get Nastee   271

Listen, I originally advertised this book as a standalone, but that made me feel like I was betraying myself because I wanted to do the popular thing, rather than the Nastee thing. I'm a series reader through-and-through, where the books have 3+ installments of the series. It's a lie, and inauthentic for me to give y'all a standalone series. I don't want to be one of those authors (no shade) that lets the readers dictate who they are. I pray y'all will follow me wherever I go, because I'm an artist, and rather than being sensitive about my shit, I wanna be authentic with my shit.

This book will explore some crazy shit, lol. This is the first part of at the least, a 3-part series. It is going to be a pinch long. This book will hop back and forth in time, because you need to know the backstory, the front story, the whole damn story. In this series, there will be profanity, the n-word will be used, nasty sex will be had. Anyway, I hope you enjoy this special read!

I am not a word-weaver. I'm a storyteller. I do not use big words. My sentences are not complicated. I don't enjoy challenging my vocabulary for the sake of writing a complex novel, and I want everyone to be able to enjoy this muhfucka. I tell it like it i-s. And I hope you receive it the way it was written.

This is not your typical or even usual romance where

the romance is always at the forefront. This is just a good read. I will not have drama in every chapter. Some chapters are for information and to build connection to the characters. Y'all don't fry me because every chapter doesn't have drama, but I promise, there won't be any "filler" chapters.

Sam & his brothers are former slaves. Until my boys get around more educated folks and learn how to communicate with others, they gon' sound like slaves, lol.

This book has mentions, whether heavily or otherwise, of the following:

- Racism
- Domestic Violence/Abuse
- Blood sharing
- Virgins
- Deepthroating
- Fuckin'
- Slavery
- Fantasy/Paranormal Realism (Meaning the setting is based on our world, and mirrors our world, but there will be differences.)

This is your last chance to turn back, lol

PROLOGUE

1759

The shrill clanking of shackles tinkering in the night gave way to the truth of the evening's events. The roaring wind around the three Brown brothers as they ran through the wooded area of what would later be known as Middle Tennessee, was the only cover shielding them from being found. Vicious hounds determinately made chase after them. They'd been thrown in the basement of their master's house just four days before for being defiant. Rather than kill them, Master Witten kept them as prisoners, hell bent on breaking the strong young men. He craved their submission, though he had no clue that the Brown brothers would rather die from starvation and cruel punishment than submit any further to their master.

The eldest brother, Sam, led the escape. He'd taken the worst of the beatings, but he was still the strongest, mentally and physically. He could go days without eating. It would take much more than lack of food, sleep, and healing to stop him from enacting his plan. From the moment they'd been taken from the field and carelessly tossed into the basement, Sam had been thinking of a way to set his brothers free.

They would have been gone days ago had they not argued about him being the one to stay behind. Sam feared nothing and no man, or so he thought, until the moment his brothers were locked in separate cells, and he could no longer control their circumstances or take care of them directly. He'd wanted to stay behind in hopes that if they got away, their master would let them be, because it was truly him that Master Witten wanted, not Taj, not Mani. They unfortunately were a part of Master Witten's cruel game against defeating Sam.

Sam garnered looks from Master Witten's wife, Angellica. His sweaty abs, strong and masculine jaw line, his hefty package that she could see from the inside of her perfectly decorated and delicate home. She'd never looked at William Witten that way, and she never would, as long as Sam was around.

William wanted his wife to love him and only him, but he was no fool. He'd heard that Angellica had affairs with the slaves on her father's plantation. Why would his be any different? Why would she respect him when she didn't respect herself? He would make her respect him, by being as awful of a human being to Sam as one person could be. Sam had no such interest in Angellica. In fact, he'd never given a white woman a direct glance in his life. He loved his black queens, and he'd hoped to have one of his own someday.

Rather than break him, Master Witten put a battery in Sam's back. He had to save his brothers, so he did the one thing he could do—he gave in to Angellica's advances. She'd often come down to the basement to speak with him.

It was always brief, and she always made an attempt to get him to touch her, to just graze her skin. She loved his "chocolatey" hands. His handsome smile. His plump and juicy lips. She wanted them for herself.

Sam would have rather choked on razor blades than to touch a white devil, but for his brothers, who he wasn't willing to let die, he had to commit a sin—his very first, in his eyes. Even if it was for a sincere cause. Angellica made him a deal, one that he could not refuse. He feared she would not hold up her end of the bargain, but with how desperate she was to feel him, to touch him with his permission, he figured she would do anything he wanted in exchange.

It was a Tuesday when Angellica had come to visit. Sam made notice of it because he'd been counting the days since she'd promised she would return, and he hadn't told his brothers what his plan was. An excited Angellica snuck down into the basement just after ten p.m. William slept like the dead, and she knew she could be gone as long as she wanted. She'd just need to beat him waking up, and he'd be asleep until at least five a.m. Angellica moseyed into the basement like she was approaching a fair—excited and ready. She'd just purchased a dainty pair of white gloves that looked like doilies against her fingers. In particularly, she'd purchased her gloves to see the contrast between Sam's skin and the purity of her clothes.

In a nightgown and robe, she happily skipped down into the basement, that was more of a dungeon, carrying a lantern, the keys to get into the cell, and nothing more. When she reached Sam's cell, he sat with his head against the moldy concrete wall. He did not move, though he knew what he had to do.

"Good evening, Sam," Angellica sweetly cooed into the night. Taj and Mani approached the doors of their cells, curious as to why Angellica would be visiting so late. She'd normally come during the workday, when Master Witten was too busy slave-driving to notice his promiscuous wife missing.

"Ms. Angellica," Sam said, his southern drawl caught Angellica's attention. She leaned forward with the lantern to get a better look at him. His glistening chest, poking out from the top of his torn shirt, looked ripe for a licking. She fanned away her roaring lust with a waving hand. Though her heat wasn't coming from the basement. It came from her hormones. In the light, she held up the keys, and Sam's face lit up.

When he'd spoken to Angellica about the deal, he wasn't sure how she would get it done, but he knew she would if she truly wanted him. The keys were proof of how deeply she wanted to lie with him.

Angellica placed the key in the keyhole and turned the cell door. She smiled, and he smiled back in kind.

"Now," Angellica held her finger up, as if she were about to teach Sam something, "I will let you go—"

"Me and both of my brothers," he corrected, and Angellica grinned, all of her teeth on display.

"I'll let you and both of your brothers go, if you give me what I want," she said, reiterating her promise. Her green eyes homed in on Sam's brown orbs, her lust returned, filling the void between them.

"And I'ma give you just what you wantin', but be clear," Sam closed the divide between them. He was so close; Angellica could smell his musky scent. She could almost taste it. "This here between us, mean nuttin' to me," Sam readdressed, flicking his hand between the two of them. Angellica nodded her head. This was all about her and what she wanted anyway. It was of no consequence to her that Sam didn't want this, just that he would do it anyway. Just as long as she got ahold of his big, strong, love-making tool, her fantasy would be fulfilled. It would be the last one she ever lived out anyway.

She placed her hands around the collar of his filthy linen shirt and untied the flimsy draw string that held it together. When it came undone, it revealed the full strength of his chest, that was covered in unhealed whip marks, deep cuts, and bruised skin. Sam stood there before her, as still as a tree in the summer, too hot, too uninterested to move.

Angellica swept her predatory hands over his chest, the keys still in between her fingers. She, like her husband, was so arrogant to believe Sam wouldn't try anything, that he was too stupid to try anything, that it never occurred to her to place the keys out of his reach.

When she leaned in, to reach for his more than sweaty crotch, he quickly leaned forward, took the keys, and spun her around, twisting her arm behind her back. For a moment, she thought this was some form of kinky foreplay. She inhaled and poked out her breasts. It wasn't until he rushed his large left hand around her mouth that she realized she was captured, and this was not going to be the pleasant experience she had mapped out.

"Now you listen here," he whispered in her ear. "I ain't got one quarrel with you, ma'am, except the fact that I think you's a nasty heathen of a woman. I ain't gon' hurt ya. I just wanna get me and my brothers free, and you goin' wit' us," he finished. Angellica squirmed under his touch. She believed the negroes of colonial America to be ignorant, uncalculated, because her people had been able to enslave them. What she didn't know was that negroes had a front row seat to deviance, had their own set of knowledge, and had they not have been captured and taken, would some day rule the world. Though slavery would forever be a mental institution that many black people would go on to cling to.

It was time for Sam to take back his and his brothers' power. Though the Brown brothers remained shackled by their feet, they were unbound at the hands, which gave them more room for movement and allowed them the space they would need to go free.

Sam, slowly and carefully, maneuvered Angellica out of his cell and down the hall to Mani and Taj's cells, which were adjacent to one another.

"Sam, I'd ask what in the hell you was doin', but I got eyes that can see a lot better than you'd think. You gon' get us all killed," Taj whispered, his head completely through the rusty cell bars.

"Then we'll die, but we'll go together," Sam retorted. He could see the desperation in his brother's eyes. The fear emanating from his brother's essence. Taj had always been one to be careful, the one who moved with a little more caution and calculation. But when he was set off, Taj's calculations turned him inside out. They made him do terrible things, but he'd done his best to keep a handle on his emotions throughout this entire ordeal, listening to Sam's command the way he always did. Now would be no different.

With a firm grip, Sam's hand tightened around Angellica's mouth, warning her not to make a sound, and he stuck the key in the door. The click of freedom sounded, and Taj carefully moseyed out of his darkened cell. Other than quick glances down the hall, Sam had not been able to see his brother, and now, under the light of the lantern, Sam's stomach twisted into knots.

Taj had been beaten badly—his face a swollen, purple and red mess. Had it not been for the need to escape, Sam would have gladly killed Master Witten with his bare hands. He had not quite given up hope on that. If they were truly able to get free, he would make sure his brothers were safe, and then return for Master Witten who deserved nothing less than death for the abuse of slaves and the abuse many a slave had to endure because of his whore of a wife.

Taj hobbled out of the cell, a nod proceeded him toward his brother—a sign that he was with him, no matter what. Sam handed the keys to Taj, and he turned to open the door for their youngest brother, Mani. Mani's eyes held a squint. For the first day they were in the basement, Mani screamed his soul to heaven in fear of the dark. Since the death of their parents years ago from a sickness that unfortunately took them both at the same time, Sam had become their father, and not an evening went by where there was not chopped wood and a fire, or a lit candlestick for Mani.

This imprisonment would be the first time. The first night, he'd nearly gone crazy with fear. The only thing Sam could do to keep him calm was sing to him. And though he was physically at a distance, his beautiful voice echoed off the stale walls and into Mani's cell, lullabying him to as sweet of a sleep as he could get under the circumstances.

Mani placed his arm over his eyes, the adjustment between the lantern and the basement stung. With his arm shielding his face, it revealed his split open skin. He'd only wanted to keep the light from shining in his eyes. He'd forgotten about his marred, semi-open flesh.

Even under the light of the lantern, Mani and Taj could see the anger in their brother's face. His tense jawline, the heaviness of his usual clear brown eyes were now raging with a storm. Mani extended his hand and placed it on his brother's shoulder, giving it an endearing squeeze.

"I'm alright, but we won't be fa' long if we don't get up outta hea'. Ms. Angellica," Mani called her name. Her eyes shifted over to his, fear began ringing through her. Would she be killed? How far would William go if he found out that she'd been taken by a negro? It was one thing for her to sneak off with them occasionally to fulfill her twisted sex fantasies, but something completely different to be carried off by one. She wouldn't be able to return without being looked at as either a victim or something dirty.

It might have been her best bet to cooperate, something she was just beginning to realize.

"This here is our ticket to freedom. Master Witten ain't gon' let his sweet little wife get into no danger, so if we get caught, we'll use her to get away," Sam made his plan clear, and his brothers would not fight him. Sam was the smartest out of the three, and he'd never let them down a day in their life. They trusted him with everything, including their freedom.

With approving head nods, Sam began steering Angellica out of the basement and up the staircase. Thankfully, there were two entrances to the basement, and one of them led directly out and into the yard. Master Witten made it that way purposely, so he could move from place to place with haste. There was no time to waste between slave-driving and abuse and torture.

The house negroes would be good and sleep by now, and the men who were meant to protect the big house would be out and about getting drunk—their favorite pastime. Trouble had never befallen the Witten Plantation. Not in the 100 years it had been standing, and as long as everyone played their part tonight, it wouldn't tonight.

Once they made it to the double-shack doors, Taj and Mani pressed their hands upward, slowly and as quietly as possible. With the doors ajar, they slowly crept out of the basement. Their heads peeked left, then right, to make sure there was no one within sight that would catch them. There were guards in the slave quarters all night. It would have been much more difficult for them to escape had they been there.

There wasn't an inch of the plantation the Brown brothers didn't know. Master Witten didn't realize it, but he would be the reason that the boys would step both feet off of that God-forsaken plantation.

Sam and Angellica followed Taj and Mani out of the basement, and with their bare feet on solid ground, the earth underneath them, the wind blowing around them… their ancestors were speaking to them. It was time to run.

And run they did. Off into the woods, away from the slave quarters, they ran and ran. Sam released Angellica once they got into the woods safely. At least ten miles away. He had not anticipated that when he released Angellica and told her to run that she would stay with them.

"Trust me, under the circumstances, William won't want me back, and if he does take me back, I'll be disregarded soon anyway."

Angellica's eyes drew downward, her hands covered her stomach. She was pregnant and had only found out a week ago. She knew it was only a matter of time when her baby came out with a brown hue, that William would do unspeakable things to her and her baby. This was just the thing she needed to get away.

Sam wasn't a cruel man. He didn't want to hurt anyone more than he and his family had been hurt. Though Angellica wasn't a part of his main plan, and she could be a hindrance, he wasn't willing to leave a pregnant woman behind. This far out in the woods, anything could happen. He had noticed how careful she was while running through the woods. He'd assumed she was afraid of what they might do to her, or what could happen in a wooded area, marked by scattered tree branches, old stumps, leaves. The ground was unclear, and so was her path. Now, he understood it was the fear of something happening to her and her unborn child.

Sam looked back to his brothers, who were heaving in deep breaths of air, trying to catch a taste of the wind. So far out in the middle of the woods, there was nothing for them to eat, unless they caught something. And with nothing but shackles to strangle an animal, and dull sticks, it was going to be a long night.

After several silent moments, Sam asked for the keys. Taj had held onto them. For what reason? Even he didn't know, but it would be their saving grace. Taj dropped them into his brother's hand, and Sam analyzed them. He knew he would not be able to release the shackles using the key in the condition it was in, but if he could alter it, it just might work. No longer concerned with Angellica, Sam had the full use of his hands.

He searched for a sharp enough rock, one with jagged edges to use. When he found one to suit his taste, he placed the basement keys against an old rock that rested in the center of the forest. The stone was flat on top, sturdy, and would be the perfect place for Sam to perform his alteration.

Taj and Mani, now with their breaths caught, came to support their brother if he needed it. Sam began clanging away at the keys. He needed to break off the tipped edges of one of the keys in order for it to be small enough to stick into the locking mechanism of the shackles and jimmy rig it loose.

Angellica held the light slightly over the rock so that Sam could see well enough to hopefully make the key give way.

They had not counted on the clanging of the keys, whistling through the wind.

Taj stood to his brother's back, staring off into the distance. The hairs on the back of his neck were standing up. Someone, or many someones, were coming. He could hear them, feel them getting closer.

"I think we need to move on," Taj said over his shoulder. Sweat cascaded across Sam's forehead. He was getting closer to getting the tips of the key off. He was almost there.

"I just need a few more minutes." Sam didn't take his eyes away from the key, or from the rock. If he was persistent, he believed he could will the tips loose.

Growling from behind them took Mani by surprise, but he knew he wasn't going crazy. He knew he heard something coming for them. Mani stood next to Taj, looking west. It was so dark, and the moon, though high in the sky, could hardly be seen through the tops of the shaded trees. Their senses though... their senses would not fail them.

Leaves crunched, and louder growling took them all by surprise. Angellica twisted around, holding the light toward the woods.

"I think they're right, Sam. We should go," Angellica whispered. Fear kept her voice from reaching its full octave.

Sam knew if he spent a moment longer attempting to

get them out of their shackles, they would be caught, and they hadn't come this far to be caught now. It didn't make any sense, though, how did they know that the Brown brothers had escaped?

Sam's thoughts wrought confusion, but for now, saving his brothers was the most important thing. He wouldn't torture himself with the details.

"Let's go," he instructed, taking the keys with him. The four of them took off deeper into the woods. Sweat pooled at their brows, leaves brushed up behind them, crinkling underneath their feet.

Master Witten had woken up in the middle of the night, with a stomachache like no other. His intestines felt like they were on their way to the outside of his body. He woke up to use the privy, and when he discovered Angellica missing, he assumed she might have gone outside to take in the cool night air. She often did that, according to her.

However, after an hour in the privy—she still hadn't returned—William went in search of his wife. Where could she have been?

William struck a match and lit one of the lanterns in the corner of their bed chamber. Stomping through the house, his stomach still full of gas, he searched high and low for Angellica on the balcony, and on the back porch, and when he reached the front porch and found his guards passed out drunk, he knew something had occurred.

He pushed and poked at them. Lazily, they shook awake. Smelling like a distillery, Master Witten held his arm against his nose and asked if they'd seen Angellica.

Neither of them had. Of course, they'd been asleep, how would they have seen her? And he still had no clue where his wife could have been, until the doors from the basement blew open as a chilling wind blew past them.

The first place he should have looked was in the basement, where he'd kept her favorite negro. Like a child running away from a swift ass-kicking, William ran down to the basement and discovered the cell doors open, the basement empty, and his wife's lingering perfume. She had in fact been down there.

Quickly, William put together a search party. He would find his wife, find his property, and set things right. The spectacle it would be if he could not recover them.

With a party of twenty men and seven hounds, he and his men took to the woods, searching for his wife and his slaves. He could tell he was gaining on them. The hounds were restless, going crazy in fact, but he had not laid eyes on any of them. Had it not been for the sound of shackles in the night, he would have never found them, and found them, he did.

When he and his men stumbled upon the Brown brothers, he was surprised to find Angellica unbound. They had run them toward the edge of a giant hole. No one knew where the hole would lead, if it led anywhere at all, but it was too large for any of them to jump over.

"Well, well, well," William taunted them, tossing his hands in his pocket as he and his men closed in on the brothers. Sam wrapped his arm around Angellica, pulling her behind him, which directly offended William. As if to say she was his. No matter what, by law, she was still

William's and belonged to him, as did the Brown brothers. "Why don't you go ahead and release my wife, and you boys come back with me," Master Witten gestured his head toward the plantation, "and we call it a night, huh?" William spoke underneath his overgrown mustache. He would later be known as the man who looked like the Monopoly Man because of his thick hairs.

Though his tone of voice was even, perhaps even friendly, neither Sam nor Angellica would be so easily fooled into believing things would go as smoothly as a bank transaction if he followed their instructions. The men behind William held their hounds at bay... for now. Their leashes were stretched to the max with fury. Sam and his brothers knew better than anyone how Master Witten kept his hounds hungry and allowed them to eat anything, once they found what they were looking for. He wouldn't let himself or his brothers become their next meal.

"I'll do ya one better. I'll come wit' ya', and you let my brothers go. Whatever Ms. Angellica choose to do, be of her own accord," Sam advised, taking a step forward, sure to keep direct eye contact with William. Angellica reached out for him, her hands begging him not to leave her behind, or leave her to make her own choice.

"Sam, you can't do this," Taj called out to him, shuffling ahead of Angellica to reach him. Master Witten became furious. To see his wife, the woman he'd unfortunately been saddled with for money, depending on Sam, a nigger? It made his blood boil.

"You think you can give me demands, boy?" Master

Witten questioned, drool, like a rabid dog, slurred from his lips.

"I think I can bargain wit' ya. You a reasonable man," Sam reasoned, though he meant none of the words. Behind him, he flicked his fingers toward the hole. Though he had no clue what was down there, he knew it would be better than watching them all get slaughtered by the hands of Master Witten. Mani took notice, though fear had him in a chokehold. He was paralyzed, completely unable to move.

Master Witten winced. How could a colored man with no education outside of how to plow a field, garner so much support, loyalty, fealty even? William would end the night having to pay his men double just to keep this quiet, and that infuriated him to no end.

"How 'bout this," Master Witten said, reaching into the leather holster on his hip and pulled out his pistol. Before Sam, or anyone else could say another word, or even react, Master Witten cocked the hammer of his Flintlock pistol and aimed it directly at Sam's head. He pulled the trigger, and when he did, the loud thud of a body dropping to the ground caught the attention of everyone.

The smoke from William's pistol covered the area momentarily, but he knew without a shadow of a doubt that he'd shot and killed Sam. He planned to do the same to his brothers, and his whore of a wife, Angellica.

Yet, when the smoke cleared, the one on the ground was Taj. He'd jumped in front of his brother just in time. He'd seen Master Witten reaching for his pistol, and he couldn't let Mani get killed. He was the youngest. It would tear his and Sam's heart apart to witness his loss. He couldn't let Sam get killed—he was the brains, brawn, and protector. Taj would be the one that could go—that no one would miss or mourn too long. He'd had enough of this world anyway. He could only hope that on the other side of the Jordan river, he'd find peace in Heaven, with life everlasting.

William was stunned—shocked to see Taj was the one who'd taken the bullet and not Sam. This would only make him stronger, make him grow in power, William thought. Angellica shouted. She'd never seen brain matter before, nor too much blood. She'd always purposely gone away when William beat the slaves, or whenever there was violence toward them. She didn't have the stomach to witness it.

But here, right now, she'd felt worse than she ever felt. Guiltier than she ever had. For the first time in her life, Angellica realized the privilege she had over others. No one would have dared shot her in the head in the middle of the woods for being... well, white. For running away from home. She finally realized how she was a part of the problem and not the solution.

She dropped to her knees, pulling Taj closer to her. There was so much blood, even with her hand covering the hole, she could not stop it. Angellica knew he was gone. Tears slid down her cheeks, and she looked up into Sam's eyes. She felt so bad for him and in a sense, guilty. Had she not gone into that basement, Taj would still be alive. Sam would not be in danger. She would not be at the helm of descension. Not yet, anyway.

Sam had never felt completely clueless, or hopeless. He

was always a man with a plan. But in that very moment, he felt helpless.

Mani screamed once it registered in his mind what happened. The scream he released penetrated Sam so deeply, it shook him from the realization that he didn't know what to do. So much so, that he knew there was only one thing he could do. The Flintlock was a one-bullet shooter. It would take time for Master Witten to reload, or even give the order to shoot the rest of them.

They had no idea what was in that hole. The only thing Sam knew was that it would be his brother's final resting place.

Sam looked behind him and back at the hole. William held his gaze on Sam, and a smile appeared. He wouldn't have to waste the gunpowder on Sam, because he knew he was going to do the unthinkable. Jump down into the earth. All he'd have to do was have them fill it in with dirt, and the others would die.

That hole had been in the ground as long as his family had the property. William's father made him promise as a young boy to stay away from it. It was a rumored snake pit, and William's father had been bitten a time or two near the hole. William always avoided it. But now, the pit would be his glory.

From behind him, William heard a shot gun cock. He held his hand up. "Put your weapons down, let the niggers jump. I just wanna watch 'em." He smiled a devious grin. Sam would have loved to rip his teeth out one by one, but his family had to take priority.

Sam tucked his arms underneath Taj's, removing him

from Angellica and pulled him toward the hole. Gently, he pulled his dead brother to the opening of the hole and let his body cascade to the bottom, which they never heard. Mani's tears were overflowing, creating little rivers on his face. When Sam looked back at Mani, it almost broke him. But even in death, he would be strong for his brother.

Sam placed his strong hands around his brother's face. He descended his forehead to his brother's.

"This ain't goodbye, you hear me? It ain't. Me, you, and Taj… that's forever, you understand me?"

Mani nodded his head, though for the first time, he could not say he believed his brother. His heart ached at the unknown of what would happen when they jumped into that pit. He was certain they would jump to their deaths. But, at least he would not be alone. He knew Taj would already be there waiting for them.

"Forever," Mani managed to say, though his voice croaked like a toad, and together, the two of them jumped into the pit, into the deepest, darkest abyss.

Angellica, too afraid for her unborn child, chose not to jump, though her heart nearly leaped out of her chest at the sentiment. William, satisfied with his victory, claimed Angellica, pulling her arm tightly away from the hole.

"I'll deal with you when we get home," William said between clenched teeth. She had no idea what she would be getting herself into. The only thing Angellica knew was that if she had the chance again, she would escape, and this time, if it came to death, she would let it take her.

CHAPTER 1

When Sam opened his eyes, he couldn't see a thing. The silence, the darkness was torture. He was positive that he and Mani had jumped to their deaths, and when they did not, Sam feared what they might have jumped into. He'd heard the whispered rumors about the "snake pit." As he laid there, still coming to the realization that he was alive, he listened, carefully, cautiously. He didn't hear snakes rattling, hissing, or even moving. He literally heard... nothing. Which made him believe he was indeed dead. Perhaps he'd jumped to Hell.

He opened his mouth, to call out for Mani, but nothing came out of his mouth. The sound of his voice was halted. He could not speak, no matter how he pushed his voice forward. No sound came out.

His mouth stretched as wide as it could. He screamed with everything in him, and yet, there was still nothing.

"If I were you, I'd stop trying to speak. You'll strain yourself," a voice reached him. It was cold, but echoed off what he could only assume were the walls of a potential cave. Footsteps followed the voice, but Sam still couldn't see anyone. Sam tried to move, to stand up, but he was still. He wasn't in control of his limp body. He could not move it no matter how he attempted to will it so.

"Yes, about that. You are most certainly paralyzed. You took a risk jumping into my pit, but now you're here," the voice laughed, but it was dark, heavy. It sounded nothing like a light-hearted chuckle. The clacking of footsteps only grew closer.

Sam's eyes shifted around him. His vision had become no clearer than when he'd first opened his eyes. Suddenly, Sam felt something, a presence getting closer to him. There was no warmth in the presence's position, but Sam could sense him nonetheless. As the clacking sound got closer, Sam's heart began to pound in his chest. Had he escaped death twice, to now only be killed in the dark?

"No, I will not kill you, though I'm not sure why someone would want to live paralyzed and alone..."

Sam mouthed the word "alone" and he took it to mean only one thing—Mani was also dead, and he alone had survived. A lone tear slid down his face as the weighted shame of letting his brothers down filled his spirit.

Sam blinked, and across from him, a ball of light flickered on, jumping inside of an iron setting, and illuminating the wall ahead of him. It was like... magic. From what he could see, there was an opening between a tepee-shaped ceiling. In the center, he could vaguely make out the silhouette of a man. The man was large, even taller than Sam's 6'6 height. He was burley, and the closer he got, the stronger the scent of cinder became. He smelled almost like... fire.

With every footstep, more balls of light illuminated the path. The red orbs of light energy settled into their iron settings. Now Sam could see the man before him, if he could even be considered that. His eyes glowed a deep cerulean color, one that Sam had never seen the likes of. He would have jumped, perhaps taken off running if he could, but as the man stated, he was paralyzed.

Moving was out of the question.

The figure stopped just short of Sam, standing directly in front of him. He lowered himself to a squat and swept his cloak behind him. His hood fell from his head, and twelve pointed horns rested atop his head. His face looked mangled, and scarred, but remained unbloody. His flesh was white, perhaps pink, with holes eaten into it. There was no doubt in Sam's mind he'd come face-to-face with a demonic entity. He was positive he'd fallen into Hell somehow.

"I can fix you. I can bring your brothers back, and all of this…" He held his arms up, showcasing the cave, "will go away. I just need one tiny thing in return." The demon held his finger up, revealing a claw as long as a pencil. He had no reason not to believe this man… this creature wasn't human.

Sam stared at the man, wondering what the tiny thing would be that he could want. Sam had nothing left to give, not that he ever had anything to give. Though, he had everything to lose, and he'd lost it.

"Your soul. In return, I will bring your brothers back. Now, that I've given you the proposition, I'll give you the voice to say yes."

He waved his clawed hand in the air, and like a deep breath, Sam was filled with his voice again.

"My soul, for our lives? You would bring back two for

the price of one?" Sam questioned. He might not have been the smartest man in the world, but he was logical, and he understood things better than most people thought.

"Your soul is worth even more than the two lives. Do you have any other requests? I would be glad to grant them for a soul so satisfying," when the demon spoke, Sam noticed his tongue flicking in and out of his mouth. He was some sort of serpent. The snake pit made more and more sense to him now.

Sam was quiet for a moment. In the event this man could truly bring his brothers back, his soul meant nothing to him. It would mean absolutely nothing. If he could see them again, alive and well, he would be happy. But what quality of life would they have? They would always be on the run. There would always be someone after them. They were runaway slaves. Where could they go to start over? They were colored—no one would help them.

"I'd rather give you my soul in exchange for death. I'd rather be dead along with my brothers," Sam honestly told the man. As much as he would love for them to all be alive, there would be more problems than solutions for them if they were.

"Tsk... tsk... tsk... that simply won't do. Allow me to paint a picture for you," the demon began, rising to his full height. He paced the floor, back and forth, pondering on how he would tell Sam the truth. He knew there was a risk in him being honest. He had superiors who would not like that he was giving up the truth, but without it, he doubted Sam would give him what he wanted, what he needed, and he was in deep need of a soul like Sam's.

"In the year 2018, you and your brothers have a destiny to fulfill, and if you do not sell me your soul now, you won't get the chance to do so." Jasper's eyes held a look of longing, as though his heart hurt at the mention.

2018! The year sounded off in Sam's head like a speeding train. He couldn't even fathom that amount of time passing by. How could he and his brothers live that long?

"That's almost 300 years from now. How could it be?" Sam's curiosity would not allow this to go without an explanation, even if it did seem completely impossible.

"Simple. I'm a time-traveling demon. I've searched the earth, the entire world for a soul to sustain me, and this is my last hope. I met you in the year 2018, and I noticed my imprint on you. I know that I survive, and I know that you survive. That could only mean that the two of us have had dealings. Taj and Mani are also there with you, though the three of you are known by different names then."

Time travel.

Demon.

2018.

Taj and Mani.

It was all so surreal, so... unbelievable. How could they live to be that old, even if this demon could bring them back to life?

"I'm sure you're wondering if there's a catch. If there's some sort of consequence. There is," he laughed, and Sam couldn't find the laughter in this situation. What was so funny?

"What consequence? I believe you might be a time

traveler. I ain't said my brothers' names, and yet, you know 'em."

This was turning out to be much easier than the demon thought it would be. Perhaps if he'd been honest during his own lifetime, he would not need to survive on collecting souls.

"The consequence is you will become immortal, destined to walk the earth for all time, unless you find yourself on the other end of pure iron, that is. Iron is the only thing that can pose a threat to you. Especially with the loss of your humanity, you won't feel any pain—"

"Loss of my humanity?"

The deal was too sweet, too good to be true. But of course, what was a soul? It made him human. Losing that would of course take his humanity from him.

"Of course. You lose your soul, you lose your humanity. I can clearly live for the next 300 years on your soul alone. I'm Jasper, by the way, Jasper Rich."

Sam didn't care one bit about this man's name. He didn't care a lick about that. What he did care about was that he was a good person, and he was positive with the loss of his soul, he would become someone else... something else. It would be the undoing of the things his mother and father taught him, what they raised him to be. His thirty years of life would be washed down the river if he did this.

Jasper could see the look on Sam's face. It led him to believe there was no way that the two of them could come to an agreement. It seemed as though Jasper was going to be out of a soul, a soul he desperately needed. He'd have to compromise, but he wasn't willing to give too much away.

"I can see you have reservations. How about this. I'll leave a part of your soul within you. A small piece, but if I do this, you will be vulnerable to more than iron. You will heal, but it will take time if you are hurt."

The pros did not outweigh the cons, but the life of his brothers, a new life… it sounded like they would find a way to survive slavery somehow. The demon was a time traveler, he could at least ask.

"My brothers and I, how will we survive slavery? Will it end?"

Jasper smiled. Sharp, pointy teeth appeared under the light of the cave on the bottom row. "From what I'm told, and from what I've seen, you and you brothers will single-handedly be the reason slavery ends.

"How's that?"

Jasper had not anticipated answering all of these questions, but the urge to tell him the truth was strong. He normally would not give in this much. He'd usually expect a yes or no answer, and then he would move on, but there was something different about Sam, something special about him.

"You'll become… in simpler terms, a vampire. You each will have a special power, a special ability gifted to you through your new vampiric embodiment. You will never age. You will never grow tired. You will survive on the blood of others…"

The more Jasper explained, the more confused Sam felt. Could he give up what made him a person for immortal life? For the lives of his brothers? Could he become a blood-sucking demon? Something he'd only heard about in his parents' horror stories?

Was it destiny? Was it fate? Sam was interested in Jasper's story, how a time-traveling demon could offer vampirism.

Rather than speak, Jasper transmitted his thoughts into Sam's mind.

I was once a vampire myself. I'm part witch, part vampire, part... demon. Until I wronged a witch, who turned me into a soul sucker. I now need souls to survive, and without them, I'll continue to deteriorate.

That made sense why the man looked like death chilled over.

I have my own special ability—telepathy. You will gain your own ability, along with your brothers as well. Super strength, speed... those are a given.

Sam had made up his mind, and whether it was the right choice or the wrong one, one thing was for certain; his brothers would be alive, and they could make the best or the worst of the situation together.

"I'll do it," Sam agreed, and the smile that stretched across Jasper's lips was chilling to the bone.

With a snap of his fingers, Sam began coughing. His lungs contracted, and he believed they were going to come through his rib cage if he wasn't careful. He coughed and coughed and coughed, until a soft blue ball of light exited his mouth. It orbed across the room, floating over to Jasper's awaiting hand. Sam watched what he realized was his soul float over to Jasper, with a tiny hole in the center of it. When it reached Jasper's hand, he put it to his mouth like a piece of candy, and tossed it in, consuming it.

His eyes closed, reveling in the taste, the feel, the warmth of the soul he was consuming. He had never tasted anything sweeter, anything so… satisfying. Jasper was a man of his word. He would not allow his word to be further tainted throughout time.

With another snap, Sam could feel his legs, the endings in his fingers slowly coming back to life. The bones in his body snapped back into place. He hadn't even realized his bones were broken, though it made sense that they would be.

Sam sat straight up, he believed he should have been in pain, but how could he be? He'd lost his soul, the majority of it. His humanity was beginning to fade. His eyes shut tight, almost as if he were trying to preserve his memory. Like lights flickering in his mind, his memories were leaving him. Things he remembered from his childhood, not that he had many happy memories to cling to. Like a picture show, his life began to flash before his very eyes, all the way up until he jumped into the pit.

By the time he opened his eyes, Jasper was on his knees, his wrist out, his vein slit.

"Drink from my wrist, and when you wake up, you will have an immortal life. You will need to pass it on to your brothers of course, but the choice will be yours."

"Wake up from what?" Sam questioned as he placed his lips to Jasper's wrist. As he drank, his question melted to the back of his mind. The blood was tangy, yet, gratifying. It was different than anything he had ever tasted. He shouldn't have felt like this. Drinking the blood of another should have been disgusting. It should have made him nauseous. Yet, it did the exact opposite. It only enticed him more.

When he'd drank enough, Sam's eyes met Jasper's just for a moment, just long enough to see Jasper place his hands around Sam's head, and in an instant, he twisted it, snapping his neck.

Sam's body thudded against the ground once more. Jasper snapped his fingers for the last time, healing Sam's brothers' wounds, and bringing them back to life. They would not wake for some time, but when they did, they'd have the choice of a lifetime to face—would they become vampires like their brother, or would they decide to remain human, and live out their miserable lives in slavery?

For Sam's sake, he hoped they would choose vampirism. Otherwise, his sacrifice would have been in vain.

CHAPTER 2

2017

"Bitch, if you touch me again, I promise, it'll be me and you rumblin' on this fuckin' ground!" Amionette screeched in her living room. She'd had enough of the constant arguing and fighting with her fiancé, Fletcher. They used to be so in love, so ready to move forward in life. Until Amionette caught him cheating, and now when she was ready to leave him, he wanted to act a fool. It made no sense to her.

Her hands were placed firmly on the handle of her suitcase, ready to drag it through the French doors of the home she and Fletcher had made, but he would not let her take her things from the house. He'd threatened that if she tried to drag the suitcase out of the house, he was going to beat her every way but loose. Something that had taken place far too often in the past, but Amionette stayed out of what she perceived was loyalty, out of what she thought to be love.

The blood seeping from her abdomen was a fair testament to what he would do to her. He'd thrusted a knife toward her earlier that day. Had she not been in so much pain at the time, she would have left the house. But, Fletcher had a plan. He would impale her to the point of her being stuck with him. When Fletcher was in the military, he was a surgeon in the field. There wasn't a wound he couldn't stitch.

When he'd seen her on the floor, lying there… her life flashed before his eyes. An opportunity arose inside of him. He thought this was his moment to prove to her that if he could hurt her, he could heal her. Like the hero he believed himself to be, he carried her to their bedroom and laid her down on the bed. She clung to her bloody flesh, wishing she would have left Fletcher a long time ago.

But love and the fear of being alone kept her there. It made her stay. After placing her in bed, Fletcher had left her, just for a moment, to retrieve his needle and thread and an antiseptic so that her wound would not get infected.

"I wish yo' ass would just learn to be still," he muttered, like it was her fault that he stabbed her. Amionette had cut her eyes in his direction. She knew that the only way she would escape from him would be to actually leave. After finding out about his baby, the one she didn't believe he deserved—the one she had tried so many times to have but continued to miscarry, that was the final straw. The two had been arguing for days.

Finally, it dawned on Amionette that she had no reason to argue with a sack of cheating shit. She was ready to go, and even with a stitched-up side, she was leaving. She hadn't imagined she'd have to fight for her life. The times they did fight, and they had fought, she'd never seen herself as a victim of abuse, as a battered woman. She fought back. She held her own. He'd never gone to using weapons. Until the proof of the leaving pudding showed itself, and he found her bags packed.

After eight hours of rest and building her mental strength, she left their luxury bedroom and carefully descended their staircase. Her suitcase was in sight, but before she could ever get to them, Fletcher passed her on the steps and guarded the door.

They'd been arguing and struggling for the last hour over her shit.

I should have slit his throat.

With all the tugging and pulling, Amionette decided to let go. It was too much strain on her tender wound, and she could feel that her stitches had somewhat busted back open. She would leave without her belongings. It wasn't like she didn't have her own money. It wasn't like she couldn't start over. When she released her grip, Fletcher fell to the ground, knocking his back against the hardwood floor of their three-bedroom single-family home. With no damn family.

Amionette gasped, but she wouldn't dare go to check on him. How many times had she been left on the floor bleeding to fend for herself? This was no different.

This was a blessing, she'd realized, and sped to the side of the door and ripped the key fob to her midnight blue Maxima off the key ring and ran out of the house like the Tazmanian devil to her car. She used the fob to unlock the door and pulled on the handle. It didn't open.

With panic rumbling through her spirit, Amionette kept clicking the unlock button, over and over, and it would not unlock. She'd be a fool to go back in the house.

From the other side of the car, she could see Fletcher getting up. Now that he was on both feet, his eyes were twitching between hazel and green, and she knew that meant only one thing. He was about to snap. Though that was a new habit he'd picked up.

Believing he wouldn't chase her, she threw down her key fob and took off running down her street. Fletcher was a real estate developer. They were the only people currently living in the neighborhood, and at a time like this, she wished she had even one neighbor. She could curse herself for leaving her phone on the damn table in the living room, but when it came down to saving her life, Amionette was no stranger. This wasn't the first time she'd had to become a track star to save her life.

Amionette was used to running from things, including men. When she was a little girl, her mother's boyfriend Azul was a little too handsy. He'd never actually done anything to her, but she didn't like his lingering hugs, his cheek kisses that seemed a little too juicy, nor the sounds that came from her mother's bedroom at night.

They scared her. So much so, that when Amionette's mother would close her bedroom door at night, rather than stay in her own room, she ran through the neighborhood. It made her feel free. It made her feel... safe. It was the reason she joined the track team in high school. She'd almost become a professional runner, but her mother's business at the funeral home and running a cemetery had taken precedence. Before her mother died, she promised she would take over the business, and she had. And now, that was her safety net.

Behind her, Amionette could hear a car coming. The lights from the front of the car illuminated her path. Her eyes stung from all the sweat dripping into them, but she was determined more than ever to get away from Fletcher. He'd done some crazy things in the past—she didn't think he was above running her over.

Her cemetery was just a few feet away. If she could just get off the main road and run through the park, she'd be there. Fletcher wouldn't drive over grass. The tires were brand new, and he was especially anal about his things getting dirty. Even if he did drive to the cemetery, he'd have to catch her on foot. Zigzagging, she ran through the park, careful to remain in the shadows of night.

Fletcher flanked a right, turning on the bright lights on the car to get a better look. He knew he hadn't lost her. Fletcher knew exactly where she'd gone—to the cemetery. If she wasn't careful, he was going to make it her final resting place. Fletcher loved Amionette, but she was too well put together. He knew dating an independent woman came at a cost. But he'd never imagined that she would try to leave him. This was the last time she was going to get away from him, and for good.

Fletcher knew that Amionette didn't need him. He'd seen it in her eyes every time she fought back. It was what drove him crazy, but also, what drove him to fight for their love. That's what he called it anyway when he'd put his hands on her. Though she was independent, he knew there was a part of Amionette that was broken, grief-stricken from her mother's passing, and too afraid to be all alone, he could cash in on her pain any time, by simply reminding her of how alone she would be if she left.

He'd cheated on her—yes. But to him, cheating was nothing but him satisfying his carnal need for pussy. Not that Amionette wasn't giving it up to him, but she wasn't giving it up nearly enough, and when he had the need to stick his pipe into something warm and tight, he did it.

This time, though, he'd gotten caught. This time, the bitch had come up pregnant. She marched into Amionette's funeral home and slapped a sonogram photo on her desk. There was nothing else for Amionette to see. She was leaving Fletcher, and he'd have to deal with that. And this was his way of doing so.

Amionette had cleared the street, racing into the cemetery. She knew hiding behind a headstone would do her no good, not if she could still easily be spotted. Her lungs were on fire with how fast she was running, with how far she'd run into the cemetery, but when she stumbled upon one of the tallest headstones in the graveyard, she knew she had a chance. She might survive the night. Fletcher would never find her here.

Amionette slid behind the headstone. The cold granite cooled her back as she used it as a shield. The loose dirt and grass tossed about the grave seemed strange. There were several craters of loose-ground. Thank God the dead couldn't crawl out of the earth, because someone had almost desecrated this grave. Something Amionette would have to worry about later if she survived. Her blood was leaking onto the headstone, into the ground. At least if she called the police, there would be plenty of forensic evidence, but she couldn't do that since she'd left her phone at the house.

Amionette was too afraid to peek around the headstone to see if his car had made it. She knew and understood how shit like that worked out from horror movies. The one thing she thought was important was for her to place her hair into a ponytail. Her thick, wet and wavy look would get her caught if her hair could be seen from a shadow.

She smoothed her hair back, placing it into a low ponytail. She'd finally caught her breath, but she wasn't ready to run again. She'd need another minute or two, and to assess where Fletcher was. It wasn't long before she heard him, heard his voice calling out to her.

"Netty, come on out. We can settle this together," Fletcher called out to her, using her nickname as though they were still going to be friendly with one another. She knew better than to answer him—though in the past, hearing her nickname always made her respond, whether negatively or positively.

Amionette looked around for a weapon, of any kind. Fletcher was bigger than her, stronger than her, and she knew he would mess her up if he got a hold of her. She found a rock and some dirt. If that was all she had, she'd have to use it, and it would have to do tonight.

"Baby, you're nothing without me. You might as well come home, let's make up. I'll leave the bitch. I ain't seen her since I fucked her anyway. You found out she was pregnant before I did. You're the only woman I want," he promised, and in his heart, he genuinely meant it. But when Amionette said she was leaving this time, in her heart, she also genuinely meant it.

She rolled her eyes at his admittance, as if hearing that he'd basically ghosted this woman was supposed to make her feel better. It didn't. His footsteps grew closer. She could hear him, feel the presence of his evil gaining on her. She wanted to run. She wanted to take off, but she was afraid if she did, he would catch her. Amionette had a plan —as he neared her, she would circle around to the front of the headstone, and then take off running. She'd run away, and hopefully be able to get far enough away to get some help. She wouldn't be able to stop moving. Not if she wanted to live.

Her nose began running. The cool night air had penetrated her sinuses, but if she even sniffled, he would hear her.

"So, you wanna do this the hard way. I said that if you wouldn't come back this time, I'd just fuckin' kill you," he threatened, and Amionette's skin goosebumped with fear. There was a harsh truth coming from Fletcher, and she knew he wouldn't hesitate to actually try to kill her. He hovered over the headstone, the one she was hiding behind. Her heart thumped in her chest, and her abdomen almost gave way to peeing on herself.

He took a step forward, and she carefully scooted around to the front. He'd thought he'd found her. He thought he had her. To his surprise, she was not there. Fletcher held his Ruger up. He was going to take her by surprise and put a hot piece of lead into her skull. She could be buried in her own cemetery.

"Please God, please help me," Amionette whispered, as she steadied herself. She was preparing to take off in a sprint back across the cemetery, and this time, to the center of town, where she would happily find the police and let them arrest this crazy muthafucka.

When he was far enough away, Amionette jumped to her feet and took off running. She had not taken into account that he had a gun, nor that in his rage, he was as fast as fucking Michael Myers chasing Jamie Lee Curtis. She ran in a jagged pattern, hoping that if he shot, his aim wouldn't be true, and she was right, for the first two shots.

It wasn't until the third shot, that when it rang out, it pierced her directly in the back, and brought her tumbling to the ground. To her surprise, she tumbled down a hill. So far, that she rolled all the way to the bottom, and into the construction zone, where there was nothing more than gravel and dirt. Only those who were certified were allowed to be in this area because of how dangerous it was.

There was no way Amionette would be able to crawl out. There was no doubt with how far of a tumble she took that she would die. Her workers weren't scheduled to come back until tomorrow.

Fletcher caught up to the open construction zone and looked inside. Amionette's blood turned the dirt to clay, and his heart broke with sadness. He fell to his knees, his eyes watering.

"Why'd you make me do that, Netty? Why?" Fletcher pounded his fists against his head, over and over again. He wanted to die alongside her. He didn't want to raise a bastard child, and he didn't even like the woman who was pregnant with his child. He loved Amionette, and if he couldn't have her in life, they would be together in death.

Fletcher reached the gun up to his head, his hand quivered with fear. It was now or never. Once they found Amionette's body, he would have nothing to live for. His life, as he knew it, would be over.

His finger itched to give him relief. He slammed his eyes shut, and with a twitch, pulled the trigger....

CHAPTER 3

1759

Taj was the first to awaken from his deep slumber. One minute, he was jumping in front of his brother to save his life, and the next... well, the next wasn't all that clear. He sat up straight, uncurling his body. The stench of blood immediately caught his attention. His gaze was drawn to his clothes, where spatters of crimson marked his shirt. Confusion filled his mind.

He placed his strong hands to his forehead, as if encasing himself inside of them would give him some sort of reminder. As if the day's events would replay in his mind like a short film, though, in 1759, he wouldn't have even known to use that reference.

He blinked back visions of what he remembered. The impact from the gun knocking him clean off his feet. He should have been dead—he thought he was. Yet, he'd never felt more alive. Taj got to his feet and looked around; Sam laid flat on his back. Taj instantly began to panic. He'd been shot for nothing if his brother still managed to somehow die. Sam was too smart for that though. He would have figured a way out.

Taj scrambled to get to his brother. His legs had never felt so heavy. His eyes began to crease with frustration, pain, and lack of understanding. Sam was the best man that Taj knew, and he would have said that even if he weren't his brother.

Sam always cared for him and Mani, and others also. He never put his own needs above another's. Sam always found ways to help other people, and in doing so, he became someone people could trust, someone people could believe in. Slave and white man alike. Contrary to what Master Witten believed, there were many humans living in the free world who liked Sam, who took well to him. He was kind, a hard-worker, and children loved him. Even white children.

Taj remembered a time that Sam saved Angellica's niece from drowning in one of the salt springs nearby. Sam couldn't swim himself, and there was a deep drop off at the end of the spring. Sam knew this because he'd been tasked with catching fish, along with several other slaves, farther down, so that they wouldn't be caught by the Indians, nor by Master Witten. Luckily for Samantha, Angellica's niece, Sam happened to be at the spring that day. Regardless of his circumstances, Sam understood that children were children.

Hate is taught—learned. It is not something children are born with. He did not hesitate to reach in to save the toddler, who would have certainly been carried to her death had Sam not stepped in.

He jumped into the spring, doing his best to stay afloat. He'd reached out for Samantha and missed her the first time as she was carried down the bubbling spring. Sam clung to a broken tree stump and allowed it to carry him to

Samantha. Her tiny head bobbed up and down in the water. She struggled to catch her breath, and the last time she went under the water, she was lucky that Sam was so long, so tall. He reached lower into the water, whipping his arm through the tunnel of liquid and reached for her. Samantha's eyes were closed, and her breath was beginning to fail her. But as anyone would, when their lungs were on their way to blowing out, she began swiping her arms, fighting to get back above the surface.

Her hand clapped against Sam's, and it took her hand slapping against him to grab her in enough time to save her. Sam pulled the pruned little girl from the water and tossed her atop the tree trunk. They floated their way to the edge, and when Sam was sure they were safe and wouldn't go tumbling down the rest of the spring, he helped Samantha climb up, reach for a hanging tree branch, and swing to dry land.

Certain that she was safe, Sam released the tree trunk and held onto one of the roots nearby. He pulled himself back to the grassy area, and just as he was getting out, another one of the men in his slave camp ran down the grassy area of the spring and found the two of them. He made sure Samantha and Sam both got back. Samantha praised the two men who saved her life, though Sam would never be properly thanked for it, and he would never ask for it either.

He was a true leader. A genuine person. Taj admired that most about his brother. He wanted to be just like him. Though, he knew he did not have the same heart as Sam. He was not gifted with true sincerity and a genuine heart.

He was constantly learning, seeking out his place beside his brother every day. He often felt Sam shined over him—that Sam was the sun, and he was the moon. Both bright in their own way, but no one ever brags on the moon. Taj wasn't jealous—he simply felt… inadequate.

And if he were going to be the eldest to survive this misfortune, he'd need to figure out how to lead. He would have to find his own way in life, so that he could protect Mani. Taj hovered his ear over his brother's face, desperate to hear breath release from Sam's nose. The air around them was completely still. Things weren't adding up.

Had he and Mani jumped into the snake pit?

How did he get down here also?

From the corner, he heard movement. He knew it wasn't Sam—he was completely unconscious. Dead, even. Mani, though, was on his feet, coming toward his brothers, rubbing the back of his head. Mani's eyes squinted as he approached his brothers. He realized his feet felt much lighter than before. The heavy weights of the shackles they'd worn were no more.

He looked down, and his ankles were battered and bruised. Dry blood and fresh cuts surrounded his ankles from the shackles he'd been carrying. When he looked around, Mani realized his shackles weren't just loosed from him, but he didn't see them anywhere in sight. They had just… vanished.

Taj's eyesight adjusted, and when he caught sight of Mani, his heart completely melted. Mani was usually the one who cried, being the sensitive one, but Taj couldn't help the mist that formed in the bottom of his lids. Taj ran over to his brother, one of his legs lagged behind him slightly from the shackles he'd previously worn. He, too, wondered when they were removed.

Pulling his brother in for a tight embrace, Taj held onto Mani as tightly as he could, giving him a loving squeeze. Taj's sizeable hand cradled the back of Mani's head. The two gingerly swayed from side to side. Tears cascaded down both of their faces.

"I-I thought you was dead," Mani stuttered, clapping his brother on the back.

"I thought you might be, too. I guess that raggedy shag on the top of your head kept you safe," Taj joked. Mani's hair was 4C, and usually all over his head. Today was no different, but his hair was not what had saved him. It was Sam, as always, who came to the rescue.

The brothers separated and turned around. Their eyes landed on Sam at the same time, and Mani's stomach began to twist with pain. Sam, the brother he knew as the mighty oak had fallen, but they survived? It seemed impossible. Unlikely. There had to be something else in the works.

Mani slid to the ground and reached for his brother's hand. It wasn't cold, though he could not see the rise and fall of his chest.

"He still warm." Mani held Sam's hand up, showing it to Taj, who was just as dumbfounded as he. Unfortunately, as slaves, they'd seen many dead bodies and felt them, too, so they knew the clearest indication of such. Though, Taj hadn't thought of it. He was too distraught to think clearly when he saw his brother in a weakened state. Even Mani seemed to be smarter than he was.

Taj lowered himself to the ground, to the other side of Sam and took his other hand in his own. He was sure that he felt him twitch, that his brother was indeed responding to his touch. But, why now? Leaning in, Taj whispered into his brother's ear, a message he felt he had to give him in order to wake him.

"I'ma be the first one to say it… We need ya', now. I ain't as smart as ya', as clever and cunnin'. I need ya'. I can't do this without ya'. Now get on up, show me you wanna be here," Taj taunted his brother. He knew that his brother's biggest fear was leaving them. He knew that Sam would spend the rest of his life, no matter how much time that was, trying to take care of them. To protect them.

He was a natural nurturer and provider. That was his M.O.

Taj released Sam's hand and tapped Sam's chest twice, tapping to let him know it was time.

"Ya' been down there long enough," Taj raised his voice. He hadn't meant to, but when Sam didn't move, his thoughts raced with anguish. He was not prepared to live in a world without his brother. That's why he jumped in front of the bullet.

"Taj, I think he gone," Mani said with reluctance. He let go of Sam and stood up, his heart breaking more and more each second.

"Ain't no gone. Sam, get ya' ass up now! Get the fuck up!" Taj began banging on his brother's chest, releasing his frustration onto him. The weight of slavery, of running away, of being shot and somehow not showing a trace of it, the weight of losing the only father he would ever know, now that his parents were gone. It was as if his soul were breaking.

Mani reached for the balled hands of his brother. The sight of him banging on Sam was horrific, and heart-wrenching. Taj tapped him on the chest once more, and Sam flew up like a passenger seat. He inhaled the deepest of breaths. His eyes were still closed, but the skin of his body felt sensitive as ever. The slight wind that blew past him tickled. No, it almost stung.

When his eyes shot open, he saw Mani standing before him with tears that resembled a rolling river rushing down his cheeks, and Taj, his right hand, with a face so red, he looked like an entire apple tree.

"Brothers." His tone was low, new in fact. His voice belonged to him, but was thick with something new, something... guttural.

"I thought—"

"We thought—"

Mani and Taj started at the same time, but speaking would have been pointless. They were both just happy to see their brother alive and well. And, as Sam gathered his faculties, got to his feet, and reached around the necks of his brothers, the thrumming sound of their blood flowing through them drove him mad. Almost as much as the fact that he was going to have to come clean with them.

How was he supposed to tell them he was now an immortal creature and offer the same to them? When Sam stood between the realms of life and death, Jasper visited him once more to tell him how to complete the transformation and gave him a few tips on how to survive and what he must do. He would have to drink blood. Human blood. The thought frightened him because that meant one thing—unless he could spring himself from the "snake pit" his first meal would have to come from one of his brothers.

CHAPTER 4

2017

The end felt like it was near for Amionette. She couldn't feel her legs, and the rich stench of iron permeated her nose. She was lying on her side, the one that hadn't been stabbed. She didn't luckily stumble into the construction hole that way; that was how she landed when the bullet pierced her back and she went tumbling down the rocky construction site. If this was how it ended, she would have no other choice but to go, underneath a beautiful sky, nearly turned light. Her breaths were shallow, but her thoughts were pensive. As badly as she wanted to let go, to let death take her, she couldn't, because her mind wouldn't allow her to.

Amionette had always been a fighter, even when she didn't want to be. Her mother had said she came from a long line of fighters, but Amionette never felt strong enough to purposely fight. No, she was a runner. When the going got tough, and the going never seemed to let up, she was always on the move. The most time she'd spent in one place was the last four years when she took over the family business. Before that, Amionette was always in one place or another, never staying in one spot too long. She never felt grounded enough to a place to stay.

What was home without her mother? Even with their strained past, her mom had done what she could. Her mother had done her best to take care of her, to love on her. Unfortunately, because Amionette's family came from a long line of fighters, they had a lot to fight for and over. Amionette's mother had gone through the ringer as the child of a single mother. And her mother in the past, though her parents were married and together, had a challenging life, and her mother before. Amionette hoped that by constantly moving, she could break the cycle. What she didn't know was that she was creating a new cycle for herself, and if she ever had children, she would be setting a new precedent—that it was better to run than face your problems, the ones that you can't see, head on.

Amionette blinked back tears. She was in so much pain, and absolutely no pain at all. She wondered if that had anything to do with her wearing a compression jumpsuit that day. There was something in the back of her mind that told her that was partially keeping her body from completely falling to pieces.

Birds chirping alerted Amionette to the presence of the morning on the horizon. She rotated slightly, hoping she'd see the sun come up one last time. She wondered what happened to Fletcher, if he'd run off after shooting her. She'd be dead soon enough anyway. Her eyes began fluttering, rolling to the back of her head.

Amionette took one final breath, but her deep inhale was interrupted. She imagined it must have been the angel of death coming her way. Though he was beautiful, what features she could make out, she had not expected to see him, or anyone for that matter. He was moving so slowly toward her, it was as if he was floating to her. She could hardly see him moving, but she knew he was getting closer because of the sharpness of his image.

Amionette had spent her life avoiding the very real realization that God existed. Because if God didn't exist, neither could the devil, and if neither existed, she didn't have to worry about Heaven or Hell. If there was no Heaven or Hell, she could live life on her own accord. Not that she was running around murdering people, but she had no obligation to answer to anyone but herself.

After all the things she'd been through, she'd convinced herself that God couldn't possibly exist. How could he let an innocent go unprotected? Come to harm? No, she refused to believe in a God like that. But in that moment, her mind rationalized that it was plausible if there was an angel of death, there might have also been a God. There might have been a devil.

Panic spread through Amionette's body like a wildfire in California. Her face stained with even more tears than before. Her heart quaked with fear. The fear of what death would be like for her. The closer the being got to her, the more afraid she became.

"I don't wanna go. I-I-I'm not ready," she rustled, her voice growing smaller by the second. Other than her new fear of death, there was a secret she was carrying. A secret that had just become clear to her. A truth that she had no claim to staking, until now. If she died, she'd never be able to tell someone. To tell someone the truth…

The dark figure pulled his pants legs up, squatting

down to her. He'd never seen such a beautiful creature, and after almost 300 years of life, he figured there was nothing left for him to see. Though, whoever dug him up from his grave must have had something else in mind. He had no idea how long he'd been buried. How much time had passed since he went underground.

The only thing he knew was that he was suddenly full, awake, and someone had dug the earth up that kept him bound. He followed the aromatic whiff of the meal he'd consumed, and it led him to what looked like an open hole in the earth. Something he was more than familiar with.

"This won't do," the angel's thick voice spilled out, filling Amionette with confusion. She loved the way his voice comforted her. Yet, his very presence frightened her.

Now that he was close to her, she could see that he was covered in something that looked like dirt. His pristine dark navy and white pinstriped suit was still sharp, yet covered in muck. That thought alone confused her. How could he have gotten so dirty? Surely the angel of death had better living accommodations that didn't concern the cemetery. Her cemetery. She knew that if someone didn't find her now, her workers would find her later. What a fright that would be.

But if this man was the grim reaper, surely he'd only come for her soul. He wouldn't have come for her body.

The angel wiped the tears from Amionette's face. A decision had to be made. Yet, as her blood continued to spill into the soil, he knew there was no choice in the matter of saving her, though he promised himself long ago that when it came to humans, he would do his best to stay out of their affairs. Every time he'd intervened, it came at a cost to him, to his brothers. That was how he'd ended up buried, waiting for his body to heal on its own, because even if he'd been given blood, this was a wound that only time could heal.

But the woman who saved him, rather accidentally, deserved a chance, did she not? He needed to pay her back for what she'd done, for what she'd given him. A second, or third chance at life.

Syncere rolled up the left sleeve of his double-breasted sack suit, revealing a long cream shirt underneath. He attentively removed his hand-made gold cufflinks, stamped with a "B" in the center of each one, and placed them in his pocket and unbuttoned the two buttons on the end of his shirt, so he wouldn't make a mess. Time was of no consequence to Syncere. His very presence slowed time.

He bit down on his wrist—the taste of his own blood awoke something in him. It was triggering, but he could fight the urge. He had to fight the urge to get more. With drops of blood trickling down his wrist he dangled his arm above her lips. Blood petals fell between the crease of her ample lips. Fluttering eyes became wide-open amber orbs. Amionette's shallow breathing quickened and came in, in deep waves.

With each drop of blood, her life force was being restored. With each moment of restoration, several things became abundantly clear; she was indeed alive, her pain was going away, and she was drinking blood.

Blood.

Her wounds were healing, rather quickly. The stitches

in her side, the few that were left, completely fell out. The bullet in her back made its way out, and she thought she could literally hear her cells weaving themselves back together, to tighten her skin.

When Amionette was no longer in immense pain, and her wit was reestablished, she slowly pushed herself upright, resting her back against one of the large dirt mounds.

She eyed the angel, realizing he was indeed no angel. She'd never heard of such healing in the way he did. She'd only known of one creature who could do such a thing.

"A vampire," she uttered.

Syncere smiled at her, his fangs had yet to retract. He suspected it would be quite some time before they did, in the presence of such a beautiful and tasty woman. It would be hard for him to make them go away.

"A human," he calmly responded. Syncere had half expected the woman to run, to jump in fear. She'd done nothing of the sort. In his time, humans shied away from the things that went bump in the night, although most of the creatures who did, played a hand in saving the world. They didn't care, though.

Much like being black in his time, being a vampire was just as bad. Yet, this woman... this deliciously tasting woman, had not cowered away from him. That was the most intriguing thing he'd ever experienced, and having lived nearly three centuries, that disturbed him.

The sun was peaking over the horizon. It had been a century since Syncere had seen the daylight. He'd wanted to embrace it, to take it in, until his senses began tingling.

There were other humans nearby. The sweat of one in particular disturbed him. The running of another, he picked up on her feet thudding against the ground. The sound of a crying baby alarmed him.

Amionette placed her hand on top of his. It temporarily grounded him. She'd seen the look in his eyes. As if he'd gone somewhere else in his mind.

"Are you okay?" she felt compelled to ask, though she didn't understand why. Why wasn't she afraid? Why wasn't screaming her head off, running for her life? This… vampire, her savior, did not make her feel fear. She could not fear him if she wanted to. Besides, after dealing with Fletcher's crazy ass, she knew nothing else on God's green Earth could scare her the way he had.

"I'm fine, and you should be, too."

Syncere yanked away from Amionette, almost as if her touch was repelling. Her eyes tensed with anger. Had she misread him as friendly?

Syncere stood up and yanked her up with him.

"Shit," she yelped, surprised that he'd touched her, but even more so that he'd tossed her over his shoulder with one arm. She knew vampires were strong, but she had not expected this.

Syncere placed his firm hand on her backside, gripping her ass cheeks to make sure she was steady.

"Watch yourself," she murmured, but she hated to admit that she liked it. Syncere held onto her steadily and climbed out of the construction zone with Amionette still over his shoulder. Déjà vu played in his mind. He'd done something similar before.

Once past the construction area, their movements seemed to be working at regular speed again. He placed Amionette onto her feet. She'd planned to thank him, to speak with him. But the vampire who saved her life would not be sticking around.

Syncere didn't say a word to her once they were back on solid ground. He frantically looked around. Amionette could not be sure of what, but she knew there was a problem, though she could not gauge it.

"Take care of yourself," were the last words Syncere mumbled before stroking the side of her cheek. His touch sent a tingling sensation through her. She blinked, only once, savoring his touch, and when she opened her eyes again, he was gone.

In one night, Amionette's life had completely changed. Fletcher had tried to kill her, and she hoped he thought she was dead. That meant she truly could start over. She could have a new life free of him. Vampires were real, and if they were, everything else she'd spent her life avoiding and ignoring probably was, too. And she, without a doubt, had to see him again.

But first, she had to figure out her own situation, and then she would set out, looking for him.

CHAPTER 5

1759

Sam would have held onto his brothers for the rest of his life if he could have. He would have held them in his arms, to keep them safe from all around them forever. But now, he was the thing he needed to safeguard them from. He needed to keep them safe from himself. In between the veil of death and life, he had a decision to make; whether to turn his brothers or leave them human. But if he didn't turn them, this decision he made would be for nothing.

Releasing his brothers, Taj and Mani waited for Sam's orders. They depended on him for everything, especially when it came to direction. Taj, at times, could find his own way, but Mani was typically and utterly confused on such matters. He was the poster child for being the younger sibling where it counted. He was the most rebellious, the wanderer, the most sensitive. He needed Sam and Taj more than anything, and they knew that. It was that fact alone that made Sam's decision for him. He would have to tell his brothers the truth and hope that they shared his sentiments—that being vampires was the only way they could be together, and that they would have the power to end slavery.

Jasper had told him that, and so far, he had no reason not to trust him. He'd seen the things Jasper could do, briefly. There was nothing telling him he couldn't believe Jasper, though he'd have to test a few theories first.

The only way for him to completely transition was to drink human blood, and with the ringing in his ears, and the way his stomach was touching his back, Sam knew he didn't have much time before he faded away into nothing if he didn't. He was lucky to have been given a heads-up, but he didn't know if he could break his brothers' necks and watch them die. Was there not a more humane way to end their lives so that they could start anew? They'd spent most of their lives in torture—perhaps a quick way of ending it wasn't as bad as it seemed.

"What happened?" Taj questioned. It had been lingering between the three from the moment each of them opened their eyes. The details were fuzzy. Sam was the only one who had the answers—he had retained what happened to him after having his neck snapped and meeting with Jasper, again. It was up to him to convey the message.

"It ain't as simple as a 1, 2, 3 kind of story there, Taj," Sam said, in preparation of gathering his thoughts. There was no way of explaining it that would come across as gentle, tender. It would be better for him to tell it like it was, and any ramifications that came after that, he would have to deal with.

When they were children, Sam used to deliver bad news by stealing sweets from the big house and gift them

to his brothers. He didn't have any sweets or even a means
to steal some, so he'd have to make it cut and dry.

"We all died. Taj, you was shot. Mani, you and me
jumped down here into this pit to get away from Master
Witten, and we jumped to our deaths."

Mani's eyes widened. The thought of him literally
jumping to die was insane, but he knew if they did, there
must have been a good reason for it.

"But why? Why would you throw yourself into a hole, a
known snake pit—"

"You see any snakes 'round hea?" Sam furrowed his
brows. He and the rest of the slaves had been told the same
thing, that this was a snake pit, and anyone who fell inside
would not make it back out without being bitten. The
rumors were clearly half right—they couldn't know what
the pit truly held, though.

Mani and Taj looked around. They didn't see anything
that resembled a snake, or even a snake's skin. As a matter
of fact, the ground was flattened earth, rock. It was more of
an underground cave, with a hole at the top. It had to lead
somewhere. Sam was curious as to how far it went, and
what it would lead them to.

"I guess I don't," Taj responded for both he and Mani.
The only thing that made sense was how far down they
had fallen. They were lucky that it was a quick death,
though neither of them would have wanted to die again.

"Right. I wasn't gon' let you die alone, and I damn sure
wasn't gon' let me and Mani go back to Witten."

"And Ms. Angellica?" Mani wondered. He hadn't seen
her and wondered if she'd gone back with Master Witten.

She seemed to want to stay with them. The way she cradled Taj when he was shot, he thought she would stay with them. But, he figured she might be just like every other white woman of their time—a colored lover behind closed doors, but when it counted, she would stand by and watch them struggle.

"Witten musta took ha. It's almost morning now. I doubt he woulda left her out for the whole world to see," Sam explained. Master Witten was undoubtedly making Angellica pay for her crimes against him. She would either become a public spectacle or a very private, miserable housewife.

"But ain't none of that mo' important than what I'm 'bout to tell you. You need to know the truth. I won't keep it from ya, and it ain't no simple way of sayin' it, but I ain't no liar, so..."

Sam began detailing the day as he knew it. What happened to him, what he saw and experienced, and how they ended up where they were now. Taj, as always, was the easiest to sway. If it would allow them the opportunity to get back at the very people who attempted to ruin their lives, he would do it. Not to mention, being told that he and his brothers would be the undoing of slavery... that was enough for him to sign up. He didn't care how much blood he had to drink. If it would help, he would do it. He was tired of being on the bottom, of being useless.

If he were a vampire, Taj believed he could make a difference. He could finally be worthy to walk alongside his big brother.

Sam rubbed his temples as he awaited a response from

Taj and Mani. His head was throbbing, and his gums ached, like someone punched him in the mouth, but in between the teeth. Jasper had told him that his body would prepare itself to complete the transformation. It was like experiencing a migraine. What he wouldn't do to chew on some lavender now. That would have helped with his headache. At least it would have when he was still completely human.

"Wherever you go, I'ma follow behind ya." Taj gave his vote. He wondered what it would be like to turn and if any of it would hurt. He couldn't imagine it would hurt worse than being shot. He hardly remembered that. Though the side of his head would always have a mark, to remind him of what he'd been through in the past. Becoming a vampire wouldn't change that.

Sam firmly placed his hand on his brother's shoulder, giving it a loving squeeze. The small doubt he had that Taj would say no had dissipated with a resounding yes.

Mani, on the other hand, had his reservations. The moment Sam uttered the word vampire Mani's mind began twisting. It frightened him, the thought of his brother becoming a creature. The only thing that sounded appealing was that if they all agreed, they would all be together. That together, they could do anything. That was how they had always done things, and he never wanted that to end.

Sam noticed the reluctance in Mani's eyes. He knew his baby brother was sensitive, fearful, even. He knew that Mani had the most growing up to do. At 19, he was extremely young, young-minded, and he relied on Mani and Sam to make his decisions, fight his battles, and take care of him. Yet, him becoming a vampire came with its own set of pros. He wouldn't need his brothers to take care of him. What would he fear, when he would become fear itself?

"But human blood? We gon' have to kill?" Mani questioned. Even with strength and potential unlimited power, the thought of killing a human… it scared him.

"We don't have to kill. We don't need to be greedy. Greed ain't somethin' we even used to. We used to rationin', bein' careful about how much we eat. Just because we got the world now, don't mean we need to take it. That's what white folk do. We ain't them," Sam reminded his brothers he meant with every fiber of his being that they would not be transformed by greed and power. They would never return to struggle, but they would respect it and give it its due. They would help their brothers and sisters in bondage rise up from damnation. They would be the representation of a savior on earth. Even if they never received praise for it.

It sounded simple enough, what they would do. How they would have to do it. Now, it was just a matter of doing it, and making sure the transformation would really take. Now that the sun had come up, Sam's physique was clearer. Sweat tabbed at the corners of his face. He was sweating, overheating. His body was close to giving up. His vision had become blurry, a thick and hazy film covered his eyes now. He was on his way out of here. Sam stumbled, barely catching himself on the wall behind him.

"Sam!" Taj and Mani both shouted. They rushed to

their brother's aide, ready to help him complete the change.

"You need blood," Taj said it both as a realization and an instruction.

Sam slowly smiled. Taj had been listening, always doting on his brother's every word.

"I don't want to have to drink the blood of my brothers," Sam spoke honestly. The thought of him frightened him, and it seemed wrong, dirty in a sense. These were his brothers, but it seemed like the only feasible option at the time. It was simple enough. He and Taj would be the first to turn. Mani would need to see the process, to understand what would happen before he completely made up his mind. Sam knew his baby brother and knew his discomforts. He knew that he would struggle with understanding and even completely wanting to join them. Anything of his own creation, Mani would trust. But this, immortality, it was new.

"Drink from me, or we're gonna lose you, and this will have been pointless," Taj said and began looking around. He found a sharp stick nearby. He figured he could poke a hole in his arm and feed his brother from it. He'd already taken a bullet for him. What was a little poke?

Taj picked it up and raised the stick high above his head. He was going to drive it directly into his arm. Sam had explained that he could heal them with his blood, so he wasn't afraid and knew it wouldn't be long before he was patched back up. Besides, for Sam, he would do whatever, whenever to help him. Giving him a little blood was small, compared to what he was prepared to do.

Driving it directly into the center of his arm, Taj stabbed his muscular bicep, and blood squirted from the round hole. Sam growled within. The scent of his brother's blood drove him wild. It smelled of iron, but also of something sweet. Something, familiar.

Sam cleared the distance between the two and pulled Taj's arm to his lips. The second the blood touched his lips, invigoration filled him. His eyes flared open. He'd thought Jasper's blood was tasty, but he had no clue that the blood of his brother would be so enjoyable.

Sam clamped down on Taj's arm, slowly sucking the resplendent sustenance. Each drop progressed his transformation. His vision improved. His headache had completely gone away, and his skin warmed up even more. He felt even more alive than he had before. The blood coursed through his body like running water. He needed it, he craved it. He wanted more.

And that's when he stopped. He understood how quickly this could get out of hand, and he wasn't willing to risk it. Not when it came to his brother's life. Sam detached himself from his brother, and when he did, petals of blood were barely hanging onto his lips. He wiped his thumb across his mouth, laying bare the apparent and curved fangs that protruded from his gums. Sam reached up to feel them. Where there was pain before to make room for them, he now felt as if he'd had them all along. As if they were a part of him.

He was strong, stronger than his usual amount. He could feel his muscles growing underneath his shirt, bulking up even more. His thighs, his calves, were growing by the millisecond. He was already as strong as a bull, and now he'd be as strong as a herd. Sam had expected that his wounds from the last few days would heal—they did. But the scars on his chest, his back, and the scars left on his heart from the experiences he'd had over the last 30 years would be stuck with him forever.

Taj looked at his brother, and the change seemed slight, underwhelming almost. Until, he started to feel light-headed from too much blood loss. His blood flowed like a stream down his arm, rushing from the wound. Sam reached for his brother, his hand extended to him to keep him from tumbling, and when he did, the blood on Taj's arm stopped moving. Along with Taj and Mani. Taj's leg was stuck in midair. Mani's torn expression was not lost on Sam, and now that he could see it in real time, completely frozen, he knew he would have to adjust himself to make sure Mani knew that Sam would support whatever decision he made. Even if it meant them not spending eternity together.

But according to Jasper, Mani would turn. He would become one of them. Otherwise, he could not have seen them in the future. In the year 2018, where Jasper claimed destiny awaited them. Though Sam wanted Mani to choose a life with his brothers, there was a matter that was a bit more pressing at the moment. How the hell was he going to unfreeze his brothers?

He knew he could expect a gift, but he hadn't expected it so soon. How was he supposed to use his power? What was the extent of it? He'd reached for his brother to freeze time, perhaps to unfreeze it, he'd need to do the same.

Before he attempted it, Sam repositioned Taj so that he would not fall or stumble. He brought his leg back down to the ground and fixed his posture to make him stand upright.

Forcefully, Sam pressed forward, expanding his fingertips, and time unfroze. Taj looked down at his arm, expecting there to still be blood running down his arm, but when he looked, it had practically dried.

"Wh-what happened?" Taj asked, looking from his arm to his brothers. Mani became perplexed. Things were changing rapidly, and he could not be sure if it was for the better.

"I-I..." Even Sam was speechless. He stared at his hands for a moment, wondering how becoming a vampire could give him magical gifts. He understood that each vampire had a gift—he didn't understand how he could freeze time.

Silence filled the space between them. There weren't enough words to speak to explain what had just happened.

"I... I'm ready," Taj rushed out. His tone was so low, had Sam's senses not been sharpened, he would not have heard what his brother said, but he hadn't missed a word of it.

Mani, on the other hand, hadn't heard him. He leaned in so that he could be a part of the conversation.

"I want some of that!" Taj slapped his knee in excitement. He was amazed by what he'd just witnessed, and he hadn't actually witnessed one thing because he was frozen, but he knew before he was frozen, he was bleeding to the point of fainting, and now that he was unfrozen, his blood flow had completely slowed.

Sam smiled, excited to share the gift. If each vampire's gift was different, he couldn't wait to see what his brother would be gifted with. Then, the realization of Mani being the one that would have to become his brother's live meal sunk in for Sam and Taj. Mani, for the moment, was none the wiser. He wasn't known to be quick-witted.

"You're the only human around to feed Taj," Sam came out with it. Beating around the bush wasn't his style, and he would need to make his decision now if he was okay with giving up his blood for his brother. If he weren't, then they would need to make arrangements, and Sam knew they would be stronger together, regardless of them not having the powers that came with vampirism.

Sam knew what real power was—the power of family. The power of love. He'd witnessed it so many times before, of course he could immediately recognize it within his family line.

Mani's heart dropped. Sam heard his heart rate quicken. He took a step toward his brother and placed his hands on his shoulders.

"Are you afraid of me, or of what will happen?"

Mani looked away from Sam's gaze. He hated that he was always afraid. That he was often so frightened of everything that he either made poor decisions or he avoided making tough decisions all together.

Sam placed his hand on the back of Mani's neck and turned him back toward him.

"Whatever you're afraid of, you can tell me. You know I

ain't gon' judge ya, I ain't gon' make fun of ya," Sam honestly stated.

This, Mani knew to be true. His brothers had never made him feel like the wuss he really was deep down. Instead, they poured into him, encouraged him to go forward. The truth was, he was afraid of the unknown. It had worked out for Sam, but what if it didn't for him? Taj was most likely to come out on top, but Mani and his fear... they couldn't know if he would come out on the other side of this okay.

He decided to keep his fears to himself. Sometimes, saying it aloud made it worse, and if he was going to be with his brothers forever, he had to follow the next steps.

"Nothing... I'm ready, too. Whatever we need to do, I'ma be ready."

Sam lowered his forehead to his brother's. Mani could not hear him, but he felt his brother's unspoken words.

"I love you, too," Mani uttered, and Sam smiled. They had a long day ahead of them. Becoming vampires, discovering their powers, and eventually, making a new life... together.

CHAPTER 6

2017

Amionette couldn't return home. And now that she knew just how crazy Fletcher was, it would not be safe for her to go anywhere. At least, nowhere near their home. Which would be difficult since her business was just a few miles away from their home.

Fletcher probably believed her to be dead, though. That might be her only saving grace. The only place she felt would be safe was her business. Every now and then, her secretary Yuzuri would come into the office on the weekends to catch up on paperwork and to assist people in the graveyard. Their cemetery was one of the biggest in the state of Tennessee. Because of that, it was easy to get lost if you didn't know where to go, and no one knew the grounds better than Yuzuri. She remembered names well, and she could see something one time, and know exactly how to get back to it.

She could only hope that she was there right now. Amionette had a spare copy of her license in her desk at work. She could use it to access her money, get a rental car, and take care of anything she needed to to get away from Fletcher. Her business was almost self-sufficient. Though she was no stranger to how to handle her business on her own. Her mother, who had done everything from start to finish in her business, taught Amionette how to do many things. She knew how to dig a grave. She knew and understood how to handle person relations when it came to losing their loved ones. Her mother was a gem, a real boss. Amionette did everything she could to walk in her mother's footsteps, but there was no way this was what her mother had in store for her.

Fletcher had turned out to be a dud, a really sexy one, but a bad one nonetheless. It was no wonder when she met him, he was single. Now, she understood how a man so "perfect" could be on his own. Because Fletcher was the exact opposite of perfect. He was a villain—the villain of her story that almost ended, and would have, if the sexy ass black vampire hadn't come to her rescue.

Amionette cautiously treaded across the cemetery and over to the office. Thankfully, Yuzuri's car was on the side of the building. Relief saturated her entire being. She swung the front door of the offices of "Hudges Cemetery and Funeral Home" open. Yuzuri gazed over at Amionette, scanning her outer appearance. Her clothes were filthy, covered in dirt.

"Uhm... Ms. Hudges, is everything alright?" Yuzuri rose from her chair, a strained look on her face. She wasn't sure what happened to Amionette, but she'd never seen her look so disheveled coming in to her office before.

"Everything will be alright if I can just get to my desk. I need a few things from you, Yuzuri. Follow me to my office please."

Amionette headed to the back where her office was

stationed. Yuzuri stalked behind her, quickly moving to keep up with Amionette's long strides. It suddenly dawned on Amionette as she reached for the door knob that she didn't have her keys. She could only hope that Yuzuri had her extra key with her.

Hesitantly, Amionette turned around to face Yuzuri, concern was etched across her gentle face.

"Yuzuri, did you bring your full set of keys? I've… misplaced my keys."

That was unlike Amionette. She was usually always so prepared, so… poised. She could tell from Amionette's appearance and demeanor something was wrong, but she also knew not to question her. Yuzuri had given up trying to make friends with Amionette a long time ago. When she was first hired, after moving to Nashville from Georgia, she couldn't wait to work for Amionette. She'd seen the powerhouse on social media, making major waves and boss moves with her own cemetery and funeral. She was a one-stop shop for the dead, and a woman, nonetheless.

Yuzuri came from corporate America. She enjoyed clerical work; she hadn't enjoyed the hustle and bustle, the poor attitudes, nor the long hours. She was paid handsomely, but her life was dwindling away. Yuzuri found that the light inside of her was being extinguished by working with major corporations. And making another white supremacist company even richer, giving her life away to them, was not on her priority list.

Things had to change, and she was ready for a new life. Moving to Nashville did just that, and her working for Amionette changed her life. She made more money, with no headache, and she was able to find a life to live. Unfortunately, the friendlier she was with Amionette, the more she felt Amionette pushed her away. Yuzuri always struggled to make friends. Her bright personality and kind words seemed to turn people off. In a society where people were no good, Yuzuri was kind, compassionate, and sweet. She was often misread and taken as fake and phony, but she was just raised properly, with a good spirit, and no matter how others treated her, she would not change who she is.

"I do have my keys." Yuzuri smiled and went to her desk. She clicked the button attached to her desk drawer, reached in, and pulled out her keys, swiping to the key to Amionette's office. When she was finished, she turned to hand her the keys, and Amionette practically snatched them from her.

Yuzuri was taken aback. While Amionette was not always friendly, she was always polite, nice even. This side of Amionette was new.

Wind picked up behind Amionette as she sped to her office. Her hands shook as she stuck the key in the door. Yuzuri came over to her and placed a sympathetic hand on top of Amionette's. "I can do it," she offered, and Amionette's hand slipped away. She realized there was a sense of urgency for her to get into her office. She did need to get away, and as calm as she wanted to be, the night's events were suddenly beginning to register to her. It felt like she was slowly going into shock. Fletcher had tried to kill her, and he believed her to be dead, she hoped. But, she didn't want to chance waiting around and letting him find her.

Yuzuri opened the door for her, and she let Amionette in. Amionette eased her way in and went straight over to her desk, ripping at the drawers. To Yuzuri, she looked like a mad woman, sliding papers across her desk, shoveling through her drawers, clearly in search of something.

"Can I find something for you?" Yuzuri suggested. She knew where most things were, and she would be happy to help.

"I... I just. I need my ID," Amionette uttered. Her throat became heavy with tears. She was such a pro at running, but the one time she'd finally let herself get comfortable, she was unprepared and out of sorts.

Amionette's eyes filled with water. Her mother had taught her not to let anyone see you sweat, but she was falling to pieces right before Yuzuri's eyes. Her heart pounded in her chest—she thought she might have a panic attack, something she experienced frequently as a teenager. She recognized the signs but could not stop it from coming. Amionette placed her hands flat on the desk, trying to find the balance between her attack and the real world.

The room started to spin, and her stomach tossed with nausea. Yuzuri flew to Amionette's side and placed her hand on top of Amionette's and squeezed it. "I'm here with you, Amionette. Can you hear me?"

Yuzuri recognized that Amionette was in the middle of a panic attack. Her younger sister Sacred struggled with anxiety on another level. Yuzuri was one of the only people who could calm her down. Her sweet voice, her calm and helpful nature always brought Sacred back to the real world. She could only hope that she would have the same effect on Amionette.

"Why don't you try having a seat?" Yuzuri advised. Had Amionette not moved, Yuzuri would have thought she didn't hear her by the way she was breathing. Amionette hadn't taken a slow breath in what seemed like minutes. But, with Yuzuri's hand over hers, she felt... tethered to earth, just enough to follow her instructions.

Amionette took a seat in her desk chair. The high-back plush seat comforted her. It felt like a hug without actually receiving one. That was the reason she got it. The top of the chair angled inward, resting comfortably just underneath her shoulders.

"I'm going to get you some water, and then I'll be right back," Yuzuri assured Amionette. She understood how important it was to give instructions and make it very clear what was going to take place to keep Amionette present in the moment so she didn't fall off the edge of her attack.

Luckily, Amionette kept a fridge in her office, and it was full of water. Yuzuri opened the smart titanium fridge and pulled out a bottle of Fiji water, unscrewed the top and placed it in front of Amionette. The bottom barely touched the desk before Amionette had it in her hands. She chugged the water, lubricating her windpipes. She had no idea what she would say when she could formulate a sentence, but she knew that she couldn't utter a word with a dry ass throat.

Once her thirst was properly quenched, and she felt her heart slow, she inhaled deeply and looked over at Yuzuri.

Yuzuri had never said a cross word to her. She'd never said or done anything that made her believe she couldn't trust her, but she wasn't a fool. She knew not to trust anyone with what happened to her the night before. She'd have to keep things as quiet as possible, but with her leaving to regather herself, she'd have to tell Yuzuri something.

"Yuzuri, thank you for your help," she started. "I will be leaving for a couple of days, and I'll need you to hold my calls. Do you feel comfortable doing tours? I know John will be in, in a few days, he can…" Amionette rambled on and on. Yuzuri took mental notes of everything Amionette said, but she got the sense that there was something wrong. The way she speed-talked through everything, without letting Yuzuri respond, she figured there must have been something wrong.

Her first thought was to ask if she was alright, but it was clear that Amionette wasn't okay. She had no problem doing anything asked of her, even if it was outside of her normal scope of things, but Amionette never took a vacation. She'd never taken time off, which would explain why she should, but she was a work-a-holic. Why would Amionette be suddenly needing to get away?

"Amionette?" Yuzuri called to her, stopping her from going on another unnecessary tangent.

"Yes?" she questioned, but her eyes were distant, almost as if she were speaking from memory, not so much from listening.

"I think it's great that you're getting away. If anyone deserves it, it's certainly you, but—" Yuzuri crossed her leg, one over the other and leaned forward. "I can sense there's something wrong. You don't have to tell me what it is, but is it something I can help you with? Do you need anything?"

Amionette couldn't stop the trembling in her lips from the tears swelling inside of her. She didn't want to show how she really felt or let on that there was something more going on, but in true Aquarius nature, her face told it all, and she'd had all she could take.

"I don't really know if anything can be done. Fletcher and I broke up last night." She'd said it so normally, like he hadn't tried to unalive her in a gruesome manner. She'd done a good job of keeping the violence of their relationship a secret, because she wasn't completely blameless in the situation herself.

"I'm sorry to hear that," Yuzuri stated resolutely, but the truth was, she had never been happier to hear this kind of news. Fletcher didn't strike her as loving. Yuzuri perceived him as controlling and a little overbearing. She'd wondered what went on in their private life, because whenever he came into the office, no matter how nice he was, no matter how often he flashed his winning million—dollar smile, Yuzuri felt uneasy around him. He had a bad vibe, bad ju-ju on him. As a praying woman, Yuzuri prayed for her boss, that anything meant to harm her would reveal itself. It sounded as if her prayers had finally been answered.

"Don't be. Right now, I'm just trying to figure things out. I need to find somewhere else to stay. I need to get some new clothes, I need—"

"I think," Yuzuri stood up, excitement twinkling

through her, "what you need is a friend. If you'll let me, I'll be there for you, Amionette. I won't ask more of you than what I'm willing to give, but as women, especially black women, I think we owe it to ourselves to stick together."

Yuzuri smiled, and it was contagious. Amionette was upset, broken, even, but Yuzuri, in just a few minutes had made her feel better by just being kind. Amionette's mother told her that friendships were for people who had time and had nothing to do. Since her mother's passing, she realized how lonely she was. How her only friend, the only person she had in her life that she trusted was her mom, and without her, at times, she felt lost.

Amionette wasn't blind to the fact that she'd iced Yuzuri out. That she'd purposely kept her on the outside. She was too afraid to let others in, too afraid that she'd end up running away from someone else. But now, she needed someone. She needed real help, and if Yuzuri could be that help, maybe it was time to stop running once and for all and let someone into her life.

"Yuzuri, I'll be honest. I've never had a friend before. I don't know the first thing about friendship. I'm not sure what to ask for, or what to give," Amionette spoke honestly. She knew how to be a good person, how to give common human decency, but in personal relationships, that involved her heart, she wasn't taught how to initiate—only how to receive.

Yuzuri smiled. She knew Amionette was lonely. It was why she was so drawn to her. Yuzuri always had a special gift of empathy. She could sense the good, bad, and indifference in people. She was often able to control her gift, but sometimes, times like right now, she couldn't turn it off even if she wanted to.

"You don't need to ask me for anything. I'll take the lead. I'll love you, and you'll love me. We'll be there for each other. Now, first thing's first. Should we go to your house and pick up your clothes?"

"No!" Amionette shrieked as she leaped to her feet, her face stunned. The last place she wanted to be was "home" if that was what she could even call it. Yuzuri felt the pain that shot through Amionette's soul. She originally thought Fletcher and Amionette breaking up was a good thing. It was painful, but good. It wasn't until Amionette nearly knocked everything off of her desk that Yuzuri figured it had to be more than that. There had to be an underlying issue there, other than the obvious.

"Okay, okay. We can just get you some new ones until you're able to retrieve your own. What about a place to stay? Did you have somewhere in mind?"

Amionette cupped her forehead. The day was getting harder and harder, it seemed. She had so many things to figure out. Clothes, she could replace. A home of her own, she could get, but being by herself, she wasn't sure if she should do that. What if Fletcher found out she was alive? Besides that, for the first time, the possibility of having a friend didn't sound so bad. She wasn't 100 % positive about the blood the vampire gave her. Something terrible might happen, and if she wasn't by herself, perhaps someone could help her in a reasonable amount of time.

"I don't know if this would be too forward, but—"

"Don't say another word." Yuzuri nodded her head.

"You can stay with me. Why don't we go to my house now. You're about my size. I'm sure I have some clothes for you to put on." Yuzuri tilted her head to the side, sizing Amionette up. Amionette was a bit curvier than Yuzuri, but even with her slender figure, she was sure she had, at the least, sweat pants and a t-shirt that Amionette could borrow until she got some more clothes.

"I don't want to put you out," Amionette mentioned, and Yuzuri smiled. This was exactly what she wanted. Well, not for Amionette to feel the way she was feeling, but to get closer to Amionette. Yuzuri had been there just after Amionette's mother passed away. She started working for Amionette just six months after her mother passed away, and she watched her pick up the pieces, alone. Yuzuri witnessed her show up full-time in her relationship, at work, and in all of her endeavors.

The one thing she always noticed, was unless it was a big deal or something that seemed important, Fletcher was nowhere to be found. Amionette had been in a relationship on her own this entire time. It was time for Amionette to be loved on a little bit, without having to give anything to get it.

"Put me out? You pay me so damn good, I've got nothing but room. We can close for the day. It's not gonna be too busy," Yuzuri suggested. Tentatively, Amionette stood up on her shaky legs. Her thighs nearly clicked like crickets with the way she was trembling. Amionette had never felt fear the way she was feeling it now, and her need to run was kicking in, but she'd grown tired of running.

Long term, she'd have to figure something out, but for

right now, she could at least go to Yuzuri's and figure out the best way to recuperate. Calling the police had of course crossed her mind, but they would want to know how she was healed quite literally overnight. She knew better than to tell anyone about the fact that she'd met a real life vampire. Television had shown her enough when it came to how the world dealt with things they didn't understand.

As a black woman, she knew all too well how people perceived and treated things and people that they didn't understand. She didn't know if she would ever see the handsome vampire ever again, though she hoped she could so she could thank him. If everything turned out okay, that is.

"Can we stop by the bank first? I need to replace my debit card and credit cards. I'll also need to withdraw some money—"

"How about we do this first." Yuzuri pointed her index finger in the air, her smile never wavering. "Let's go to my house, get you into something clean, and then we can run errands, together."

Amionette's heart hitched in her chest. A lump formed in her throat. She wasn't the type of person to show affection, nor let her emotions easily slip out. But, as she rounded the corner of her desk and wrapped her arms around Yuzuri, she knew the old her hadn't served her well. And, the new her, the one who was bursting at the seams, pushing out of her like a newborn baby, needed a friend, and desperately needed a hug.

Yuzuri enveloped her in a loving hug, embracing her with all of the power inside of her. "It's okay. You're okay,"

Yuzuri assured her. Though it had not completely seemed like things would be alright, being held by another black woman, who seemed to care for her, for a moment made the world stand still, where she wished she could be held forever...

# CHAPTER 7

Mani would be the last to turn. Sam turned Taj, and Taj successfully completed the change. He expected to feel extremely different. The only difference he felt right away was his physical strength. But that was a given. He wondered what his special power would be. Sam was gifted with time manipulation. What would his be? He could only hope it would be half as good as his brother's. Even in death, he wanted to be as good, if not better than Sam.

"We'll go down the path there, and see where it leads. We gotta find somebody for Mani. That's the only way he'll be able to join us," Sam pointed out, and though Mani felt a pinch of nerves, he wanted nothing more than to be just like his brothers, in every way he could.

Sam and Taj's vision adjusted in the underground cave. Now that they were vampires, they could see beyond their sight directly in front of them. Each of them could see the path a mile ahead, but they were uncertain where the rest of the path led.

Before taking down the pathway, Sam grabbed one of the iron settings that held fire inside of it and handed it to Mani. As they traveled down the path, Sam anticipated it would be dark, and even with two vampire brothers who would die for him, Sam knew Mani needed his own set of comfort, for himself.

Mani politely smiled at Sam and took the light from him.

"Together," Sam said, and the three of them lined up beside one another. Sam in the center, Mani on his left, and Taj on his right. They trailed down the path, slowly creeping through it, uncertain of what they might find. The cave seemed to become narrower the further inward they traveled.

"I don't too good like this," Mani spoke, keeping his tone low, as if some thing or someone else could hear them. He was exhausted. They'd taken frequent stopping breaks, and each time they stopped, he felt more and more tired. Taj and Sam had not experienced being tired. Their new vampire bodies could go for quite some time without requiring rest. Even though Mani was used to being pushed past his physical limits, he'd just about had it. Without water, he was becoming thirsty. Sweat bunched around his forehead, underneath his shirt. He was wet all over.

"If we stumble upon something, I think we can handle it," Taj retorted. His eyes would have rolled if he weren't doing his best to keep them from doing so. He loved his brother, but at times, his incessant fear drove him crazy. This was the first time he noticed just how badly it bothered him.

Sam heard the disdain in his brother's voice. He usually exercised patience, care, and understanding for Mani. He could only hope that becoming a vampire hadn't completely twisted him inside. That it hadn't made him into something new.

Sticking his elbow out purposely, Sam gave his brother a warning. There was no need for him to be mean to Mani, especially when currently, he was much stronger, and capable of much more than Mani. Before vampirism, on their best day, Sam was always stronger. Next to him was Taj, and then of course, Mani. Physically, they were all fit as fiddles, but Sam never allowed his physical body to rule over his brothers, and he wouldn't let Taj, now being a vampire, control or rule over Mani.

Taj turned to Sam, bearing his fangs slightly. Sam's eyebrows upturned. Vampire or not, Taj knew he didn't want to go there with Sam. He figured he must have been out of line and swallowed the feelings he was having. The last thing they needed was to be at one another's throats.

Defeated, Mani trudged alongside his brothers. Their shoulders began bumping the further inward they went.

"I think we should turn back," Mani suggested. They were squeezing tighter and tighter.

"No, we should keep going this way. It'll open back up in a minute," Sam proposed as they advanced. Up ahead, he could see a tiny sliver of light peeking through a spiral. Taj smiled; he understood why their brother wanted them to keep going. Mani, though, didn't have the same amount of sight as they did, and soon, his light wasn't going to be able to go with him if they continued. There wouldn't be enough room for it.

Once they reached a space too tight for the three of

them, Sam proposed that he should be the one to check out the crawl space in front of them. It was just big enough for one at a time, but he knew for certain, there was light on the other side, which meant they might have been coming out and into the open. Which would also mean they had to be careful. Not knowing where they were headed would be troublesome, but they didn't know how else they would get out of this cave if they didn't.

"We should all go together, one-by-one," Taj offered, hoping his suggestion would be head.

"No, you need to stay behind for just in case," Sam's ominous prediction weighed heavily on his two little brothers. He knew what that meant. The trio had been put in too many life or death situations, where one (Sam) risked their lives so the other two could survive. This was a recurring theme in their lives, and the cycle would not be broken for at least another century.

"I'ma go up ahead and see what's on the other side. I'll be back quick. I got a couple of tricks up my sleeve now," Sam said, referring to him being able to manipulate time. "I'll be safe, don't worry."

Sam didn't give either of them the opportunity to speak. He squeezed into the tight hole and crawled inside. Around him, he could hear the earth moving, filled with insects, breathing even. The smell of dirt was so strong, it almost made him turn around. Being a vampire so far had seemed easy enough, though he could understand how it wasn't all glitz and glam. Already he was starting to get hungry again, but he wasn't exactly sure how he would go about getting food for himself, or for his brothers. But he knew that if they did not drink blood, they would die.

Taking another human life was off the table. Sam did not profess to be God or even godlike. He knew taking a human life, unjustly, was wrong. That was the reason that when he came across Angellica, even though she was a super freak, he knew better than to harm her. It was not in Sam's nature to be cruel for no reason, and he would not allow himself to change just because he became a vampire.

His fangs protruded as he got closer to the light. The scent of honey filled his nostrils, and he could not control himself. The scent was so powerful, he could taste the honey in his mouth. He licked his lips, salivating for a taste. When he reached the end of the tunnel, the light peeking through was indeed daylight. Sam poked his head out slightly, and he recognized where he was slightly.

The boys had traveled further than they realized underground. They'd traveled nearly forty miles, into Fort Nashborough. Sam had spent time traveling between Middle Tennessee and Forth Nashborough when Master Witten made him trade goods with the Indians or other plantation owners.

He laid eyes on the Cumberland River. There was only one major plantation lined along the river and several other large homes. This would be perfect for them to get a bite to eat and turn Mani. They could return to the cave once they were done and figure out their next move.

From the looks of it, there was a party taking place along the river. There were boats and tents lined up, chairs and tables. Slaves were setting up and bringing pitchers and glasses out on trays. He wondered what they were celebrating. Not that anyone would ever invite him. But perhaps one day he would be allowed to attend fancy parties. He couldn't imagine so far in the future, in the year 2018 that he wouldn't be welcome, especially since Jasper told him they would end slavery. He wondered what would lead to that. How he and his brothers would facilitate that. One day, though, he'd figure it out.

Sam quickly began formulating a plan in his mind. He knew that if he left it up to his brothers, there would be an argument. It was just easier for him to say what they were going to do, rather than ask what they thought was best. It cut down on confusion and arguing.

Sam sat sideways in the tunnel, watching people come and go. The women were dressed in fine and vibrant petticoats. The men were showing off their rings and necklaces, made of ivory and the teeth of his people. His flesh rippled with anger. He wanted to tear their heads off, but that would not be who he was, he reminded himself.

Women and men alike frolicked along the water. Some of them slightly undressing to take a swim. There was laughter, music, and what looked to be joy. Sam hated them for having such a good time. He hated them for having the privilege to do so while he and his people weren't allowed to breathe the same air as they were, simply because of their beautifully melanated skin.

Swallowing his hatred, he figured out what they should do. It would be easy enough once they all got drunk to take a human. There was plenty of blood in one person to drink from them and still return them to the party. The problem would be making them forget. That was his only fear. How were they supposed to keep the fact that they were vampires a secret from others without killing?

Sam had only come up with threatening their victims. Who would believe them anyway? They were runaway slaves after all—who would have left them alive? Their chances were looking better and better.

Swinging his long legs around behind him, Sam began crawling back to his brothers to convey his plan. By nightfall, they would all be the same—vampires, full, and completely free.

Hours had gone by, and the Brown brothers were waiting for the perfect opportunity to strike. Mani's stomach roared of starvation. If he could just get a potato from one of the tables, he would be okay. Even a glass of water. He was famished and had been for days. He had no idea how long he could go without food. The longest he'd ever gone without eating was four days. Today would make his third day. He'd hate to see what another day of hunger would do to him. Mani was living on willpower at this point.

Taj had become anxious. His patience was wearing thin, and the small amount of blood he'd consumed from Mani had worn off. He needed to replenish himself, but he wouldn't take another bite out of Mani. He'd nearly had a panic attack the first time, and he wouldn't put his brother through that again. Watching everyone enjoying themselves at a close distance, he could hear their hearts beating, their protruding veins that he couldn't wait to sink his fangs into.

Sam recognized the looks on his brother's faces. He knew they were hungry. He was, too, but he could always curb his cravings by singing. Music saved him, he felt. Sam believed Negro Spirituals were meant to be uplifting. God had blessed them with windpipes that bellowed all the way to Heaven, and they should use their voices, to remind them of who they served, and to whom they belonged.

Even in slavery, with all the pain he'd experienced, while he did not understand why things happened. He had no clue why bad things seemed to happen to good people, but in his case, he was beginning to see his life turn around. Perhaps it was the fact that bad things had to happen, so balance could be restored to the good.

In a quiet, and low register, Sam began singing his favorite comfort Negro Spiritual,

"I held my brother with a trembling hand I would not let him go,

I held my sister with a trembling hand I would not let her go."

He placed his hand on the shoulders of his brothers, singing, witnessing to them.

"Wrestle on, Jacob,
Jacob, day is a breakin'
Wrestle on, Jacob,

Oh, I will not let you go."

Taj and Mani smiled as their brother sang. He had a powerful voice that resonated inside of them. Tears lined Mani's eyes, and his hunger pains went away. He knew his brother had his back, his front, and both of his sides. He would not let them go without. Patience, they just needed to exercise a little more patience.

Taj and Mani's heads hung low in reverence as they took in their brother's voice. He sang the song for three rounds, and when he finished, the brothers' spirits were renewed, and any hunger they felt had been filled with the spirit. The party had been going on for quite some time. There were case bottles littered near the docks. White women and men, married and single, sprinkled about, laying on the ground. Their guards were down, and all they would have to do was snatch someone who was already out of place.

Under the cover of nightfall, Sam and Taj climbed out of the cave.

"You stay here and wait for us to come back. Do not come out, for any reason. Do you understand?" Sam bent over, looking into Mani's eyes. Mani was much shorter than Sam, and he often felt he towered over his brother. Yet, he did his best to constantly get on his level so that he would understand that while he was the eldest, he was not better than him nor did he regard himself as above him.

Mani nodded his head in agreement, and Sam and Taj climbed out of the cave together. They were thankful to no longer have their shackles on. They would be able to easily sneak up on their victim. Taj and Sam scouted the area visually before putting together an attack strategy. To the far right of the docks, there was a man, lying on his back, staring up at the sky. While he was glancing upward, peacefully, Sam nor Taj cared about his peace, when their peace had been disturbed for generations. They would not kill him, but they were going to feast on him. But first, they would turn Mani, and then use him as their meal for the night.

"You see 'em? Layin' there, not a care in the world," Taj tilted his head toward the far right, his voice laced with ill intent.

"I do. Here's what we do. I'll stop time, and we can carry him back to the cave. I don't know how long I can hold it, though, but I guess I could keep freezing time if necessary."

Sam's eyes were on the prize, and he was willing to take all the risk. "If the plan don't work out, you take Mani and get out of here. We ain't all the way immortal," Sam warned Taj. He had remembered what Jasper told him. Since he maintained a piece of his soul, and Taj still had his entirely, they would be vulnerable to the weapons of this world.

But, Sam would protect his family until his dying breath, no matter when or how that came.

"I ain't gon' leave ya. Get that out ya head now," Taj reminded him. He placed his hand on Sam's shoulder, and Sam reached across his chest and clapped his brother's hand. He loved him in life, and he loved him even more in death. Sam had begun realizing the differences in the way he felt when he was alive, and now how he felt in his afterlife. He'd loved his family with all he had before. Now, he loved them to the point of possession. They belonged to him, and him alone.

Sam thrusted his hands outward, and the music decrescendoed as time began to stand still. When they were positive Sam's power had worked, they began making their move. Quickly, they rushed over to the man lying on his back. His face was calm, like he'd never seen a hard day. With one arm placed behind his arm, and the other across his stomach, Sam could see that he wasn't a careful man. Why would he have to be? There was no way Sam would have ever been caught slipping like this. His arrogance would be his demise.

Sam placed one hand underneath his arm, and Taj did the other, and together, they drug his dead weight back to the cave. They placed the man inside, and Taj drug him backwards to where Mani was.

Stupefied, Mani stood frozen in the cave. It was in that moment that Sam realized that he could freeze humans only, and not vampires, and at varying ranges as well. It would take time to understand his power and truly utilize it to its full potential, but he could in fact do it, with enough time.

Climbing in behind them, Sam entered the cave and found his brothers standing there.

"What now?" Taj asked, as he looked between the meal and his older brother.

"I'll unfreeze time, we'll turn Mani, and then we feed."

Taj knew it would not be that easy, and so did Sam, but

if any trouble should arise in the meantime, surely the two of them together could handle it. Sam wafted his hands in the air, and the man lying on the ground looked around, dumbfounded. Confusion sifted through his mind. He was relaxing near the dock, and now he was in a cave, surrounded by colored folks.

He scooted against he wall of the cave, frightened. Mani stood there, fear pulsing through him. He would kill if he had to, but taking a human life was not something he enjoyed or wanted to do. Mani had only done so once. It was an unfortunate evening. He was just twelve years old, and he caught a man raping one of the slave women whose quarters were directly across from theirs. Rather than let it happen, he went inside the room and stabbed him with a makeshift knife. While he did it for the right reasons, it didn't make him feel any better. He'd only done what he had to do.

The brothers had not said a word. Taj and Sam moved toward him, prepared to restrain him. The blue-eyed man held fear within him. He feared black people because he was told he had to. He'd been told they were untrustworthy and that they were dirty. Unfortunately, his pea-sized mind couldn't help but believe it. He opened his mouth to scream. His voice rumbled upward and spewed out.

"Help!" he shouted, his voice echoed off the cave walls. Sam went to freeze him. They couldn't have this man screaming his soul out and letting everyone know they were in the cave.

"Shut up!" Taj called out to him. The man immediately shut his mouth. The quickness of his silence was shocking.

The fear in his face hadn't gone anywhere, but he had closed his mouth.

Taj had a theory. "Stand up," he demanded, and the man got to his feet. "Scratch your head," he further instructed, and the man began scratching at his head. It was then that the three brothers realized, Taj had the power of mind control. He could make someone do his bidding simply by just telling them.

"That right dea' might just work in our favor," Sam pointed out. He'd been wondering how they would survive long-term. He now knew how and understood. With their powers to freeze and mind control, they would be impossible to stop if they learned to hone their skills.

Sam and Taj quickly went to work preparing things for Mani. Taj made a tiny incision on his wrist. His blood slowly leaked out and into the palm of his hand.

"Drink." Taj tilted his head in the direction of his bleeding wrist, extending his arm out to Mani. He swallowed hard, gulping down his fear. He'd made his decision, and the only thing left was for him to take the next steps. What scared him was how he would die. Even though he would come back, the fear of the pain of his death frightened him nearly to it.

Mani placed his lips to his brother's wrist and drank deeply from him. He wasn't sure how much it would take for him to drink, so he took deep pulls until his stomach began to turn. Unlike Sam's experience, he did not like the taste of blood. It tasted rotten to him.

He wiped at the corners of his mouth. His stomach turned in swirls, and for a moment, he was afraid that his system couldn't handle the blood mixing with his own. He'd had his doubts, and now one of his worst fears was about to come true—being without his brothers.

Sam took a hold of his brother. It was easy for him to notice the signs of him being about to have a meltdown.

"Have you changed your mind?"

As badly as Mani wanted to say yes, he was more afraid to say it aloud, because he knew deep down he didn't mean it.

"Uhn-uhn," he said, staring Sam into the eyes. His brother had taught him that you always looked a man in the eye, no matter the situation. It would earn him the respect he deserved, even if he faced an opponent he couldn't win against. Respect was important, no matter the time period.

"Good. Keep your eyes on me." Sam gave his order, and Mani nodded his head. He wasn't sure what would come next, well, how it would come. But, at least it was going to be Sam taking care of it.

Close by, there was a rock that glimmered in Sam's peripheral. Almost as if it was beckoning him to pick it up. He chose it for the deed. He wouldn't snap his brother's neck. That seemed entirely too harsh. He wasn't a monster. Leaning to his right, Sam grabbed the rock with jagged, sharp edges. He would make this quick.

With the rock in hand, Sam gazed at Mani, a smile on his face, and then waved his hands in the air, freezing Mani and the gentleman they'd snatched.

"What you gon' do? I think he'll be scared no matter what," Taj interjected, but Sam didn't bother turning around. He needn't explain himself or what he was doing. Mani was suspended in time, but it was for his own good. Sam took the rock and slid it across his brother's neck. Taj deeply inhaled, gasped even, shocked at what he was seeing. This seemed much more cruel to him, but Sam felt he was doing his brother a courtesy by doing it this way.

When he unfroze time, his brother would quickly bleed to death, rather than have a slow death. It was a favor, considering he could see and smell the fear coming from Mani's body.

With another wave of his hands, Sam unfroze time, and Mani's knees buckled. Sam reached around him in the knick of time and helped to lay him down on the ground. Mani spat up blood, only once. He'd hardly had enough time to reach for his neck to hold the wound before he was completely bleeding out. Within minutes, Mani was dead, in between the in between, preparing for his transition.

Sam and Taj eyed one another, knowing exactly what time it was for the two of them.

"I think it's time you have your first meal," Sam recommended, moving toward their victim.

"I couldn't agree more," Taj said, licking his tongue across his teeth. His fangs popped out of his gums, ready to sink them into something so he could finally eat.

"You won't scream. You won't make a noise," Taj compelled their victim. When he did not speak, Taj knew his gift had worked. Though Sam was the eldest, he was used to going last at all things. He took a step back and let Taj have his fill first. As the eldest, it was his job to provide, and sometimes, that meant making sacrifices, and going last.

Everything he did was for Taj and Mani. He just hoped they'd made the right decision.

"That's enough. We need to save some for Mani," Sam reminded Taj. He had taken plenty of blood for himself. Taj was as swollen as a mosquito, and though their victim's heart was still steadily beating, there was no reason to be greedy. They could literally have any meal they wanted now. There was no need to become a glutton.

When Taj didn't stop, Sam placed his hand on his brother's shoulder to ground him and bring him back to reality. "We don't kill," Sam stated. The word we suddenly sounded foreign to him. Yet, when Taj felt his brother's firm, authoritative grip, he knew it was time for him to pull away. He took one last deep gulp, and then took a step away.

His chest heaved up and down from the thrill and sheer excitement of getting full. He could genuinely say he'd never experienced a meal like that. A rush of ecstasy washed over him. Taj had only experienced his own brother's blood. It wasn't nearly as delicious as someone else's. He figured that it must have had something to do with the fact that they shared the same blood. Like a chef who prefers someone else's cooking to their own. It was probably just a mind thing. But, the stranger's blood was invigorating.

They had been waiting for Mani to wake up for some time now, and they'd healed their victim and put him to sleep, so that he too would be rested for Mani when he woke up. Taj was becoming restless. He wanted more, to indulge even more. His eyes were set on the end of the tunnel, leaving to ravage the entire party of humans.

Sam didn't need to hear his brother's thoughts to know when he was up to something, or when his thoughts were anywhere but where they should be.

"Taj, everything alright?" Sam dipped his head, raising a brow of curiosity at his brother.

Taj didn't turn out. His eyes jet back and forth between the humans. Drunk, gluttonous, sexual, jailers that they were, Taj felt no remorse for what he wanted to do, for what he planned to do. Hearing his brother call out to him infuriated him, where in the past, it gave him comfort. He hated Sam's innate ability to always know when something wasn't right. For once, Taj wanted to do something that would make him happy. Something that had little to no consequences without the guilt-trip of his brother.

"Everything just fine," Taj said, sarcasm in his tone.

Sam came up behind his brother, and he knew something was off. When Taj turned around, his eyes were bloodshot red, and his fangs were protruding.

"What's the matta?" Sam asked with concern. Regardless of what he'd said, he knew his brother, and even before looking at him, he knew he must have been messed up. Now, looking into his eyes, his suspicions had been confirmed.

"I'm tired of following rules. Your rules. Why can't we kill? They been killin' us for centuries. Don't we deserve a little vengeance?" Taj crossed his arms, leaning back against the wall of the cave. His relaxed demeanor unnerved Sam, considering the words Taj was saying and his bulging red eyes.

"We don't kill because we not them. They abuse the power they created. Why should we?"

"We betta than them—even without being vampires! That's why they hate us Sam, because we betta! We always been betta than them."

"And the only way for us to keep bein' betta," Sam stopped and looked his brother deeply in the eyes, "is if we choose betta. We can be monsters without bein' monsters."

Taj's chest swelled with fury. He wanted to put his brother in his place. At times, Taj felt Sam could be a bit righteous, but he'd never led them astray, and he knew that his brother wouldn't now. But he was frustrated and overwhelmed. A bit overstimulated too, not realizing that vampirism would only heighten what they already felt and thought.

Sam closed his eyes, blinking away the crimson blood lust. When he opened his eyes back up, he saw something to his left moving. It was Mani. He sprung up, reaching for his neck. He didn't quite remember his death, but he did remember the way it felt, for just a brief moment. He'd seen himself, an out-of-body experience, bleed to death. His neck was leaking blood.

He placed his hands in front of him, and the blood wasn't there. It was, however, all over his shirt. When he looked up at his brothers, they both held smiles for him.

"You should eat," Sam said, a twinge of excitement in his voice. His brother was now awake, and together, the three of them would find their destinies. It wouldn't be easy, but now that the trio were completely together and whole, there would be nothing standing in their way of figuring things out.

Sam, of course, would be the one to put a full plan into place. But for now, he would enjoy being free with his brothers. He'd only wished his parents were still alive to see them. How proud they would be.

CHAPTER 8

2017

It was an extremely shocking experience for Amionette to walk into Yuzuri's house and see that her home was laid. She really was paying Yuzuri extremely well. She knew better than anyone else that Yuzuri deserved it with all she had to put up with. Death had a way of bringing the worst out in people. You could see behind the masks people lived in on a daily when someone close to them died.

Amionette's mother had taught her that she could always tell how a person was loved by the way they were treated in death. She believed that and watched it play out every day. Another reason she had to get and stay away from Fletcher. Amionette wondered who would attend her funeral if she had died besides the people employed by her. She'd moved so much, purposely, and never really made a friend, there wouldn't be anyone to attend.

"Follow me to the back. You can pick out something to wear. I'll get you a towel and washcloth."

Yuzuri waved a welcoming hand for Amionette to follow. Amionette had lived in many nice places, but nowhere ever felt cozy and warm. She'd never felt like she needed to return to something. Yuzuri's home, though, blasted Amionette with warmth and light the moment she stepped into her foyer. The warm tan and deep browns of her living room lounge and couch set were inviting, just like Yuzuri's personality. Everything seemed to have its own spot—flower vases were meticulously placed where they could easily be viewed on end tables, and at the edge of her breakfast nook.

Amionette didn't want to seem like an uncultured swine or an orphan as she let Yuzuri lead the way through her home, but she felt, in a sense, inadequate as a woman walking passed all of her things. Yuzuri had pictures hanging up on her walls, of people, who she assumed were her family. There was even a picture with Yuzuri and a little shots in a large, golden picture frame at the end of the wall, just before they entered Yuzuri's bedroom.

When she opened the door, Amionette was floored by how lovely and feminine Yuzuri's room was. She had a beautiful purple and gold decorum as the color scheme. Her beset was purple satin, with gold fringe around the edges. Her king-sized bed sat up on a platform, almost like it was being showcased.

"This is my room," Yuzuri said, wide-eyed and bushy-tailed. She had a smile a mile wide on her face. Amionette didn't understand why she'd let her into her space like this. Into what seemed like something so special with how filthy she was.

"It's beautiful, Yuzuri, should I—"

"Oh! You can also just call me Zuri, if we're gonna be friends. Only my mama says Yuzuri when she's trying to get my attention," Yuzuri corrected her. The name felt strange as she repeated it in her mind, but she knew that Zuri just wanted to make her feel comfortable. That she was being kind on purpose.

"I will keep that in mind," she said, and then looked around. "Are you sure you want me in here? I'm filthy," Amionette pointed out, like it was not already obvious that she was filthy from head to toe. Zuri was just so happy to be having company, she didn't care if Amionette was butt naked, as long as she was here.

"I don't mind at all. Plus, you're about to get in the bath. This is my closet," Zuri said and slid open a hanging door. Inside was a walk-in closet. It was big enough to be another room entirely. Amionette had always thought Zuri was well-dressed, but she figured she was just well put together. She didn't have a clue as to how true that was until she looked inside.

Her cardigans were separated by length. Her dresses were all put together neatly, hung, and separated by color scheme. Even her shoes, and she had many, were perfectly placed in order of style and color, on eight shelves. Amionette had always thought Zuri dressed like a kindergarten teacher, and she was right, but she was a very fashionable one.

Zuri always dressed in color explosions that typically made Amionette's mind hurt, but now she realized that she was only dressing to match her personality.

"Pick out anything that suits your liking," she suggested, but Amionette couldn't see herself wearing any of those dresses. Not to run errands, or even go on a date. She didn't want to hurt Zuri's feelings, but nothing in her closet looked remotely comfortable, and that was the honest truth.

Amionette loved Zuri's slender figure, the way her clothes clung to her body, accentuating her toned but feminine body, but Amionette had curves that would make water weep—she would have to squeeze into those dresses, and even then, she'd be contorting her body trying to walk around in them.

Zuri noticed Amionette stalling, her eyes scanning each row of clothes.

"In the drawers, there are lounge clothes, more comfy clothes." Zuri knowingly smiled and pointed to the drawers underneath one of the dress sections. When Amionette didn't advance toward the drawers, Zuri stepped in front of her and pulled out two drawers. One had lounge pants, leggings, and yoga pants. The other had shirts, long-sleeved and short, sports bras and no-wire bras. Enamored by the organization, Amionette reached into the drawers, sifting through the clothes.

"I'll get your towel and wash rag," Zuri mentioned before walking away. Though somewhat overwhelmed, Amionette felt much safer in Zuri's place than she did being in the outside world. She wondered if Fletcher would come to look at what was supposed to be her gravesite. She hated him for what he did to her, but vengeance was something she could not seek. Not if she wanted to remain safe and under the radar. She wished her mother was still alive—she could certainly use a hug from her.

Amionette's fingers landed on a black and gold pair of leggings, and there seemed to be a matching sweatshirt in the other drawer. They looked large enough for her to fit. By the time she'd popped back up with clothes in her hands, Zuri had reappeared with a matching towel and wash cloth set. Amionette had never realized just how anal Zuri was about color patterns and things that went together. She'd just thought she was well-put together. Now, she realized Zuri might have a touch of OCD.

She reached the towel set across to her and Amionette graciously took them.

"Thank you, Zuri, for everything."

Zuri, with an understanding smile, nodded her head. "Let me show you to the bathroom."

Amionette followed Zuri out of the closet and back into her bedroom. Across from her bed was another sliding door. Zuri pulled the door to the side, and she touched her hand to the wall. The entire bathroom lit up. Overhead lights shined down onto the both of them, and it was so bright, Amionette thought she had just walked into heaven, or an insane asylum. The shower was encased in glass, a touchscreen panel on the wall, three smart showerheads.

"How the fuck much do I pay you again?" Amionette asked. Even her place with Fletcher wasn't that nice, and they had the money to do it. She just couldn't see herself setting up such a nice house with Fletcher because of how much they fought. It was in that moment that she realized even being engaged to Fletcher, she might have been thinking of running from him. From this life.

The only thing she couldn't leave behind was her family's business. It had been passed down generation to generation, for quite some time. Losing or leaving the family business would be the equivalent of losing her heritage, her legacy. It was the only thing she actually had to her name. It was her saving grace, her constant.

Zuri giggled. "You pay me really well, and I'm thankful for that. That means I just do my job the right way." Zuri winked and pat her on the shoulder. "I'll be in the living room when you're done. We'll figure out our next steps from there."

Amionette waited until Zuri left the bathroom before getting herself set up. She had never received this kind of kindness from anyone. In school, she was always treated differently, as a separate entity. She often felt she stuck out like a sore thumb. Even when she wasn't running from town to town, she couldn't make a friend to save her life. Women often disregarded her, thought she had an attitude, and thought she was stuck up.

She was anything but.

Amionette was just careful. No one ever gave her the chance to be nice or to see who she really was. No one, until Zuri came along.

CHAPTER 9

1760

It had been one year since the brothers had become vampires. Their adjustment period had been long and hard, but finally, the trio were happy and living their lives. They stayed in the cave for six months, marking the time only by the moon descending and the sun rising. They had been fortunate that they were not marred by the sun, and they could still enjoy the daylight as they saw fit.

With Taj's power of compulsion, he could make people do his bidding. People saw them and never told a soul about seeing them because they didn't remember what had occurred by the time they were gone. Sam had several rules, and one of them, the most important one, was that they did not kill, unless they absolutely had to. It wasn't just about them being better than their oppressors; it had everything to do with keeping people off of their trail.

Sam knew that he would be vulnerable to human weapons because he'd kept a part of his soul. He was strong and almost invulnerable, but his brothers would fall easily because they still had their souls in tact. He was careful for them. Even though Taj and Mani were hungry for blood, Sam kept them in check and wouldn't allow them to over indulge. Sam figured they'd live best under the radar.

And he was right.

A year later, the brothers were living in one of the nicest, abandoned mansions in the city of Nashborough. It was sequestered in the woods, obviously forgotten about. The only people they saw from time-to-time were the Indians, and they stayed away from the Brown brothers, because they suspected who they were. Though the Brown brothers respected them and their land and stayed out of their way, the Native Americans had a way of knowing things others possibly wouldn't. Not to mention the fact that three, very black men were living free, with no one to stop them or call them property. But they would never belong to anyone else, ever again. To nobody but themselves.

Taj's 25th birthday was only a week away. They'd never been able to celebrate their birthdays in an important or special way. Every one in a while, they had small celebrations in the slave quarters, but they were quick and short lived. This birthday, Sam would not begrudge his brother a special celebration. He wanted him to be happy, and since they had many more birthdays to celebrate, there was no reason they couldn't start now.

Sam sat in the corner on the embroidered sofa, thinking about the perfect birthday gift for this brother. As a child, he requested toys. Year after year, he always wanted toys. They weren't allowed to have nice things as slaves, and any toys they had were hand-made. Taj was entirely too old for toys now. As adults, he wanted his freedom, and he had been given it. The only other thing Taj wanted was a woman to call his own. He'd been expressing his want for a woman for a very long time. Taj had no idea how he would procure a woman for his brother. The woman he'd had a crush on in the slave quarters had jumped the broom with another, and she was with someone else.

He could always allow his brother to use his powers to compel himself a woman, but that would not be genuine. He wouldn't even know the first place to find black women to begin with without spilling their secret. Their secret was the one thing keeping them from living a truly free life.

The Native Americans were the only people who knew their secret, and while they weren't afraid of one another, they purposely avoided each other.

Maybe we can have a party...

Sam had never even been to a real party, but he understood the makings of a party. He'd seen what it meant and what it was like to have a party. All they needed were guests, food, and entertainment. Since they'd maintained their humanity, the brothers could survive on blood or food, though their craving for blood was strong, and it was sweeter than food to them. It was more like a delicacy.

Taj and Mani were wrestling on the ground, having a strength contest. They'd been challenging one another for days, questioning who was stronger, faster, and who, in the event of trouble, could defend them.

Sam figured this was the best time for him to step away and try to plan his brother's birthday party. He rose from his seat and headed for the door. It was the dead of winter, but the 20 degree weather hardly bothered him. When he opened the door, the wind blowing caressed his hickory skin. He welcomed it as he walked through the front door and into the great outdoors.

Taj and Mani were none the wiser. Sam crossed the land that separated their abandoned home to the Native American's territory. As he crossed the boundary, he heard leaves rustling against the ground. He'd already expected to be met with a bow and arrow. Though he did not see them, he could hear them. They were circling him. Sam loved how protective the Native Americans were about their land and their tribe. He felt the same about his own brothers.

Sam wouldn't kill unless it called for it, and if the Native Americans attacked him he was willing to di for his, or get as close to death as he could be.

The Native Americans slowly began to reveal themselves, one at a time. Their heavy deer skin coats covered them, their furs a representation of their native culture to the land.

Sam raised his hands in the air in surrender, hoping they'd see his hands up as a sign of peace. He meant them no harm. He needed their help if he was going to create the perfect party for Taj.

"I wanna strike a deal with you," Sam said, unsure if they could understand one another. He wasn't sure if they spoke English or not. He knew that some of the Native Americans spoke English because of the trades they'd made back and forth. But there were typically only a few who did. It wasn't something widespread throughout the tribe.

A bronze-skinned man, directly ahead of him stepped out of the circular formation, advancing toward Sam, his arms righteously crossed against his chest. His feet thudded loudly against the ground. Sam's eyes shuddered momentarily as the man neared him. Sounds, colors, and at times, even people's heart beats still astounded him, overstimulating his heightened senses. He wondered when that feeling would wear off, if it ever would.

"What deal do you speak of?" The man's voice was strong, as strong as his beating heart that struck a thirst inside of Sam. He swallowed hard before speaking, doing his best to drown out the beating hearts around him.

"Me and my brothers ain't neva had no party before. I wanna have 'em one, up there at the house."

Sam turned around, tossing his head over his shoulder and in the direction of their home. The Native Americans looked through the trees, assessing the house.

"This has what, to do with my people?" The bronze man spoke, golden bangles shook from his wrists as questioned Sam.

"Not a thang. I was hopin', seein' as how we both colored by my book, you might be willin' to help me out."

The Cherokees closed ranks, inching closer to Sam. Fear, he should have felt was not there. Though Sam didn't want to hurt anyone, he would if necessary. He only hoped they wouldn't try anything.

"Colored?" The bronze man's brow furrowed. He was unsure of whether or not to feel slighted. Given the opportunity, he could re-enslave Sam and his brothers, and sell them for a pretty penny. Yet, he also knew that there was something different about the brothers. He'd felt it from a distance, making sure to keep his people at a safe distance. A war wasn't something he wanted. A fight, where he might lose too many of his own people, certainly wasn't something he wanted.

"Of brown-skin nature. Yes-suh," Sam spoke, looking directly into the man's eyes. "And in the future, if you be needin' us to… help ya in anyway, we'd be happy to oblige," Sam spoke honestly. He recognized that though they shared similar melanations, they would not help him on the strength of the both of them being colored. He'd have to offer the one thing the Native Americans were also fighting to get—protection. The palm-skinned giants were taking everything from everyone. They needed to join forces and help one another.

The bronze-skinned man smirked. He liked Sam's directness. He also liked his proposition. He'd had the unfortunate task of doing business with the white man. He'd wanted to make things easier for his people, on the land they helped craft. To share, hopefully meant peace, but it seemed to have meant anything, but. His people were still going missing in the night. Women were being raped. Children were being murdered. The resources were becoming harder to find.

He knew that with Sam's help, he could do something. His ancestors had given him warning to stay away, because a monster lurked within him and his brothers. The bronze-skinned man recognized the monster. He could sense it, feel it, even now, within Sam. Yet, they had been nothing but polite, stayed out of their way, and he'd had no trouble out of them. It was the palm-skins they struggled with.

"A deal is a deal," the man agreed, and Sam smiled harder. He'd never given his brother a birthday party before. He'd never attended one, but tonight, for the very first time, Taj would have one, and it would be the first of many gifts to give to his brothers.

Sam reached his hand out to the bronze-skinned man and introduced himself. "Sam," he stated plainly, waiting for the man to take his hand. Rather than give it a shake, the man gripped his arm in response. "Ahuli," he introduced himself, a smile covering his lips, and the two began planning a night that none of the Brown brothers would ever forget.

Hours later, Sam had his brothers preparing for Taj's party. Though excitement hung in the air, nerves swirled in the same capacity. None of them was exactly sure of what to expect.

"And how you know they ain't gon' betray us?" Taj asked, looking himself over in the mirror. He'd compelled them an entire wardrobe—the only thing he'd been able to use his gift for on a wide scale. The three of them were dressed to impress. Because it was Taj's birthday, he'd opted for a scarlet petticoat, a matching scarlet waistcoat, paired with velvet black trousers and long black stockings. Sam, never one to purposely outdo his brothers, chose a black petticoat, with a round-collared black and gold embroidered waistcoat. His pants, were chocolate, and lined with black and gold embroidered flower petals.

Standing behind Taj, Sam placed his hands on the back of his brothers shoulders, squeezing lightly. "We don't, but I ain't got no reason to thank they would. They'll be as dumb as a donkey to go 'gainst us," Sam established and clapped his brother on the back. "Tonight's all 'bout you. Just enjoy it. Now, where's Mani?"

Sam left Taj standing in front of the mirror, obsessing over his attire. He was the reason they had the new attire. He remembered compelling the tailor, who had just received a shipment of imported textiles from England, to give him and his brothers all new ensembles, fit just for them, and their personalities. Thomison had done well making sure the boys were fresh and properly dressed.

Taj, though, hadn't thought what he'd feel like in these new clothes. A part of him felt like he was betraying his people, betraying himself even by wearing the clothes of a white man, but he deserved nice things. He deserved to feel this sense of worthiness, of belonging. He wondered if this was the armor of a white man. Privilege, thrill. In his clothes, they were like a costume, a mask.to hide the monster within. To hide the black man within.

He'd thought several times of ripping his clothes from his muscular body. In shreds he'd scatter them across their ridiculously large home, but when he saw Mani entering the room, with his head down, Taj knew he had to exude confidence. There couldn't have been a worse time than now, for him to suffer through his own personal existential crisis when it was clear his younger brother was struggling with his own crisis.

Mani had been suffering the hardest with their transition. While he enjoyed being strong, and he hardly felt fear anymore, he often felt unsure of himself. Like he was only pretending to be strong. Mani hadn't discovered his gift yet, and he was beginning to believe he didn't have one. He would forever be the left-behind and forgotten about little brother, in his eyes.

Yet, he had no idea how Taj and Sam truly viewed him. He was a burden, but no more than any other sibling. They loved him, and taking care of him was an honor, a privilege. To have one another, to risk it all for one another; it would be their saving grace. And though Taj didn't quite feel like celebrating in his new clothes, when he saw his brother, his suave and debonair little brother, it became abundantly clear to him just how much he needed to encourage him and cheer him on.

"Them rags sho' do turn to riches," Taj teased his brother. Mani's hands sweat in the pockets of his trousers, his eyes holding a staring contest with the ground.

"Eh... I done my best," Mani smirked, slowly dragging his eyes from the hardwood floor over to his brother. When his eyes met Taj's, he was instantly stunned by how nice his brother looked. If only he felt the same way about himself.

"You done better than your best. Tell 'em, Sam." Taj placed his hands in his pockets and leaned against the mantle above the fireplace.

Sam entered the room, looking at both of his brothers. How handsome they were. Pride swelled in his chest. He wished he could have painted a picture of them. But he wouldn't need one—this moment would be forever etched in his mind for all time. It would be impossible for him to forget what he was witnessing.

Back excellence.

"You both look good. Even your hair look good pulled back like that," Sam pointed out, referring to Mani's thick and course hair, that he'd pulled into a low ponytail that brushed the top of his coat collar.

Mani's darkened cheeks turned a rose color, and he smiled. Of the three, Mani's smile could change the air in the room. It brightened even the darkest of days. Sam knew Mani questioned if he'd received a gift of sorts. Sam couldn't put his finger on one just yet, but if he had to guess, he would have thought it was his innate ability to make people feel better. He just knew how to make people feel good.

"Let's get goin'." Sam's ears were tingling. He was drawn to the sound of drums deep in the forest. "They're ready for us," Sam grinned and opened the door to the quiet home they shared.

Mani looked over at Taj, who was also smiling, and together, the brothers left the house, heading into the forest.

As they approached the Cherokee's land, there were lights staked into the ground, leading them down a path, where the sound of drums and piccolo flutes could be heard. At the end of the aisle of lights was a large teepee, the length of four teepees, connected to one another, made of bison hides and wooden poles. There were several Cherokee women, besmeared in red and white paints on their faces, and across their chests. Wearing nothing more than long cloth joined at the waist to cover their nether regions. Their shirts, an animal's hide, wrapped and crossed around their necks.

Taj nearly growled. He had not been this close to a woman of color in so long, his britches nearly suffocated his growing erection.

As the men got closer, the women smiled, waiting to greet them.

"Evenin'," Taj was the first to speak, the most eager to join the party. The Cherokee women spoke little to no English, but they understood most phrases. Each woman took turns bowing their heads. When they'd greeted each of the men, the door to the teepee opened, and two of the women stepped to the side to help usher them in.

"Afta' you," Sam leaned in and whispered to Taj. Smoothly, he took several steps toward the teepee, dipping his head low to enter through the door. As he did, he scented one of the Cherokee women. His stomach twisted into knots with desire, hunger. He had not had a drop of blood since the day before, and though he could survive on blood and human food, he would always have a deep hankering for blood.

Mani and Sam followed after him. Mani made eyes with one of the Cherokee women. She was just as young, just as shy, and though neither of the two could communicate verbally, their eyes said everything their mouths couldn't.

He's handsome.

She's gorgeous.

I want her-

I want him…

Sam, on the other hand, would not be interested in any woman for quite some time. Knowing that he would live for at least another two centuries, he was in no hurry to find someone to spend his time with. Besides, the women he'd encountered in this time period had all been sexual deviants, eager to get married and settle down. He felt he had nothing, just yet, to offer a bride, a woman of any stature, and he wouldn't search for a woman until he did.

However, that would not stop him from having some kind of fun tonight. Upon entering the teepee, there were wooden tables lined up and a great feast for Taj's birthday lined up. Roasted chicken, vegetables, grilled rabbit, and plenty of ale to go around.

Around the table, there were several white women and men sitting at the tables. None of who could be recognized, but they were nonetheless in attendance.

Sam, Taj, and Mani stilled. Sam thought he had enough discernment to know if he was being tricked or not. He hadn't believed he would be. Yet, with these white people sitting around the table, he couldn't help but wonder if he had been foolish.

Ahuli appeared from a dark corner in the back, a friendly smile and open arms greeted the brothers. "Do not fear—they are friends," Ahuli quickly defended the pale faces to Sam, whose squinted eyes told Ahuli everything he needed to know. If he did not receive an explanation, a strong enough explanation for why they were here, he and his brothers would tear the party to pieces in a matter of minutes.

Ahuli held up his hands, several warriors gathered around the brothers. "Please, we only wanted to make the party special. Sarah, Stephen, James, Hannah, and Katherine are family. Katherine is to be my bride. These are her siblings." Ahuli opened his hand, pointing to each as he spoke their names.

Sam was the most surprised. He hadn't seen any white people here before. When he'd looked down into the forest weekly, he'd only seen the Cherokee. He couldn't understand why Ahuli hadn't mentioned this earlier in the day when they'd spoken. Were they not just as traumatized by white people as they were? Sam didn't understand.

"I see the look in your eyes. Falling for Katherine is an accident. I would not have even met her if—"

"If it weren't for my cousin, Angellica. She has been known to be a bit… free-spirited," Katherine finished Ahuli's sentence, and Sam stiffened in his stance.

"Angellica Whitten?" he questioned, wondering how much of a coincidence it would be if their Angellica was the same as the one he knew.

"The one and only. We were coming to visit her, and she took us off into the slave quarters. We don't see a lot of slaves where we're from. Papa says it's downright wrong how they treat y'all..."

Katherine dragged her story out in a contradictory southern drawl. She'd seen black people as pets almost, not as an enslaved people. At least, not until she saw the living conditions. Until her suspicions and the rumors had rang true to her eyes. It was from there, Katherine wanted to know more. She often snuck out on her own, leaving her siblings to wander after her and hopefully find her before something bad happened.

"But something bad did happen to me. I came across a Native American tribe further up the river. They were going to...." She swallowed down her tears. Sam was not amused, nor did he feel sympathy for the woman before him, although he had been known to be the most compassionate. He didn't feel the sincerity in her story. He didn't feel like she was in love with Ahuli. He believed she was like Angellica—amazed by the circumstances and situation. But she could go along to get along. This would not last.

Ahuli came to Katherine's side, holding onto her by the waist. He doted on her, pulling her close for comfort. "Well, they were going to do unspeakable things to me. Angellica came after me, thank God. She used the name and word of her husband to save me. Anyway, on the way back, Ahuli and his tribe members found us. Angellica was about to give birth, and she couldn't very well give birth in the middle of the forest. I thought.

"Until she did, with the help of Ahuli and his wise medicine women."

Taj, Sam, and Mani were stunned by this elaborate story. Neither of them could have fathomed that something so horrific could occur, and that their paths would all cross again, especially not in this way. Sam often thought about Angellica in a platonic way. He wondered if she survived that fateful night. He wondered if she had her child. If the baby came out as brown as he'd imagined it would. Considering they were sequestered, and purposely stayed away from the plantation, he would have no one to ask. No way of finding out. Until now.

"And the baby?" Sam curiously inquired, wondering what came of the child, or of his skin, should he say.

"As dark is night. She never went back to Witten of course, for obvious reasons. As I heard it, she's gone up to north Tennessee to stay with some of our other family members. Last I heard, she and the child were doing just fine." Katherine tapped Ahuli's arm like she'd just told a joke, laughter following the end of her sentence. It was a relief to find out that Angellica and her child were doing well, but in a world like they lived in, there was no telling what kind of life the child or Angellica would have.

"Well, sound like everythin' worked out fa' the best," Sam said, and he and his brothers took a seat around the table. If for nothing else but for Taj, Sam would put on a brave and happy face. He'd gone through a lot of trouble, after all, to make sure that Taj had a great birthday. He didn't want to spoil it now.

And if his brothers senses weren't tingling, he figured he should chalk it up to being overprotective.

With a nod of approval from Ahuli, the brothers relaxed, began drinking, and started to enjoy the night.

CHAPTER 10

2017

While Amionette showered and changed into a clean outfit, Yuzuri made tea. Pressing the issue of what happened with Amionette and Fletcher blared in her mind like sirens on a firetruck, but she knew better than to pry. Rather than do so, she would stick to what she said she would do. Help her run her errands.

Yuzuri lived almost 30 minutes away from the funeral home, which meant she lived the same amount away from Fletcher. In Antioch, Tn, Yuzuri was close enough to Nashville that she could easily get there, but far enough away, that unless someone knew where to look, they wouldn't want to come out to that part of town. Though, everything Amionette needed, as far as a bank and perhaps some clothes, they could certainly find on that side of town.

When Amionette stepped out of the shower, though her body felt renewed, her spirit was broken. Her thoughts raced, and though she had Zuri's help, she didn't want to be too much of a hassle. Especially since their friendship was extremely new. The last thing she wanted to do was upset her friend by being too needy. That was the exact reason she needed to get by herself and handle her business. Depending on others had brought her nothing but upset and descension. Fletcher was one of the few people she'd allowed herself to depend on, and it turned out to be the biggest mistake of her life.

She was thankful that her wig hadn't taken on any of the damage that her body had, even though there was no visible evidence of the trauma. Amionette would carry what happened with her for the rest of her life. If she was lucky enough to even make it to the next day.

As Amionette exited Zuri's bedroom, her gaze was drawn to the walls once more. She wished that she had a picture of her mother to hang on her walls in any home she'd ever know. But, with all of the moving around she did, and her inconsistent behaviors, she was never around long enough to get a good photo. The last picture she saw of her mother was the one she had for her obituary—her mother had chosen her own photo and had all of her affairs in order. When Amionette came home for her mother's funeral, there was nothing for her to do but show up, and of course, take care of the family business.

Which she'd done with style and grace.

From the kitchen, Zuri heard Amionette's footsteps and greeted her in the hallway with a special edition teacup from the classic movie "Beauty and the Beast." Amionette stifled a smile, surprised to see something so uniquely charming in the hands of Zuri, though she shouldn't have been shocked at all. There was something special about Zuri, a light inside of her that made Amionette feel like she could trust her. She wondered what Zuri's upbringing must have been like for her to be so kind, so... easy going.

Zuri reached the cup out to Amionette, who reluctantly took it. A glance down gave way to a blue-ish, almost purple tinted liquid in the cup.

"This Fabuloso?" Amionette questioned, her brows furrowed.

Zuri's hand shot up to her mouth. "Absolutely not. It's butterfly tea, with a few other things. I like to call it dragonfly tea. Drink it, it's good," Zuri urged. Normally, if someone were trying to give Amionette something, she would have turned it down, feigning a poisoned item or something she shouldn't have, but coming from Zuri, in her cute little Beauty and the Beast cup, she couldn't tell her now.

Amionette tilted the cup slightly to her lip. The steam from the warm cup tickled her face, but it was not off putting. A drop of the liquid touched her top lip, and Amionette nearly moaned. She'd never had tea that tasted so good. It was the perfect mixture of sweet and sour, and it had a certain soothing effect that she'd never experienced, not even with herbal tea when she was sick.

"That's some good ass tea," Amionette chuckled, and Zuri nodded her head, knowing about her mean brewing skills. She'd learned from her own mother, who'd been taught by her grandmother. It was a long line of passed down recipes.

"That's what I know." Zuri winked, and placed a gentle hand on the back of Amionette's arm and led her to the long sectional couch in the living room. The moment

Amionette set down on the plush couch, her body began forming to the cushions. She could have fallen asleep right there the way the fabric melded to her body, but Amionette felt eager to finish the considerate cup of tea Zuri made for her.

Amionette took a few more sips of her tea before placing her cup down onto the Dregan Coffee table, that lit in the center with a light blue light. Amionette could see how having something like that could come in handy, especially in the dark.

"So, you said you had errands?" Zuri mentioned, and Amionette nodded her head. She had a list of things she needed to do, but her mind suddenly didn't seem to be running a special race of its own. She was calm enough that she now had a sharp perspective of what she should be doing.

"Yeah, I need to go to the bank. Then I need to go to the phone store," she said, a new realization popping into her mind. She'd left her phone at home, but she wasn't going to be returning to get it. Instead, she'd start anew—a new phone, a new number, maybe even a new cell service.

"Okay, we can make that happen. Then we can go and pick you up some clothes from the store. Although, you're more than welcome to borrow more clothes from my closet," Zuri excitedly offered. She'd thought about things she'd do with a best friend if she ever got one. Sharing clothes when the other needed something to wear, or desperately wanted to borrow an outfit from the other. She figured this situation didn't fall short of her hopes and expectations.

"I would rather have some things more my style," Amionette spoke honestly. When she noticed disappointment creeping onto Zuri's face, she quickly remedied her statement by saying, "But I'm so thankful for these clothes you let me borrow, and once we get new clothes, I'll still need to wash them before putting them on, so I'll probably need another outfit or two before I—"

"Absolutely!" Zuri almost jumped up from her seat. She was so happy to be of help, and though she didn't have the courage, quite yet, to tell Amionette why it was important for her to give her something to wear, she hoped one day they would be close enough to do so.

"Good. So, if you don't mind giving me a ride. After we go to get me a new phone, I need to look at the schedule for arrangements coming up. I think I need to get away for a few days…" Amionette pondered. She simply needed a break to gather her life. She hadn't thought about running away again. No, she was tired of that.

Especially now more than ever. With the secret that had just come to light in her mind, when she found herself dying in a construction zone, it became abundantly clear to Amionette that leaving was the last thing she needed to do. No, she needed to stay and reveal a secret that she didn't even know she was keeping. A secret she thought must have been a lie before. A rumor could still be a lie, if it couldn't be proven, right?

"I'll give you a ride wherever. Let's head over to the bank before it gets busy with people. The construction workers should just be getting to work, and that side of the street will be running a little slower," Zuri reminded

Amionette, and she nodded in agreement. The sight of blood turning the mud a deep red crossed her mind. She could only hope the construction workers thought nothing of it. The last thing she needed was a scandal on her hands. And if the ground was tested, it would come out that, that was her blood staining the dirt. There wouldn't be a story great enough for her to explain the blood, and how there was so much, and yet, she didn't have the marks on her body to prove it.

Zuri and Amionette headed to Zuri's lavender and cream Mini Cooper S, Zuri extending her key fob toward the driver's side door to unlock the car, and they both slid into the front seat, ready to see to the day ahead. Zuri turned over the ignition, and her phone automatically connected to the Bluetooth in the car.

"President Howard is set to honor the end of slavery, January 1st, 2018, which is in just under a month's time. With the turn of the recent heat spike in weather, the event is scheduled to be outside and open to the public in the capital of Nashville, Tn. President Howard…"

Zuri turned down the radio and looked over at Amionette, whose eyes were set out of the window. Hoping to make conversation, Zuri started speaking about the excitement nearing, with the End of Slavery celebration in their town.

"Can you believe it's been 200 years since slavery ended?" Zuri's face lit up. She loved history, and the story of how it ended always intrigued her. She highly doubted that it was as simple as the historians had made it sound.

"Back then, they couldn't even fathom a black president. Now, we've had like six—"

"Seven, if you count Humphreys," Amionette corrected. She didn't count him, though, because she felt he had speculative heritage and he sided with the white community entirely too much.

Amionette's attention was drawn back to the car, but this wasn't the conversation she wanted to have. To Amionette's understanding, slavery had been brought to a halt when President Monroe had a compelling conversation with three slaves, who changed his entire outlook on the world, and it was because of his new outlook, that black people now had rights they weren't previously given. It was the reason that there was a mix of president types—Asian, White, but more predominately since 1818, blacks.

That one conversation helped to reshape the world. What she would have done to be a fly on the wall for that conversation. Beyond the end of slavery and how their world had forever been reshaped by it, slavery brought up uncomfortable feelings for Amionette. For her family, even, because it was during slavery that one of her ancestors made a grievous mistake, that Amionette often wondered if it shaped the reason she was a runner. Why, when things became overwhelming for her, she'd rather take off.

It was... a curse almost, one that she felt was rooted deeply in slavery, in her ancestor's mistake, that she passed down, generation to generation. Her mother was the only one who somewhat managed to not let the curse weigh her down. Who hadn't let it completely affect her, though she'd seen her mother run proverbially, while she was more of a physical runner.

Though the reasons she ran were very similar to her mother's, and her grandmother's. None of the women in her family seemed to have any luck in the love department, the life department, or any department, for that matter. The only thing they seemed to be able to hang onto was money. And what was all the money in the world without someone to spend it on or with?

"I don't think much about slavery, even when they broadcast it all over the internet and the radio. We live in a different world now, where black people are equal, and at times, seen as a bit more superior. We're the precedence. Whether that was because of slavery or not, I cannot say. I try to live in the now. In the present," Amionette stated proudly, only being halfway truthful.

She did often live in the present moment, but she did think about slavery, often, almost everyday. She couldn't help but wonder more about the truth about her ancestor during that time. She wished she knew someone from that time period, or knew of records that could be accessed to tell her more about her family history, other than finding out the women from her family had to survive the best they could.

Amionette was done surviving—she wanted to live. For whatever reason, she'd been given another chance, and rather than waste it, she wanted to look forward—not just at the present, but to the future.

"That's... noble I suppose. I plan to go right down to the capital. They'll have lots of artifacts, and things to see from that time period. I heard they'll be unlocking the vault and showing items from that period that were never before seen."

Zuri wafted her hand through the air, like she was painting an invisible line for the "never before seen" items that would be laid out. Amionette didn't want to, but she smiled. Zuri seemed so passionate about it. Amionette didn't have anything in her life like that, that she felt passionate about. Something that she could speak with so much conviction about that it made others excited at the thought.

"If you're still around, I'd love to take you with me. We can be present in that moment together," Zuri suggested. Normally, when invited anywhere by someone who wasn't Fletcher, Amionette found herself saying no. But, Zuri made her intentions clear for her and Amionette. She'd made it clear that they were forming a friendship, and she figured they couldn't do that if she wasn't willing to make compromises.

"I guess we can start thinking about it. But first, we'll have to get through the excitement of Christmas," Amionette huffed. It was her least favorite time of the year. Christmas, for whatever reason, hadn't felt like Christmas for quite some time. At least not for her. Even though, there were several houses in town that were perfectly decorated with snowmen in the front yard, enough Christmas lights to light up the entire town, and Christmas shoppers would be going wild soon, between the loss of her mother, the weather that was almost 80 degrees, and the fact that she'd been separated from society, living in a developing neighborhood and could see none of those things for miles… Amionette felt completely segregated from the Christmas holiday.

"Not big on Christmas?" Zuri queried as they exited her subdivision. Zuri wondered where Amionette went during Christmas break or how she celebrated, but never pushed the issue because they'd never had so much "outside of work" conversation than they were having now. Zuri could feel Amionette's emotional exhaustion from the driver's seat, and she wondered if it came from work or from her personal life.

Zuri loved Christmas. She often went home to celebrate with her family. It was the experience, the time of Christmas she loved. Not so much the holiday itself.

"I'd rather be doing anything else," Amionette said honestly, not realizing she would potentially offend Zuri.

Zuri had forced herself to believe that Amionette was just the kind of person who didn't enjoy human interaction, or that she was too busy to mingle. Perhaps she already had her own set of friends. She was now beginning to understand that Amionette was jaded, more than likely due to a traumatic past. She wasn't unfriendly, nor was she someone who would truly rather be to herself. It probably seemed better for her survival.

"Well," Zuri began her proposition, "rather than spend it alone, or doing anything else, you're more than welcome to celebrate with my family and me. We don't have a huge celebration, but we do take pride in spending time together. Something I think you would like."

Zuri presented an alternative to being alone. Without

Fletcher, Zuri was now positive she'd have no one to celebrate with. Though Zuri had never spent a holiday alone, she understood how lonely the holidays could be without family or without people who seemingly cared about you.

If it was the last thing Zuri did, she would make sure Amionette knew that she was cared for and even loved. That even outside of work, she was someone that deserved time and attention—happiness and friendship.

"I'll think about it," Amionette responded. She surprised herself at how optimistic she sounded.

Zuri nodded her head and switched to her Apple Music app on her phone. The popular song "Loyalty" by Kendrick Lamar filled Zuri's Mini Coop as the two made their way to the bank. Amionette turned up the volume, unearthing a hidden talent of hers as she began harmonizing the lyrics. Zuri nearly wrecked the car listening to Amionette sing.

She slammed on the brakes in just enough time for them not to hit the bumper of the car in front of them.

"Bitch," Amionette laughed. There was something about the dramatic stopping of the car that made her giggle, though she wasn't exactly sure if it was the car or Zuri's jaw hanging.

"I'm sorry, I think you might have chosen the wrong career. Why the hell are you taking care of dead people instead of making a career of singing!"

Amionette shook her head. She knew she had a talent for singing, but she lacked passion, the desire to want to make anything of it. Besides that, she always knew if she blew up for singing, in the event she wanted to change her life and do anything else, she wouldn't be able to. She'd always be in the limelight, and she would never be able to disappear when she was ready to do so.

She'd seen, in recent years, how more and more female artists were struggling, openly, with their mental health and how the world clowned them for it. There was no way she could survive something like that, and she wouldn't make it possible for anyone else to make her life any harder than it had to be.

"I'm not really into that sort of thing. It's a hobby—"

"A talent… it's okay to say talent," Zuri corrected as traffic began moving again.

"Fine," Amionette dipped her head in agreement, "a talent that I'm okay with keeping hidden. I've actually never sang in front of anyone else before," Amionette realized, but then she was reminded of her first-grade choir recital that ended in her peeing on herself from the nervous breakdown she had on stage.

Perhaps it was fear that kept her from singing? She didn't know, nor did she give herself time to think about it. That was her super power—never dwelling on something too long. That way she could protect herself from getting hurt. She didn't realize, though, she was doing the opposite.

She was making deposits into her "I'll worry about it later" vault, not realizing that eventually, her vault would become full, and it would all have to spill out. Whether she was ready for it to, or not.

"You just sang in front of me, and I loved it. I hope you'll sing at my wedding," Zuri snickered, and

Amionette's forehead wrinkled. She'd never known for Zuri to have a man of any type around her. She'd never mentioned having a boyfriend or fiancé. At least Amionette didn't believe her to have mentioned such. A twinge of guilt rang through her body. She felt horrified at the thought that Zuri had divulged personal information to her that she either didn't listen to, or had forgotten.

Zuri slapped her hand on top of Amionette's, and a laugh rang through the car. "I haven't met him yet, of course, but I have the damndest feeling, that my soulmate... meeting him is just around the corner," Zuri prophesied.

Amionette loved how sure she was of herself, and what her future might hold. Though Amionette had not been so lucky in the relationship area, hearing Zuri's assurance almost made her forget about how the man she'd thought to be her soulmate turned out to be a serial murderer... almost.

"Well, in the event you find yourself on the other end of that arrangement, I would be happy to sing for you," Amionette found herself saying, and it was an honest truth.

Unknowingly, Zuri was breaking down walls within Amionette that she'd put up as a teenager, and now as a grown woman, the walls she hopelessly fought to keep in tact were falling like the walls of Jericho.

"I'll hold you to it." Zuri double tapped Amionette's leg as they pulled into the parking lot of the bank. Amionette hesitated to get out of the car. Her original plan was to come and withdraw some money and get out of town, but now she felt drawn to a different purpose. To do something else.

Zuri's hand was readily placed on her doorhandle, ready to step out, but she couldn't help but notice the apprehension in Amionette's movement. "Everything okay?"

Amionette thought about it, and for once, in a very real way, everything was okay. She figured confiding in Zuri might help her make her decisions, rather than avoiding talking to someone. She needed advice, but more importantly she needed a guarantee that she was making the right decision.

"I need to tell you something," Amionette spat out.

"Okay," Zuri said, a comforting warmth thick in her voice. "Anything," she reiterated, and though Amionette knew whatever she was going to say, however she was going to say it, was going to sound crazy to anyone who hadn't experienced it.

But aside from the vampire saving her life, the rest would just sound like a Lifetime movie. Mentioning the vampire would mean that Amionette trusted Zuri in a way that even she didn't think she could trust someone.

Would she tell her? Would she tell the deepest part of this secret to Zuri?

As she leaned in and began retelling the events of the last day, the question hung in the air like a very uncomfortable fog clouding her judgement.

CHAPTER II

1760

Taj's party had been a success, and he and his brothers were as drunk as drunk could be. It had taken many bottle of ale and wine to get them there, but the Brown brothers were inebriated beyond their wildest dreams.

To celebrate his birthday, Taj was in the corner with a beautiful Cherokee woman named Catori. She'd seductively whispered into Taj's ear that her name meant "beyond words" and he could see how fitting that name was for her. She was gorgeous, with hair nearly to her feet, braided into three stitched braids, slanted, deep brown eyes that made him feel as if he were swimming in an abyss, and a set of lips shaped into the perfect cupid's bow. She looked so good, Taj could eat her, if he were hungry.

Now, in his drunken state, the only thing he wanted to do was feel the inside of her. Taj ran his finger along her bottom lip. Under the shadows of the teepee, no one could see them. They were well out of the way, and any prying eyes would have to strain themselves to see one another.

"I know what you are." Catori's voice was but a whisper as Taj's thumb spread across her lip.

"And what that be?" he retorted, wondering if she'd

really known. Sam said that the Cherokee might have suspicions of what they were, but they'd never done anything to show them any real proof of what they could do. It would all just be rumor and hearsay.

"Child of Jumlin," she eerily vocalized. Jumlin was the father of vampires, at least that's what the Cherokee believed. Though they had never seen Jumlin, nor had they come across any of his offspring before, whispers of him being the first vampire throughout their tribes was something to be taken seriously. And when the Native Americans found that the colored men living alone, in an abandoned mansion, hardly came out of their home for food, to mingle, or for anything else, they grew suspicious.

Their clothes, at night, were stained in blood, along with their mocha lips. Catori kept watch at night, for intruders or outsiders, or anyone and anything that meant them harm. She was a beast with a bow and arrow, and since trading with the unmelanated, she'd learned how to aim and shoot a gun properly.

She, along with several others, had seen the Brown brothers. They were thankful that they were not targets, meals, nor on the other side or at risk of turning.

"Chile of Jumlin?" Taj asked, cocking his neck to the side, waiting for her to give an explanation.

"Those who are not Cherokee call them vam-pire," she broke the word into syllables for emphasis, her lips separated, giving Taj a full view of her very wet tongue. Her eyes searched his, wondering if he was a vicious killer, if he would attack her. She was surrounded by family and had a knife just in the top of her boot if he tried anything.

Though, she wasn't sure if the knife would do anything to a child of Jumlin.

Taj heard the steadiness of her heart. She didn't seem afraid, which turned him on even more. The husky smell of musk and arousal infiltrated his senses, driving him temporarily mad. Taj had only been with a few women, but none since he'd become a vampire, and he'd been—quite literally—dying to sink his teeth into a woman and make love to her.

"And you ain't afraid?" He leaned in, his lips nearing her neck. A protruding vein caught his attention, and he licked the length of it, from the nape of her neck to her jawline. She shuddered, anticipating... a bite... a kiss... another lick. She could not be sure.

"Tla," she spoke, the Cherokee word for no, and smiled.

Taj liked that. He only wanted to inspire fear in those who meant him and his family hard—mainly white people. He had no quarrels with the Native Americans, especially not Catori.

"And if I bite ya?" his thick, dark eyebrows tugged inward with inquisition, and she puffed her chest out, a welcome invitation.

"Do it," she whispered, and Taj's senses came alive.

He ran his hands underneath the flap of her cloth, that just barely covered her throbbing center. She inhaled a deep breath, the touch of his warm fingertips tickled her inner thigh as they traveled up to her awaiting wetness.

He separated her vaginal lips just enough to reach her swollen clit. With his middle finger, he carefully flicked it back and forth. She became wetter and wetter with each flicker of his finger. Catori's head leaned backwards, her ajar lips begging Taj for more clitoral stimulation. Taj got closer to her, placing his legs between hers to open them up farther. With her legs completely spread, he had much more access to her pulsing button.

Catori moaned for him, her hips grinding toward his finger as he continued fondling her nether region. She placed her hands on his shoulders as her legs became wobbly. She had no idea a man could make her feel this type of pleasure from just using his finger.

The farther back her head went, the more prominent the vein in her neck became, and Taj refused to ignore the need to sink his fangs into her. They stung at the thought of not biting her. Taj slanted his neck, moving forward and toward the juicy vein. Her breath caught as Taj drug his fangs up her neck. The anticipation of being bitten made Catori's thighs clench. She'd wondered if it would hurt, and if so, to what extent? Would her mind be changed what she was bitten? Would she—

Catori's worries were quelled the moment Taj's fangs broke her skin. His plush lips and tongue soft were pillows cushioning the stinging pleasure-pains she felt from Taj's gentle sucking. If she were going to die, it would be okay. She would go within the peaceful serenity of blood-sharing, something she would have never thought would feel so good or arouse her so much.

Catori raised her leg—Taj instinctively caught her leg, helping her to raise it. His pulls were slow, yet feverish, as his eyes glazed over to crimson, matching the shade of blood he was in-taking.

His finger was wet with Catori's love, an erection extending through his britches. "Mmm…" she moaned at the recognition of his thick penis pressing against her.

She reached her hand between them, heatedly freeing him from the confines of his pants.

Her heart began slowing, though she felt nothing but pure bliss. If he didn't stop soon, she would certainly die. Their most important rule was that they could not kill. And even though on his birthday he felt he should have been given a reprieve from that, just once, he chose to obey the rule.

Taj removed himself from Catori, breathlessly he stood before her, his pants now down to his ankles. Catori leaped into the air, and Taj caught her in his arms and pressed her back against the wall of the teepee. Her legs wrapped around his waist, and he angled his dick at her opening. Drenched in her own juice, she leaned forward, rocking her hips toward Taj, egging him on to take full advantage of her warm nectar.

Taj eased himself into Catori. She had the tightest walls he'd ever experienced, and had she not been so experienced, he would have thought she was a virgin.

"Oh my…" he fell short of saying God when his mind emptied and became full of visions of him thrashing Catori for everyone to see. Though they were covered in darkness, Catori's rising moans echoed against the hollow sticks of the teepee.

"More, more!" Catori demanded, and without caution,

Taj shoved his solid dick inside of her, leaving indents in her walls that would never leave from the digging he was doing into her.

Taj, using his vamp speed, flipped her to the ground and ripped off the cloth wrapped around her neck that shielded her breasts. Her titties bounced, her nipples hardened as they were freed. Taj's muscular and rippled body showed no signs of tiring any time soon, and the way Catori's areolas moved to their own tune made Taj hungry again. He clamped down around her nipple, pricking the tiniest of holes on the outside of her areola.

"MMMM…." Was the only sound Catori could make as she willingly became a blood bag for Taj's birthday.

While Taj and Catori were occupied inside the teepee, on the outside, Mani was nervously sitting beside Hannah, who was immediately enamored by Mani's kinky coarse hair. She wanted to stick her fingers in it and see how soft it was. His head reminded her of a pillow—equal parts tough, equal parts soft.

The two were sitting on the ground together, laughing and exchanging sibling stories, the one thing they seemed to both be able to bond over. Hannah was the youngest in the family, just like Mani, and she understood what it was like to never be taken seriously and to always be viewed as someone who was weaker, even if it were by accident.

Her kind blue eyes and her wide smile made him feel at ease amongst her. She was beautiful, nice, and she seemed to like conversing with him. Something he also enjoyed. She'd been a bit handsy, but nothing too inappropriate. She'd stroked his arm, a light pat on the back of the shoulder in between laughs. He'd considered her to be very... friendly.

"Once, Katherine threw all of my clothes over the balcony in the rain simply because I'd forgotten to return her favorite hairbrush. She can be a bit of a menace, you know?" Hannah laughed, and her giggly nature made Mani happy. He liked speaking with her. He liked that on a night where they were supposed to be celebrating, enjoying the night, they could actually do that, and no one had to hide. They didn't have to go inside early for the fear of being seen. They didn't have to creep out of the house late to find blood, or eat what they had at home, because Sam didn't want them overindulging. It was the perfect evening.

Silence fell between them, comfortable, befitting. It was a wonderful night, until the pleasant quiet turned into awkward discomfort. Hannah placed her hand on the center of Mani's britches, grabbing at his flaccid penis.

Mani moved away from her, only slightly. He didn't want to make it a big deal that she'd touched him. They had, in fact, been enjoying a nice evening together. Sam was wrapped up learning a new game called "Basket Play" which would later be named Dominoes, and Taj was too concerned about how he could drain himself while also draining Catori, to notice that Mani had snuck off with Hannah.

Hannah hadn't picked up on the hint that Mani didn't want her touching him in that way. That, or she just didn't care. She leaned in, this time with a smile, her hand grabbing for his penis again. This time, Mani politely grabbed her hand and shook his head. "No," he said, firmly enough for her to get that he wasn't joking, but not in a way that should have offended her.

Her facial expression changed, from a smile to a grimace as she examined his hand on her wrist. She snatched away from him and muttered something under her breath.

"What did you say?" he asked, noticing she'd spoken underneath her breath. He often did the same when he was saying something he was too much of a coward to say aloud to his brothers.

"I said, you must prefer the company of young men," she said, with a little more of an edge in her voice. Mani knew he didn't prefer the company of other men. He'd spent his life around other men. He would have loved to have found a nice girl to settle down with, but Hannah was a little too forward for him. He wanted someone who would move slowly with him. The most Mani had found himself doing was kissing a girl. He'd never been touched like that, and he knew without a shadow of a doubt that he wasn't ready to be, not yet.

And certainly not by a white woman. Under her gaze, he felt... fear. That doing anything with her outside of having a friendly conversation and maybe even a hug would be a deep betrayal. After all, it was the glances of Angellica that got them into this mess. For the fear of repeating the mistake, that hadn't been Sam's fault to begin with, Mani would not fall into the same trap.

"I like women. I just like 'em like me," Mani said in a

matter-of-fact way, to make sure there would be no confusion between the two of them.

"So, you're prejudice against someone with different skin? That's certainly rich comin' from someone of your kind," Hannah shot, and Mani's heart and pride became wounded. Something in him in that moment changed. The rhythm of her heart, the scent she gave off. She was afraid, but of what? What would she be afraid of while also talking so much shit, that she clearly had the upper hand.

"You afraid of somethin'... what is it?" Mani looked closer, narrowing his eyes on her. She looked away from him, but it was only for a moment. Mani clamped his hand slightly and pulled her face back around to him.

Her blue irises and pupils began to swirl, turning into a circular pool of liquid. Mani honed in on her eyes, and before his very eyes, Hannah's began showing images. Images of people he'd never seen before. There was a man standing before her. He was well-dressed in a brown and tan embroidered suit. He removed his hat and held it to his stomach as he approached Hannah. She had a smile so wide on her face, it could have broken her teeth if she would have moved another inch.

She reached out her arms to hug the man, and he took a step back, shielding himself and separating himself with his hat. He'd shook his head no, swatting Hannah's hands away from him.

Her baby blue eyes turned sad, tears filled them. He read her lips "What about the baby?"

"I... I can't be with you. My father chose another bride for me," the man had said.

The more Mani focused, he could swear he could hear the visuals as if they were playing out right in front of him.

"We can just run away. I love you," Hannah had said, and she reached up to touch his face. He leaned into her embrace for just a moment, just long enough to kiss the palm of her hand before looking away and saying, "I can't, Hannah. Goodbye."

Hannah stood there, watching the gentleman leave her behind. Her hands reluctantly moved down to her stomach. She gripped onto her slightly protruding belly. "But what about the baby?" Her voice became a whisper in the wind, and tears slid down her grief-stricken face. Mani understood then why she'd taken a cruel approach with her. Why she hurt so badly.

She feared being rejected. It had crippled her so gratefully that when Mani told her no, it turned her upside down. Mani could feel her pain. He wanted to fix it for her, though he knew he should not, even if he could. But, there was something inside of him that told him he could. That he could fix the fear inside of her.

When her eyes had finished swirling, Mani felt compelled to kiss her. To kiss away her pain. Tears streaked her pale cheeks, tears that Mani planned to relieve her of. Mani leaned over toward her, studying her face. She sniffled, doing her best to hold back more tears. She seemed none the wiser to what Mani saw. She didn't know that he'd seen just what she'd been through, nor did she know that he could feel what she felt in that moment and in this one.

Mani stretched his hand around the back of Hannah's

neck with care and pulled her to him. Her tears salted his lips the closer he got to her face. Mani placed his lips against hers, and they were both transported to a different vision. Their tongues twirled, and in the eye of their minds, they both began to see something beautiful.

Hannah was sitting on a long porch, rocking a beautiful baby girl in her arms. White rocking chairs decorated the length of the porch. The sound of wind chimes blowing in the wind comforted her and the baby. She sang a lullaby, unpeeling the wrapped blanket from around her baby to reveal the little girl's larger than life smile, that which matched her mother's.

A screen door opened, and a handsome gentleman, with a kind face and honest demeanor stepped onto the porch. He leaned down, placing a kiss on Hannah's cheek, and placing another to the baby's forehead.

"I love you, Hannah, and being married to you is everything I imagined it would be," the man had said, tears filling his eyes behind a pair of round spectacles. Hannah reached across the baby and up to take the man's hand, revealing a beautiful solitaire diamond ring inside of a gold setting. It sat up on her hand like the pyramids in Egypt, with a sharp point at the top.

The man took her hand and placed a loving kiss to each of her knuckles before the vision faded away.

Hannah blinked away tears as she looked over at Mani. "Did you see…" her words trailed off as Mani nodded his head. He had seen her past, and then he'd seen what he could only assume was her future, and not so distant in the future by the way she looked.

He had so many questions. He wanted to know about her past, more about where she came from. What happened to her baby that she clung so tightly to her stomach. Mani wanted to know more, but he didn't want to upset her further. Rather than intrude on her privacy any further than he already had, Mani simply gave her a hug.

Since becoming a vampire, he believed that he didn't have a gift, that he would just be a blood hungry demon for the rest of his life. Forever the brother who wasn't special, but he was wrong. He had the gift of sight, premonitions. He could see the past and the future. He had no idea how to turn it on and turn it off. Forever the eternal little brother, but he was wrong.

He had a gift, a very special gift, and together, the three of their gifts would aide them in fulfilling their destinies—separately and together.

CHAPTER 12

1918

Wars had been fought, lost, and won on American soil and in foreign territories, and the brothers were no closer to seeing their people be freed from the shackles of slavery. Sam had come to think that Jasper lied to him, that he'd given him false hope about what he and his brothers were supposed to do, about their future together. He'd told them that they would end slavery, that the three of them together would put an end to slavery, but almost a half a century later, they had no clues as to how they were supposed to do so.

Sam, Taj, and Mani had watched many humans grow old, and they were aging with grace. To be senior citizens, they still looked like they were in their mid 20's, and at the most, the earliest of their 30's.

The brothers were now living in Edgefield, just two short years after "the fire of the century." The coined time that destroyed nearly 650 homes, and because of this, the purchase value of real estate had never been lower. The Brown brothers had just moved into Edgefield. It was a much better time to be black, with over a century's worth of freedom and reorganizing the United States, the neighborhoods were much safer for black people to live in.

On the corner of Fatherland Street, the brothers had opened their hotel, Brown Hotel, where many famous artists, musicians, and regular folk alike were known to come to enjoy Nashville and all it had to offer. The Parthenon "the Athens of the south" drew people from miles away to visit, along with Centennial Park and Rock Castle. Nashville was bustling with people ready to explore the city. New people meant more people to hide their secret from. It had become more dangerous for the brothers to be out and about in the city after a certain time.

There had been mention of creatures of the night, who weren't as fortunate as they were, to walk amongst the day light. There were pale vampires who burned easily in the sun, to a crisp. The Brown brothers had, had a run in with them a time or two, and now, to get their vengeance, they were doing everything they could to take out their revenge on them.

Brown Hotel housed 100 rooms, room-service accessible, and everyone who worked for the hotel was friendly, kind-spirited, and would never dare say an untoward word to a guest. And though slavery had ended, and black people had many more opportunities than they had before, there were still those who felt unnerved by "niggers" running the country, running the world, and having anything to call their own.

Hatred is a learned trait, and racism was something easily passed down.

It was August, 1918. The Fisk Jubilee singers were

staying overnight at the hotel on their way to a singing engagement. They liked to treat themselves, and the Brown brothers loved their company. The singers had a way of bringing the whole city out to listen to them perform, and they often blessed the hotel with surprise performances when they stayed.

This evening would be no different.

And because the entertainment was open to the public, something the brothers would later regret and regulate, anyone could stroll into the hotel.

"I think tonight gon' be amazin'," Taj stated as he and his brothers came down the grand staircase in their fabulous hotel. Chandeliers hung above their heads, bell boys jumped from the front door to the receptionist desk to check guests in.

Sam looked over his shoulder, past his brothers, pride emanating from his very being. He and his brothers had accomplished so very much, he couldn't wait to see what was coming next for them.

"Evenin', Mr. Syncere, the night is young. What you boys up to?" Emilee, their receptionist asked. She was a young woman with skin the same color as vanilla ice cream, but she was a hard worker, always on time, and she was damn good at her job. They couldn't have asked for a better worker.

"Emilee, the night is young and so are you. You stickin' around for the Jubilee?"

Emilee gazed on as Sam got closer to her. He would always be Sam Brown, the slave, to himself, but to others, who knew and loved him and had come to know him, he would be Syncere Brown. Strong, powerful, wealthy black man of Nashville. Emilee's tongue slid across her bottom lip as she took Syncere in. He was gorgeous, and she'd flirted with him, harmlessly in the past. But he nipped that in the bud the moment he realized what she was doing.

"I think you're a beautiful woman," he'd told her. "But, I'm waitin' on an ebony queen. No disrespect to you or the way you were raised, Emilee."

Even though he was honest, he was polite, and even being rejected by him was sexy. She'd opted to just have a friendship with him. That seemed simple enough. He was a good guy to have by your side, and he made for good company.

"I'm gonna head out before the Jubilee starts cutting up. My daddy wants me home as soon as my shift is over tonight," Emilee told him honestly. Syncere admired the respect she had for her parents. At twenty-one, he appreciated how she was a family woman, and it wasn't uncommon for women and men alike to continue living with their families back then until they were married or had children. Sam had intended to live with his brothers for the rest of his life if he could. They'd always been close. Being separated, he couldn't imagine anything of the sort.

"You be safe now. When you get off, come get me or one of the boys. We'll be glad to get you a ride—"

"Syncere, Malicio, and Tyrian Brown. Sound like nigga names to me," a cold voice crept up behind the brothers.

Syncere was the first to turn around, his brothers not far behind him. "How can I help you... gentleman, tonight?" Syncere asked, eyeing the four gentlemen up and down. They were dressed to impress, bow ties as tight as jock straps around their necks, but they were laced in money—the new fad around town.

"Sound like Italian names to me, George," one of them said. Between his teeth was a gap as wide as the Cumberland River.

Syncere, nor his brothers, had ever seen any of the men around town. They wondered who they were, to be coming around them so casually, as though they knew one another.

"My brother asked y'all a question," Tyrian came forward, standing to the left of Syncere. If there was anyone who would snap first, ask questions never, it was him, and that, at times, had put them in bad positions.

"Oh, you think because y'all are somewhat civilized we gotta answer to you?" The one called George titled his head. Syncere knew right away from all the talking he was doing that he wasn't the leader. No, their leader was standing directly behind them, silent. He'd let the others do his dirty work for him.

"What I think is..." Tyrian began, but Syncere placed his hand in front of his brother's chest. He was the eldest, and as such, he would speak for them.

"What's your name," Syncere questioned, pointing his finger adorned in silver and opal ring toward the man in the back, in the center.

He smirked and took a few steps in front of the men he'd come in with. "My name is Clinton. Clinton Samuels. I've come to discuss business with you, Mr. Brown," he explained, and though his gesture seemed friendly enough, there was a deadness in his eyes, a coldness that would have made Syncere shudder if he too were not a bit dead himself.

"Office hours are between 9 a.m. and 5 p.m., Mr. Samuels. You're more than welcome to come back with you… business partners, and discuss it then," Syncere advised them, and Clinton didn't like hearing no. He'd come that night specifically for one reason, and one reason only.

"I don't think I've made myself very clear, and to show you how serious I am, let me show you how quickly I handle business. Emilee, dear?" he called out. Emilee's attention was immediately drawn to the man.

Robotically, she walked over to him, as if he'd commanded her to do so. She stood before Clinton, staring into his eyes. He leaned in to whisper something to her, and she nodded her head in agreement. Syncere, Tyrian, and Malicio were on guard in case trouble befell them this night. Something was off, and it was clear to each of them. Luckily, the guests were in the entertainment room, being serenaded by the live band before the Jubilee singers did their "surprise" live performance.

Emilee turned toward the brothers; there was no recognition in her eyes for them. It was almost as if they were strangers, though she'd just addressed Syncere only moments before.

Emilee reached into the pocket of her barrel line dress and retrieved a letter opener. In the blink of an eye, she'd stabbed it directly into her neck. Syncere, of course, was the first to rush to her before she could hit the ground.

Shock echoed through his body as he put his hands to her neck. In that moment, Emilee blinked back tears, and her memory restored. She saw Syncere, and fear covered her face. She was remembering what happened.

It became clear to the Brown brothers that these four fools were vampires. It was a condition that was becoming more and more common these days, but the Brown brothers weren't going around turning people. They didn't believe in it, and if they did, the last people they would have turned were white people.

There was something about having the power of everlasting life that not everyone could handle, and they were currently faced with that problem now.

"Why?" Malicio questioned, staring down at Emilee. They'd come to know and care for her. She was a part of the hotel, a very important part of the hotel. Syncere did not believe in saving people. He thought that when it was their time to die, God called him home. He and his brothers were special, they were different. They were meant to stop traumatic events before they occurred, or intercept them. They were the exception to the rule.

But Emilee, sweet Emilee. She did not deserve this fate. She didn't deserve to die, and he would not let her. Just as Syncere slit his wrist to feed her his blood several police officers, white police officers, invaded the place. They came in, billy clubs, pistols up, ready to take down the Brown Brothers, and now, they had the proof they needed.

The police had been watching the Brown brothers for some time now, waiting to get proof that they were vampires. Each and every time they were observed, they were able to go outside in the sunlight, a known clue that someone wasn't a vampire. The sun should have burned them. They were scene eating regular food. Why would a vampire need to eat such things? It wouldn't. They could never be caught.

What Syncere and his brothers didn't know, was that rather than the Ku Klux Klan parade around in white hoods and white robes, they did the exact opposite—they turned their members into vampires, so that they might have an everlasting bloodline of people to stop black people from being great. No matter how hard they tried, though, they could not stop them. The only reason Clinton Samuels knew about the Brown brothers was because of his own origin story.

He'd heard all about the men who single-handedly ended slavery with their "conversation" with President Monroe. He had gifts of his own that he'd been using to keep slavery going, along with the pawns he'd embedded directly in the government. Vampirism was an all-white society, before the Brown brothers. They were the first black vampires ever known. What Clinton didn't know was how they survived on food and blood. He'd sold his soul years ago for everything he wanted in the world, and so far, it had worked out. But the Brown brothers stood to gain too much power. Too much influence, and they were gaining entirely too much support from and within the white community.

They. Had. To. Be. Stopped.

And stopped them he did.

Malicio looked to the edges of the billy clubs. There

were wooden, pointed stakes at the end. The police knew they were vampires. Syncere reached out his hands to stop time. The police stood frozen before them, along with Emilee, who was in the process of healing before he'd frozen time. Syncere could only slow and freeze time for humans. Vampires could fight his gift.

The Brown brothers weren't afraid of a fight. They weren't afraid to die again either. They had already ended the greatest tragedy the United States had ever seen. Everything else was just a privilege, a gift they'd been fortunate enough to have. The gift of time.

However, Syncere didn't want to risk his brothers lives if he didn't have to. Clinton stared into Syncere's eyes. He felt he'd read him for filth in that moment. Pulled his number and dialed it twice. He knew that Syncere was a caring individual. It was the reason that he'd come into the hotel, and one-by-one, had compelled them to kill themselves unless Syncere turned himself in.

Syncere crouched, ready for battle, his slit wrist had already begun to heal.

Clinton grinned. There was nothing more that he would love than a big fight, except for the fact that he knew he would indeed die at the hands of a nigger, and that, he could not justify. It was why he had taken such severe measures, by compelling the police force, the humans in the hotel, and had come at just the right time.

"I wouldn't attack if I were you," Clinton warned. "You will have saved Emilee's life, but everyone else in this hotel will die." Clinton bore his fangs. They were much longer than the Brown brothers' fangs. Syncere wondered if there was any significance to that. Their fangs were small in comparison, not nearly as sharp. Syncere figured that was so that even if they were around other people, they could still blend in. These vampires looked like monsters. Real creeps.

Syncere stood in front of his brothers. His eyes had turned crimson from anguish and the fear of what might happen next. He had no reason to fear for himself, but the other humans in his hotel, whom he considered to be under his care. He cared a great deal about them. They were in his charge, and he didn't want to see anything happen to them.

"And why's that?" Syncere asked, his deep brown orbs squinted at Clinton as he waited for an answer.

"Everybody in your quaint little hotel has been compelled. They'll all start killin' themselves, one-by-one at 8 p.m. Including the police. The last thing, I think you'd need is to be blamed for the death of several officers of the law and other human casualties. That wouldn't be good for business. Not at all."

Malicio, with all the anger in the world understood the truth of Clinton's statement. He wanted nothing more than to figure out Clinton's future and show it to him. Or end whatever future he might have, but he knew recklessly jumping to murder would get them all killed.

Syncere looked to his wrist, checking the time. It was 7:54, just six minutes to the hour. He didn't know how long he could keep them frozen, though he would try his best to keep them in place. At least then, no one would be harmed.

"You can watch the time if you want, but not even stopping time will stop me. By my count, you only got about four minutes left."

Panic rose in Syncere's body. How was he going to save everyone from getting hurt? Were these humans more important than he and his brothers? No, he wouldn't think like that. He never had in the past. He didn't believe himself or his brothers to be "above" the humans. He'd risked everything for them, and now would be no different. They wouldn't be pawns in this game.

"So, what do you want? What was all of this for?" Syncere asked, his mind on the time.

"I want you out of here. I want you and your nigger brothers to pack up and leave town and never look back."

"That ain't gonna happen," Tyrian laughed, his crooked smile even more crooked now that he'd become furious.

"Oh, it will, because—"

"It won't, because if we leave town, we'll just go and come back stronger. We'd never let you have everything we worked for, you wicked cracker," Tyrian shot back, taking another step forward, prompting the other three vampires with Clinton to come forward.

"Mm... well then, I propose we work together. But, he goes," Clinton demanded, pointing his self-righteous finger at Syncere.

There was no way either of those options were going to work, and they were wasting time. Unfortunately, Syncere knew some of the humans would die. They would all die because he couldn't let Emilee die. Had he let her die, Clinton and his minions would be dead already.

The ticking of the grandfather clock in the atrium tick-tocked in Syncere's ears. He'd have to fight, if for nothing else, to try and save a few humans, but losing the hotel, letting it be run by Clinton and the Klan, was unacceptable, and he wouldn't allow it.

"Save as many as you can," Syncere murmered to his brothers, barely looking over his shoulder. At 8 p.m. on the dot, time unfroze, and Syncere realized just how strong Clinton's powers were. His compulsion power was stronger than that of Syncere and his time freezing powers, but his will, his drive and determination were not stronger than the Brown brothers.

Tyrian and Malicio took off running toward the entertainment room. There would be the most people in there. Hopefully, with Tyrian's mind control power, he could stop several people. Syncere was willing to face off with Clinton and his goons, but when the goons left his side, it was just him, Clinton, and the now unfrozen police officers.

Syncere unbuttoned his cuffs and rolled his sleeves up. His gorgeous locs were thankfully pulled into a neat top knot bun, and no matter what tonight, he was going to get down in style.

Clinton raised his hand in the air, and the troop of police officers stormed Syncere. It had been many, many years since he had to fight this way, but some things, you just never forgot. With Syncere's fangs on full display, he growled as the officers trampled over to him. With his vamp strength, he twisted both arms to the left, knocking the officers flanking toward him out of the way and into the brass banister of the staircase. Their bodies soared through the air, groans and high-pitched howls screeched through the air.

The second wave of officers came toward Syncere, and though he'd been lucky to subdue the first wave of men, the second would be a part of his undoing. With wooden stakes at the tips, they jabbed and stuck their clubs in Syncere's direction. He shuffled around, doing his best to get out of the way, but he couldn't ignore each pointed tip. Especially the ones currently being poked into his rib cage.

Syncere inhaled deeply, his anger rose to an ultimate high. He grabbed one of the officers, who'd been over zealous about poking his billy club at Syncere, and lifted him to the sky. Slobber flew from his mouth as he furiously shook the man around and then threw him into several of the other officers. Had he been paying attention to the other officer lunging directly at him, he would have noticed that he came in with a staked spear. It was the blow that would ultimately ruin Syncere and put him into the ground.

In the entertainment room, Malicio and Tyrian were doing everything they could to save the guests and the staff, though they had not quite been successful. They had unfortunately lost several people, at least twenty, and the harder they tried to save people, the harder it became to protect the ones they saved.

Malicio knew he had to do something. His premonitions gave insight to people's pasts and futures. He'd seen how several of these people were supposed to die, and it was not by the hands of themselves. Malicio got up onto the stage, kicking over the microphones and several instruments that were in his way.

He outstretched his hands, allowing the energy in the room to fuel his visions, to allow him to see into the people who were before him. Each of their futures was glim, disturbing in a sense. None of them would live to be old. They would die of heart disease, cancer, car accidents. He was close to giving up hope until he found one… one future that if he could project would give everyone a clear mind, a sense of hope, and a reason to live.

Tyrian had run himself around the room. One by one, he'd done his best to control the guests' actions by telling them what not to do, but he was exhausted. Using his mind so much had its limits, and he had just about reached his.

Malicio used his gift to channel the perfect future. The future of a young woman by the name of Selma Higgins. She came from a family of slaves, raised hard, on the farm, who never got a chance to live, until tonight. Her future, though, was brighter than ever. It catalogued her standing in the center of Union Station, trains chugging through, dark smoke blowing in the wind. People boarding the trains. Children smiling, laughing, families carrying luggage.

She'd step onto the train and remove her gloves. The chill from outside should have kept her from removing them, but she liked her hands to be free. On her way to her seat, she'd brush shoulders with a handsome stranger. A tall, lanky fellow, with a smile that warmed her soul. He'd apologize, asking her name. She'd giggle out "Selma," and they'd spend the train ride together. After the ride, he'd finally say his name, "Anderson Todd." Before leaving the train station, he'd ask her to dinner, to which she'd give a resounding yes. She was supposed to be going to see her parents. Instead, she fell in love.

The vision cleared, and in the next frame, Anderson and Selma were old and gray, children with their likenesses running around, calling them "Grandma" and "G-Pop." Her heart swelled, growing twice in size. The depiction before Malicio was the same as everyone else's. They were all able to see what life could be like. There is no greater vision, no greater future, than that of one with love in it.

The frenzy of guests and workers trying to kill themselves instantly stopped, smiles creasing their faces. When Malicio dropped his hands, exhaustion overwhelmed him, and he fell to the ground. His knees slapped against the waxed floors. Tyrian looked over to his brother, the feeling of victory shared between them. The guests, in a haze of confusion, stammered in their places, seeking understanding in the eyes of one another. It was like they had all been in a bad dream, a nightmare. The same nightmare.

The musicians had tossed their instruments aside. The dancing guests had come to a complete halt, all in the name of compulsion. And now, they were supposed to just go back to normal, like nothing had just happened.

Tyrian rushed to his brother's side, hopping with both legs up onto the stage. "You alright?" Tyrian placed his hands on both sides of his brother's face to get a better look at him. He was so used to worrying about his brother, worrying about his well-being, that even as a vampire, his role as an older brother would not die.

"I'm alright, don't fuss over me…" Malicio's words began to fail him as he thought about the reason all of this was occurring. "Sam," Malicio breathlessly voiced. In the time of fear, he'd reverted back to his brother's original name, and the thought of something happening to him was earth shattering.

Malicio and Tyrian got to their feet and ran back to the atrium of the hotel. It was a blood bath. Splatters of blood were strewn across the walls and the floors. Humans were left broken, their legs and arms turned every way but right. Clinton Samuels, the vampire who thought he had a plan, was decapitated. His head was near the door, and his body, a running and bloody mess.

Tyrian knew if his brother got angry enough what he was capable of. He was always the strongest, and the scene before them had clearly taken place in part, due to his strength. The other part was sheer anger.

Several officers, thankfully, were left alive. But many lost their lives that night. They had been compelled to do the unthinkable, and now that their mission was complete, those who had been left alive, were left in horror. The sight before them was as gruesome as it could possibly get. Their fellow comrades had been ripped to shreds. This night would be known as the Ku Klux Klan Massacre, and they would never stop coming.

When they found Syncere, he was beaten into submission. Though he'd taken many down with him, he'd also taken the brunt of their attacks. With more holes than the moon has craters, Syncere bled from every open wound in his body. Thank God the police, and Clinton for that matter, didn't know about the iron being the only real thing that could kill him. Otherwise, he would have been dead. From the looks of it, he was on his way out.

Maroon shaded blood seeped from Syncere's lips, staining his mocha skin and the mahogany floor beneath him. Tyrian slid over to Syncere on his knees, propping his head up in his lap. He stroked the thick locs that had fallen into his brother's face away so he could get a good look at him.

"You're gonna be okay. You're gonna be okay," Tyrian repeated, though he wasn't sure he believed it. Malicio stared off from the side, still taking in the terror before him. All the blood made him feel like he was going crazy. Had he lost his humanity, he would have lost his mind in a blood frenzy.

Syncere's eyes were so swollen, he could hardly see out of them, but he could hear his brother's voice. He could pick it out of a crowded room with his eyes closed. With the strength Syncere had, he placed his hands over the top of his brother's. He ached so badly he could not speak. It was the only thing he could do to let his brother know that he was holding on.

Tears rolled from Tyrian's eyes at the thought of losing Sam. They had been through so much together. They had literally survived slavery, ended it, managed to save an entire race of people, start and make a good life for themselves, and this was how it would end? Impossible.

Tyrian had a thought. The brothers became vampires in

the darkness of a cave. The cave, though dark and glib at times, kept them hidden. It kept them safe in the early years of vampirism. When Mani had been shot in 1901, they kept him in the basement of their home to heal. He'd said the darkness made him feel safe. It made him feel… better. It was in darkness they were reborn, each and every time. And if darkness saved them once before, it could save them again.

"Help me," Tyrian instructed Malicio. The sight was so horrific, he couldn't hear anything around him but the blood oozing from people's wounds, spreading across the floor.

"Mani!" Tyrian called his birth name, jolting him from the tunnel of chaos around them. "Help me!" Tyrian shouted, his face a total mess from the tears he'd shed.

Malicio, running to his brother's beckoning, helped him lift up his brother. Malicio carried his feet, while Tyrian carried him by the arms. Shifting his weight through the hotel, they carried him through the back door. Under the guise of night, Tyrian had a plan.

He and Malicio carried their brother, like soldiers, through town, catching alleyways and back streets, until they reached "Hudges Cemetery and Funeral Home." It was the only black-owned graveyard in the city, and Tyrian had no doubts about being able to pay off the woman who owned it.

She and her husband were the kind of people who liked to lay low. Out of sight, only seen when necessary. If they could not pay them off, Tyrian was prepared to force them into it. Their brother needed to rest, to recuperate. His injuries were so grave, the only thing that would help him was rest, the kind he could not get above ground.

The brothers arrived at Hudges Cemetery and Funeral Home just after 10 p.m. Amelia and Harold Hudges, and their daughter, Anya, lived a few houses away from their business. While their offices were technically closed, they were in a sense, always open. There seemed to always be someone dying, which was what made their business so lucrative.

Amelia had just pulled the covers up over their ten-year-old daughter, Anya, as she slept on the couch, when there was a banging on the doors of the funeral home. Harold, who had been preparing to go over some paperwork jumped at the sound of the banging doors. While black people had many opportunities now, and it wasn't as common to be on the wrong end of a hate crime, with all the success they were seeing in a predominately white area of town, there would always be a twinge of fear in the back of his mind.

Stories of slavery would always be passed down, generation after generation, no matter the fact that it was over. Slavery was a system, a system created for others to get ahead, to oppress an entire race of people. Slavery might have ended, but the mindsets did not change.

Another knock at the door shook him from his office. Harold reached underneath his desk and pulled out the shotgun he had resting underneath. As he approached the door, he saw Amelia hovering over Anya. She reached under the couch for the pistol she'd kept hidden there in case of emergencies. She would not wake her daughter unless she had to, but she was ready to bust a cap if necessary.

She and Harold exchanged glances. He gave her a head nod, and she smiled at him, letting him know she had his back no matter what. Harold parted the curtains to the right side with the barrel of the shotgun to see who it was. There were two men holding another who seemed badly beaten, bloody, and completely bruised. They were three young-looking black brothers, who seemed somewhat familiar.

Harold pulled the door open, still holding the shotgun, but he had not aimed it.

"We need to bury our brother," Tyrian rushed out.

Harold recognized the man they were carrying. He had seen Syncere around time. Respected and revered the way he took care of business. He was a sharp youngster, and his brothers were as loyal they came. He could see that in passing, and he could see it even now. Yet, with them on his front porch like this, it begged to question what these brothers were really into. Especially since he could see that Syncere was still breathing.

"That's usually not how we do things around here, son. You need to—"

"We ain't goin' to no hospital. From our arms to the grave is what we gon' do. You need money? We got plenty of it. It's no problem!" Malicio yelled, his chest heavily rose and fell with each word.

Though Harold was confused, and slightly frightened, he let them in. They came into the funeral home, and Harold led them into the show room, where they kept the caskets. Tyrian and Malicio placed Syncere inside of a cherry veneer casket, lined in satin.

"Hey, you can't—" Harold began, but when Malicio flashed his fangs at Harold, he nearly fell to the ground.

There had been rumors in town that there were vampires, creatures of the night, but to his understanding, they were white. He'd never suspected the brothers—they walked in sunlight.

"Stop," Malicio ordered. If Tyrian scared this man away, they'd lose time trying to figure out somewhere else to take their brother. Malicio retracted his fangs, doing his best to calm down. He paced the floor, ingesting worry with each breath.

"Look, I don't think I need to tell you—"

"Harold, everything alright in here?" Amelia appeared in the walkway between the comforting room and the showroom, the pistol behind her back. She observed the two brothers, who were both covered in their brother's blood. From the looks of it, she could tell whatever was going on was severe, and these young men needed help.

"Go on back in the comforting room, MeMe. I got this," Harold assured his wife, but she knew better than anyone that at times, her husband could be harsh, not in the slightest bit sensitive. Amelia found herself drawn to to Tyrian's tear-stricken face. She found herself wanting to help him, wanting to shield him from whatever pain was on the horizon.

"Son, why don't you tell me what's going on. How can we help you?" Slowly, Amelia approached Tyrian, a kind smile that reached her eyes rested on her face. Tyrian looked to her, her kind voice calmed the stress and worry inside of him.

"My brother… he needs to rest. You see, he's… we're not like others," he whispered. Upon entering the funeral home, he'd had so much gusto. Yet, in front of Amelia, he'd found himself diminished to that of a little boy. Under her motherly gaze, he couldn't help but to relax.

"I understand," she softly spoke. She'd witnessed Malicio's fangs just moments before, and though she didn't quite understand what she'd witnessed, it was clear that he and his brothers were indeed different, and they'd need to be handled as such. "I'm sorry for your loss," she whispered, and extended a hand to Tyrian, and then one to Malicio. They both submitted to her kind heart. Her kindness stilled Malicio in his tracks.

It had been a long time since they'd been in the presence of a woman who made them feel this way. They both felt the sting of missing their mother in that moment. As Syncere in-took shallow breaths, he could overhear the interaction. That was the one thing he knew his brothers were missing—the love of a good woman. The tender, sweetness that only a woman could provide. On the inside, he was smiling.

"Thank you, ma'am," Malicio stated, as Amelia rubbed the top of Malicio's hand with her thumb.

She smiled and dipped her head slightly. "Now, tell us how we can help you—"

"Amelia—" Harold called out to his wife, but the look she gave him over her shoulder was silencing. Harold knew long ago when his wife said something, whether verbally or otherwise, not to go against her.

Harold tossed his hands into the air and took a step back. He did not want to upset her any more that he possibly already had.

"Ma'am, we need to bury our brother, and we need to keep it a secret. We'll pay you however much it costs, but our brother needs to be in the ground, where he can rest, undisturbed."

Amelia placed her hand on Tyrian's cheek. She didn't need to understand fully to help these boys.

"We have a hole dug for a funeral coming up. We can put your brother in it and just dig another hole—"

"But the family—"

"Harold," Amelia cut her eyes at her husband, "so help me God, if you don't hush," she warned him, and with a shake of the head, he turned around and headed over to the corner, where he could be alone. If Amelia was going to directly undermine him, he would let her handle every detail. "Now, let's discuss process," Amelia directed, and she led them over to the wall to hand select the special details of Syncere's burial.

Within an hour's time, they'd decided on Syncere's headstone, plot, and a price point that would keep them quiet through the ages to come.

Malicio and Tyrian carried Syncere, in the casket, to the hole that had been dug, surprising Amelia and Harold by their strength. Though the word vampire had crossed her mind, it had not left her lips. It wasn't for her to say or worry about. She and her husband would be given enough money, that even if they never buried another soul, they'd be just fine.

When they had Syncere safely in the ground, Tyrian promised his brother that this would not be forever. They would retrieve him, and when they did, they would live out their lives together. Malicio hovered over his brother in the grave, his casket top wide open. "I don't want to leave you here," he said, tears swiftly rolling down his cheeks.

"When it's time," Syncere curdled out. "I will come to you,"Syncere whispered, between breaths. He felt like a 500-pound person was sitting on his chest. It was hard for him to breathe, let alone talk.

"How? You'll be buried. We'll have to come and get you. We'll have to—"

Syncere partially raised his hand. He was exerting too much energy, and with each passing moment, he was getting closer to death. He could feel it. "I'm the strongest person you know. I'll see you again, I promise, and it will be of my own choosing. Leave me, live your lives. Make me... make me..."

The word "proud" was on the tip of his tongue, but he was growing more and more tired by the second. His eyes fluttered. He needed his rest. When his eyes closed, it felt like the equivalent of a casket closing. Their brother, who had always carried light in his eyes, had darkened the city of Nashville that night with his leave.

Malicio and Tyrian filled the hole with dirt, leaving their brother to rest, and rest he did. They had no idea it would take 100 years for their brother to get up. For their brother to come home, but they made sure, that when their brother was ready, he'd have something to come home to. They built a life for themselves. They'd made sure that when Syncere made it back home, and they believed it was a matter of when, not if, that they would make him proud.

Diligently they worked over time, to make their names ring through the streets of Nashville. They sold their hotel to a worthy black brother, who took it to the next level, and they remained partners in the hotel group, allowing them to still make money from their original investment. They used that money to open boarding houses for people of color, which later turned into renting houses, and much later, turned into them buying and selling houses.

They were in league with some of the richest people in the city, and their homes sold fast, sold well, and sold high. Syncere would be proud, and he would see that in his absence, his brothers had not only survived, but they had thrived, the way he'd always intended.

CHAPTER 13

2017

Sam had run off so quickly, he didn't even ask the young lady who he'd saved if she would be alright without him. His first task would be making sure he was alright. Over the years, he'd become somewhat... blood crazy. He swore it off a century before to make sure he didn't harm anyone after the last incident that landed him underground, in a casket.

As he fled the scene, trying with all of his might to get away from the thrumming heartbeats sounding in his ears, his memories came flooding back. Memories he didn't want to think of. Memories, that for the last century he'd been able to hold at bay because he was desiccating in his grave. Thinking too much made him drowsy, and he feared going to sleep for too long. He might mummify and never wake back up.

He'd had a taste of blood, several drops of it, and it almost drove him mad. Getting out of his grave shouldn't have been so easy. Him getting the blood shouldn't have come so easily, and yet, it did. It nearly dripped right into his mouth, seeping through the ground.

Now that he had a clear mind, and he wasn't starving, he'd heard strange noises, something that sounded like shifting dirt, moving soil, but Sam thought he might have been going crazy when he heard that. He'd thought it was wishful thinking.

He was supposed to be underground, healing from an injury. He and his brothers had no idea how long it would take for him to heal, but they were certain it would take some time. Mani had been shot in 1901, by a nearby hunter trying to hunt an animal, while Mani was also hunting... for a meal, and even with him being a vampire, with human blood, it had taken nearly a year for him to heal fully. Jasper had told him the ramifications of holding onto their humanity. Clinging it to it had made them, in a sense, vulnerable.

What Sam experienced in 1918, caused him so much bodily harm, it broke his body, it injured his soul, and even with him being underground for a century, he wasn't sure he was completely healed. It wasn't until he realized he could slow time again that he believed he was healed. He would not and could not fault his brothers for not coming to get him. He'd made them promise to stay away from him, to live full lives, and when the time was right, he would find them.

And he would indeed find them. He knew his brothers. They would be in the nicest house, somewhere gaudy for sure, somewhere they could easily be seen. They had not mastered, nor wanted to master the art of laying low. That was partially what landed Sam in the ground for a century.

But waking up in a new time, it had its advantages, but plenty of disadvantages as well. The sun had completely come up, something he didn't have to fear or worry about, thanks to his beautiful melanated skin. Unlike most vampire lore, Sam and his brothers were safe from the sun. They didn't sparkle in the daylight, and they damn sure wouldn't burn to a crisp because of the sunlight.

It was all tied to their humanity. Clinging to it had been a blessing and a curse. Today, it would prove to be a blessing. The city of Nashville had changed since 1918, but Sam knew he was home nonetheless. There were large billboards, showcased in the sky, flashing advertisements for downtown Nashville. One minute the picture on the billboard was inviting people to enjoy festivities down on Broadway, and then the next, another picture appeared, showcasing the most popular hotels.

Though Sam was no stranger to the way times would and did change, it always amazed him to see the extreme progression technology made as time went on. The most advance piece of technology before Sam went down was the telephone, which was very exciting, to be able to reach out to others, who were miles away, by just picking up a device to reach them.

Sam and his brothers had very seldom been able to use a telephone. Back then, they were just getting their hotel up and running, and they only had two telephones in the entire hotel, to start, that is. They were proud of their achievement. Brown Hotel was a place for all kinds of people to come and rest their heads, enjoy music from live musicians, and they hosted some of the most amazing chefs of their time.

As Sam walked down the road, what he could only surmise were cars whizzed past him. They were quiet, compact, and didn't take up nearly as much space as he remembered them taking up before. There were women and men jogging along the sidewalk, carrying small, white circular pod shaped devices in their ears, attached to a wire as they ran.

There were buildings as big as the sky surrounding him, and even if he didn't want to be amazed, he was. In such a thriving area, he couldn't help but wonder if his and his brothers' hotel was still standing. If somehow, their business was able to stand the tests of time.

Based on his location, if he was right, Church Street would be just a few miles away. Sam was no stranger to walking, though he wanted to change his clothes, since he was, after all, covered in graveyard dirt. No one had given him any strange looks just yet though. On his stroll, he had to keep his thoughts occupied, so he wouldn't rip out someone's throat. He was starving, and the slight meal he'd had was starting to wear off. His stomach was growling.

It would have been easy enough for him to freeze time and sneak and get something eat, but Sam had done his best to remain an honest person, to remain someone that he and his brothers could be proud of, and stealing wasn't something he would willingly do if he could help it. As he neared Church Street, the cars that drove by him were nicer, more expensive-looking. The buildings were even better, and the hum of the city was truly alive. Sam swallowed, his throat felt like sandpaper, but that was better than sinking his teeth into someone if he could help it.

He'd made it to Church Street and Rosa Parks Blvd,

where he could see a building with large letters on it that read "AT&T." A building he was positive wasn't there in 1918, but it was a building that would forever be etched into his mind by the two points on either side of the building, pointing straight up and to the sky. If he was right, the hotel should only be a few blocks from here. His muscle memory kicked in. Even with a new atmosphere, he knew his way around his city. He'd always know the way home.

Sam hung a right on Church Street, and just a few blocks away, he'd run into a building with a small signage on the outside, that read "Brown Brothers Homes." A prideful smile creased his lips. He knew for sure this was his family's headquarters, and he'd finally made it home.

Sam pulled the door open to the office, and tears filled his eyes upon looking at the wall. The last photo he and his brothers took together, the same day he was buried, hung on the wall. He was still in the same suit as well.

There were other photos lining the wall, in color. Something that almost made his jaw fall off. He couldn't believe they'd finally captured the essence of real pictures. He was drawn to the frames like a moth to a flame. His ashen fingers rubbed over the frames, each finger memorizing the photo in front of him. Before him were his brothers, Mani and Taj, shaking hands with other people. Signs that said "Welcome Home" in people's hands. His heart warmed at the thought of his brothers providing homes for others.

That was their dream in the end, to provide stable housing for people who needed it, especially people of color, and from what he could see, his brothers had carried out that dream. Each photo captured a moment of people of color finding their forever home.

Behind him, someone's throat clearing caught his attention. "Good morning, sir, welcome to Brown Brothers Homes, how can I help you?" the woman asked. She was a young and beautiful black woman with braids so long they surpassed the height of the desk, even with her sitting down. She had such a big smile on her face, it was hard for Sam not to match it.

"Yes, good morning to you…" Sam came closer to get a better look at her name tag. "Sanya," he said slowly, waiting for the approval that he'd said her name right. She nodded her head, patiently waiting for him to continue. "I was wondering if you could help me. I'm looking for… well, the Brown Brothers. Are they here?"

Sanya looked into Sam's eyes, something about them seemed familiar, safe. Though he was filthy and looked like he had just climbed through mud. She would never know, but he literally had. She normally wouldn't give their whereabouts so easily, but in this situation, she felt led to tell him the truth.

"Yes, can I tell them who's asking?" she queried. If nothing else, she could find out if this person's name was on the "no fly" list for meetings.

"You may. My name is Syncere Brown." He grinned deviously. Syncere was the name he'd picked up when he and his brothers ended slavery. President Monroe had named them Syncere, for Sin, Malicio, for Malice, and Tyrian, for Tyrant.

Sam believed his first sin was tricking Angellica into freeing them, but he hadn't actually done anything wrong. He'd done what he had to, to free him and his brothers. That was for safety. His first, true sin was murdering President Monroe's bodyguards and freezing time, and letting him see it and live. The brothers had never done that—let someone live after bearing witness to their power, minus a few women. But, Sam was positive that had President Monroe not seen what they were capable of, he would not have put an end to slavery when he did.

Taj, the tyrant, was the one who gave the demands. He tried making President Monroe simply relinquish power, in the most unconventional ways. What other choice did he have? Taj killed President Monroe's advisement team, state officials, and took down, single-handedly, anyone who would come after President Monroe to undo what they were aiming to do.

Mani, malice in its truest form, the sweetest of all, had learned to use his gift to help and hurt others, and President Monroe was no stranger to that. Because Mani could see the past and the future, and make his victims see the same, he was sure to show President Monroe what his future would become if he did not free the slaves. If he did not create a decree so absolute, enough to change history, how generations after him, his bloodline specifically, would be affected.

Syncere's mouth watered at how much blood they consumed over the course of that week. It was deviously delightful.

Sanya took a deep breath. She'd heard rumors about

Syncere Brown from her employers. How if he ever returned, from what Sanya could only assume was a long vacation, or perhaps prison stay, how their family would be made whole, and there was nothing the three brothers could not accomplish. She was positive she had already witnessed black excellence in the flesh. Their company morphed from a hotel franchise, now to real estate for people of color.

It was the FUBU of real estate.

Sanya jumped to her feet, her heart pounding in her chest. She'd always thought the Brown brothers were fine, but standing before Syn, her coochie thumped and her underwear felt a little too tight for her own liking.

"L-let me go get them now. One moment, Mr.—"

"Syncere is fine." His smile almost brought Sanya to her knees. She had never experienced this type of magnetism toward a man before, and if she wasn't careful, she would lose her job behind this much physical excitement.

Sashaying to the back where there were two closed doors, Sanya knocked on the one on the left. She was thankful she didn't have her press-on nails today. She'd just got a fresh pink and white acrylic set, thankfully. Otherwise, she would have definitely popped them off knocking on the door.

"Mr. Brown, uhm, there's a man out here. Claiming to be—"

"Sanya, I've asked you more than once to call me Malicio. Mr. Brown makes me feel so..." As Malicio came to the door, his slow beating heart thudded in his chest. He had not felt it beat quite as fast in centuries, but standing before his brother, his eldest brother, he was starstruck, nearly paralyzed with excitement, fear, concern.

"Sam," he whispered, his voice so low you would have had to be right up on him to hear him utter the name.

"Brother," Syncere nodded, heading to the back of the office to embrace him. With dirt particles falling off of him, he glided back toward his brother. To Tyrian, he was still as pristine as he had always been. The dirt changed nothing for him. Because in his eyes, his brother would always be that nigga.

Tyrian, in his $1,000 suit, reached out and embraced his brother, happily slapping him on the back. The moment they hugged, questions began swirling in his mind about how his brother got out of his casket. How was he able to climb out of the grave on his own. But now wasn't the time for questions. For now, they would celebrate their brother's return.

"Sanya, break out a bottle of champagne. The best one we have—"

"I think all we have is the Prosecco left, sir—"

"Not good enough," Tyrian interjected. "Go to the liquor store. Use the company card, get the most expensive bottle they got! My big brother's home," Tyrian instructed, embracing his brother once again. Syncere laughed at his brother's enthusiasm. He was usually the more calm and subtle one, never one to express his excitement and happiness. But sometimes, even if you wanted to hide how happy you were, you simply just couldn't help it.

"Yes sir, I will. I'll go now," Sanya agreed, turned quickly on her heels and did her best to head out of the office. Her heel got stuck on the carpet, and she was set to fall, when Syncere sped over to her, breaking her fall. Sanya's eyes grew wide—shocked to have seen him move so quickly, though she shouldn't have been.

For a while, she'd had her suspicions about her employers. They were fine as hell, fast as hell, always came in dressed nice, smelling nice. They kept strange eating habits, never had women around them. They were private, very secret. She'd assumed they might be a part of the Illuminati the way they acted.

But, she was paid handsomely not to question what they did. She'd even signed a confidentiality agreement, a damn NDA just to work for them. Whatever she saw, or was paid not to see, she figured must have been pretty serious. But she didn't mind as long as they were paying.

"Are you alright?" Syncere asked. He'd caught her just around the waist, and with his sturdy hands around her, she'd never felt so safe, so protected in her life.

"I'm-I'm more than alright, thank you, Mr. Brown," she blushed, and Syncere smiled.

"You can call me Syncere. I, like my brothers, don't take pride in being called Mr. anything," he corrected. Sanya swallowed hard, nodding, as if she were in a trance each time he moved his lips.

Foregoing further embarrassment, Sanya pulled down her rising dress that was inching up her thighs, calmed herself by taking a deep breath, and went over to her desk to get the company card and her car keys.

As she was exiting the building, the second office door swung open. Malicio casually walked out of his office. His head face down toward the buttons on his suit jacket that he was trying his best to button. He'd need to speak with Fransisco, the tailor about his loose buttons. When he looked up, before him, he saw not one, but two of his brothers, with their arms around one another. Malicio swallowed hard. He, unlike Tyrian, could easily express his emotions and had at times been coined the sensitive one.

When it came to physical expression, he had no qualms with showing how he truly felt. Tears instantly covered his cheeks as he went up to Syncere to hug him. Tyrian took a step backwards, allowing his baby brother to hang onto the elder one.

After several minutes of hanging onto one another, Malicio released his brother and gave him a once over. He was filthy, and now the three of them were covered in muck.

"What year is it?" Syncere asked. Everything around him let him know that he was clearly in the distant future. He just wasn't sure how far in the future that was.

Tyrian placed his hands on his brother's shoulders, squeezing them for dramatic effect.

"2017... Can you believe it?"

Syncere indeed could not believe that it had been so many years, nor that they were living in the 21st century.

"I can but cannot believe it," Syncere said, more to himself than to his brothers. A deafening reminder flooded his mind. Next year would be the year that Jasper said he and his brothers had a destiny to fulfill. He'd had no clue what that might be, and he'd kept the fact hidden from his brothers that Jasper told him this. He wondered what it would be.

"We've got a lot to catch you up on, and it seems, that you might have the same. How the fuck did you get out of your grave?" Malicio wondered, now that the initial shock of seeing his brother had worn off.

"It's an interesting story, actually," Sam pondered and headed back into the front of the office to take Sanya's seat. Malicio and Tyrian followed their brother, as they always had. Dutifully, with purpose.

Syncere told his brothers of what happened. About how, just before he'd heard the soil moving, he was thinking about letting go. How he was okay with dying since it seemed he might from desiccation. And then, out of nowhere, he tasted the most satisfying and fulfilling blood he'd ever had. It had given him enough sustenance to find his brothers, and the last time he'd had such a hearty meal was the first time he'd had Chicken Alfredo, and that was a delicacy. The blood he'd had, was an absolutely gratifying form of nourishment.

By the time Syncere had finished explaining what he knew about the events of the day, they were left with more questions.

"What about the girl?"

"Is she okay?"

"Are you mad at us?"

Question after question, they fired off. Syncere was delighted to know that things had not changed that much since he'd gone underground. It seemed like they would still be depending on their brother after all.

"I'm not mad. Who could have known how long it would take me to recover? I'm not certain myself that had it not been for that girl's blood, if I would even be moving right now. Who's to say if you would have come to dig me up, I would have even been healed?" Syncere rationalized. His body, though sore, did not hurt nearly as much as it had, even in the last few days. Whatever that young woman had in her blood stream, he knew he needed to stay away from it. She would become a source of food for him—nothing else, and since he'd vowed not to get involved in human affairs, or involved with humans at all, and he'd already broken that rule, he needed to renew it.

He was officially done with humans, outside of using them for food, again.

"Sounds like this girl was the star of the show," Tyrian pointed out, and Syncere smiled slightly. If he were being honest, she was the one piece of the day that truly blew his mind. He wanted to find her, to know more about her, but doing so, he knew would only lead to trouble. Humans were often more trouble than they were worth, and getting involved with her, even to find out who she was, would bring more issues. Of that, he could be certain.

"She was something, if I'm being honest, but I have no true desire to figure out who she was. I would instead like a bath, fresh clothes—"

"Enough said!" Malicio jumped to speak. "We'll go home, and then we can go see Francisco. I need to speak with him anyway. I've got a couple of loose buttons on my jacket." Malicio smoothed his hands over his jacket, and Syncere's heart began tingling.

From what he could see, even his baby brother had come into his own. That he was more confident than ever. His charcoal gray suit, obsidian black shirt underneath, and enough gold on his person to be considered a jewelry store, he could see his brother had gained much self-confidence over the years. Perhaps him being gone was not so bad after all.

"Home, and where is home exactly?" Syncere asked, and Tyrian smiled.

"We live in the former area known as Eastland—"

"Now known," Malicio cut his brother off, "as East Nashville, or as the locals call it, out east," Malicio laughed, and Tyrian joined him. Things had changed so much since their brother had last been alive. They were excited to show him around and introduce him to the privileged side of life.

"Very interesting," Syncere said, remembering the land as being rich in farmland and agriculture. "Well, let's not dally. Take me... home," Syncere advised.

"What about Sanya? Let's at least wait for her to get back," Malicio stated, and Tyrian's eyebrow shot up.

"I'm sure you do want to wait for Sanya to come back."

Syncere chuckled, picking up on what Tyrian was suggesting. "Is Sanya your..."

"She's my nothin'," Malicio said sharply, his throat going dry. He liked Sanya, but had not worked up the courage to tell her. Though he'd hoped it would be obvious by the flowers he brought into the office and placed directly on her desk daily.

"We'll wait for Sanya. Afterward, we'll go get cleaned up and put together some things for my new wardrobe."

Malicio and Tyrian agreed and waited for Sanya to return. In the meantime, the brothers caught up on everything from the year their brother was put down, all the way to now. Including an exchange of how Amionette's blood saved him and he in turn, saved her. He'd made it sound transactional, though there was something lingering, something else, just below the surface.

Syncere would be a liar to say that he was not impressed. And even with the impact their stories had, the lingering wonder of what destiny they would fulfill next year seemed troublesome and took the place, temporarily, of the happiness he felt in returning to his brothers.

The Present

Amionette woke up in a colorful bedroom in Yuzuri's home. She'd been sleeping in the guest bedroom since her ordeal with Frederick, and the bedroom's colorful décor scheme lifted her spirits. With shades of coral and turquoise equivalently tossed about the room, with accents of silver in the room, she had no choice but to wake up feeling... happy? She almost hated to admit to herself that she felt anything that wasn't anguish, depression, or loneliness. But whether she admitted it or not, she did feel excited and ready to take her life in a new direction.

The only problem with that was Fletcher. There had been no signs of him anywhere. Supposedly being "dead," she thought she would have heard something on the news, through the police or something about her being missing or him having reported her dead. He'd done something similar before, but she was different. Amionette figured she either wasn't worth him mentioning that he killed her or wanted anyone to know, or he was somewhere running for his life.

She couldn't be sure. He had a business to run, and she

did, too. But her business, thanks to Zuri, would be just fine. Zuri had been handling her day-to-day operations, and that was one less thing to find stressful in her life.

However, her stress level was about to go straight through the roof. When her alarm clock went off just ten minutes before, it was a reminder of what she had to do that day. When Zuri invited her to spend Christmas with her, she'd agreed. It had been a long time since she celebrated Christmas, and with everything Zuri had done for her, and would probably do, she couldn't tell her no. She hadn't realized she'd grow to regret that.

Zuri's mom sent out a text decree that they should all wear ballgowns. This Christmas, they'd be celebrating at the governor's mansion. Zuri's father was a very important, prestigious man. Her father owned his own dental practice, and he'd rubbed elbows with some of Nashville's finest business owners, men, and politicians. He hadn't mentioned it, but he planned to run for senator next term, and in order for him to do so, he needed to start getting into certain rooms with certain people.

Politicians valued family and appearances above all. For Zuri and her family, though, it wouldn't be a stretch. She was close to her father—forever a daddy's girl. She was the best sister to her younger protégé, Sacred, whom she loved dearly, and the relationship she had with her mother was solid. It wouldn't be a stretch to convey the strength of their family. And now with Amionette on her arm, a true friend, someone she was becoming more and more fond of by the second, she was beginning to consider her family as well.

When Zuri found out about the change, she feared Amionette's response, knowing that she hadn't wanted to make a big deal of the pagan holiday, but Amionette was surprisingly pliable. Her response was a smooth "I'm not thrilled, but we'll do it," leaving Zuri feeling happier than ever. Up until recently, Sacred had pretty much been the only friend she had, and now, to have Amionette, she was nearly complete.

The only thing Zuri was missing in her life was someone to call her own, but she'd never admitted it to anyone except her father. He just understood her in a different way. That was one of the reasons she was happy to stand at his side at the governor's Christmas ball, because there was nothing he'd ever denied her, or would, and he always had her back. Now, she would have his.

Zuri lightly knocked on Amionette's door. She'd learned her lesson the last few days knocking too loudly got her nowhere with Amionette but looked at crazy and talked bad to. Amionette was a late riser, someone who preferred to sleep in rather than get up early, but if she and Zuri were going to find the perfect gowns, they would have to get their behinds up and get out of the house.

"Come in," Amionette called out to Zuri, who she knew would be on the other side of the door with a smile as wide as all outside. When Zuri opened the door, she entered the room with a breakfast tray. The scent of eggs, bacon, French toast, and dragonfly tea percolated in the air. Amionette's eyes popped shut, and she inhaled the aroma that made her wish she would have eaten something a little later last night. The way her stomach was touching her back, she was ready to snap.

Zuri, fully dressed, took a seat on Amionette's bed and sat the food tray down on the bed.

"You know you don't have to do this every day, right?" Amionette smirked as she reached for a piece of French toast.

"She says, as she begins to ravage the food," Zuri snickered, her bright smile igniting the entire room.

"Okay, the food is good, what you expect? But seriously, every day, you don't have to. You're not my servant, and—"

"Enough already. We can be like the modern-day Golden Girls, but just the two of us. Maybe three when you meet my sister Sacred. She's gonna join us today. Is that okay?"

Zuri hadn't thought to ask if Amionette would be okay with someone joining them. With how skittish she had been, Zuri wasn't sure if she should be inviting anyone else around them, but she would meet her sooner or later.

Amionette observed the look of worry on Zuri's face. Her eyebrows tensed, and though things had been strange for Amionette recently, and she was learning how to start over, healthily, she didn't want to completely disrupt what Zuri had going on or make her feel uncomfortable.

"Of course. I can't wait to meet her. You talk about her so much, does she look just like you?" Amionette probed. Wishing she'd always had a sibling, Amionette wondered what it was like to have someone to grow up alongside, but with the way she lived her life, she was somewhat glad that she hadn't had to worry about someone else. But, when things were lonely, especially after her mother died, she wished she had someone to care for, and to care for her.

Perhaps that was why God had brought Zuri into her life now. HE knew she wouldn't be able to take another traumatic event without the help of someone.

"She does look kind of like me, but kind of not like me," Zuri tilted her head to the ceiling, envisioning a mental photo of her sister. She leaned over and took a piece of bacon from Amionette's plate and snapped into it. "She loves to wear braids just like me. Uhm... her nose is kind of like mine, like how mine is sharp, I guess you could say. And, she's... well, that actually sums it up," Zuri laughed. Describing a person, even though she saw her in her mind's eye was still just as difficult.

"Well, then I'm sure she's beautiful. I can't wait to meet her. Where are we going to get dresses again?" Amionette asked as she dug into her meal. Zuri was such a good cook. She wondered if she made her a meal would she enjoy it as much as she had enjoyed Zuri's well-thought out meals.

Zuri began filling Amionette in on the day's events. They would be going to Spring Hill, a smaller town just an hour outside of Nashville, that housed many expensive boutiques, shoppes, and restaurants, to get their dresses and shoes. With the party just two weeks away, it was important for them to get everything now, since technically their invite was already so late.

Amionette finished up her breakfast and hopped into the shower. She figured since they were going to Spring

Hill, dressing down wasn't going to be the best option. One thing she hated was being judged, and even though she had money, she didn't like dressing like it. Something about flaunting her money made her feel mildly uncomfortable. She'd rather pretend to be broke than floss the fact that she was in a sense, well-off. Some might even say rich.

Wanting to blend in with the crowd, Amionette chose a pair of light-wash distressed blue jeans, a white, button-down boyfriend shirt, that she tied at the bottom, and rather than putting back on her wig, that she was sure was tore up beyond repair, she wet her hair in the shower, put in a little Shea Moisture curl cream conditioner, and went on about her day, letting her voluptuous hair rest naturally on her shoulders.

She met Zuri, the punctual, in the living room by the front door. Zuri, as always, had on a pleated olive green and cream dress, with neon flowers printed all over her dress and a matching cardigan to go over the top. Amionette laughed at how perfectly dressed she was and how well she would fit in with the big spenders in Spring Hill. Amionette worried about the shopping trip as they headed to the car. She didn't want to cause problems with her up and down emotional outbursts, that for the most part, she'd been able to keep to herself.

But the thought of having to control herself struck something inside of her. She just didn't want to let Zuri down or leave a bad impression on Sacred. Zuri's sister meant everything to her, and having just made a friend for the first time ever, she didn't want to scare her or her sister away.

On the way to Spring Hill, Amionette figured her best bet would be to just inhale deep breaths. Take it one second at a time. She could do this. She wasn't a social pariah, and she refused to believe that everyone around her wanted to treat her terribly. That everyone around her was a bad person, simply because Fletcher was.

Amionette and Zuri landed at Spring Hill Formals, where Sacred was there waiting for them. Amionette gripped the strap of her purse close to her as she exited the car, straggling behind Zuri and into the shop. A loud squeal escaped Zuri's lips as she laid eyes on her sister. It had been months since she'd seen Sacred, and her heart stirred with happiness when she laid eyes on her.

Sacred, with a smile unmatched by even a pageant queen, threw her arms around Zuri. The two teetered in a circle, embracing one another, which brought a smile to Amionette's otherwise nervous-looking face.

"Sacred, I want you to meet Amionette. Amionette, this is my sister, Sacred," she said as she released Sacred from her grip. Inwardly, she hoped that Amionette would feel just as comfortable with Sacred as she was starting to feel with her.

"Hi," Amionette reached her hand out to Sacred, who

was thankful for less contact. With the way her anxiety was set up, too much physical touch too soon made her extremely uncomfortable.

"It's nice to meet you," Sacred quietly uttered, shaking her hand also. The two instantly separated, standing to either side of Zuri, who couldn't have been happier. In her mind, she had just enough sugar, spice, and everything nice to balance the two of them out. She would be the glue to bring the two of them together if it was the last thing she did.

"Hi, ladies, can I help you find anything?" one of the Springhill Formals associates asked. She approached them with glasses of sparkling cider on a silver platter.

"Oh, this place is fancy-fancy," Amionette joked, nudging Zuri in the arm. Zuri laughed, swatting her hand away.

"We're looking for ball gowns, for the governor's Christmas celebration. Where could we find ballgowns?" Zuri queried, looking past the associate to see if she could find it on her own.

"The showroom is pretty large. Let me lead you ladies to the back, and I'd be happy to start some rooms for you. We also have sparkling cider as well," the associate informed the girls. "My name is Janelle, and I'll be happy to help you find whatever you're looking for."

Sacred grinned and took a glass from the tray. "Got anything stronger?" she joked, and Zuri's eyes widened. Sacred was usually very reserved, hardly ever even drank alcohol, so she was shocked to hear her make such a request.

"Yeah, if we're gonna do this, I'ma definitely need a little something extra." Amionette bounced her shoulders when she said "extra," and the associate chuckled.

"Let me see what I can dig up for you ladies. I know we have a little wine—"

"Pull it out!" Zuri said, wanting to join in on the fun. She linked arms with Sacred and Amionette and followed behind Janelle and into a much larger showroom, filled with gowns fit for queens.

Each display held something fit for a princess, a queen, even. Zuri's mouth dropped open as she took in the dresses. There were so many, it would be difficult to settle on just one dress.

"These are all of our ballgowns. I'll go ahead and start dressing rooms for you, and then I'll go check on that wine," Janelle announced and placed the platter of cider on one of the end tables resting near the opulent coffee table in the center of the dressing room.

Janelle disappeared and started their rooms, as promised, and the girls began scanning the dresses. They separated, heading toward dresses that caught their eye. Zuri found an exemplary plum dress that spoke to her soul. It was held together at the bust with a large bow, had a tight-bodice and jewels on the bottom that flared out. She had to try it on.

Sacred had no idea what she was looking for, but her main goal was to wear something striking. To help with her anxiety, she wanted to take chances on her own terms. Do things that got her out of her comfort zone that she was comfortable with, and wearing a bold and daring dress was something she'd always wanted to do. She just had to figure out exactly what that meant for her.

Amionette's eyes landed on several dresses that would have fit the bill for her. With her shape, there wasn't much she couldn't wear, but she'd never been to an event of this caliber, and she didn't know what kind of dress would best suit her. She'd never worn a dress as nice as the ones in these stores. She'd skipped out on prom, never ever thought of homecoming, and since she hadn't even begun looking at wedding dresses during her and Fletcher's engagement, dresses like these seemed simply out of her gaze, out of her depth.

Her fingers grazed against the delicate fabric of several dresses. She'd picked up a gorgeous powder blue dress, with a high-split that inched up the thigh and would land directly underneath her hip bone. It was beautiful, but she wasn't sure if it was a dress for her.

The bell at the door ringing caught Amionette's attention. She looked over her shoulder, and her stomach nearly dropped into her asshole. She couldn't believe what, or rather, who she was seeing entering the store. She'd promised herself that she would find him. Though, she had no idea how she was going to go about it. But she knew that she would find him at some point.

It just so happened, that she was lucky enough to be found by him.

When Syncere entered the store, he floated across the marble-tiled floor, and over to the men's side of the formal shoppe. Amionette dropped the dress to the ground, stalking the areas near him, just so she could get a closer glimpse. A part of her mind felt she was just seeing what she wanted to see. She'd been desperate to figure out where he was or where he might be, but she hadn't the slightest clue on where to begin looking.

"We're here to see Francisco," she'd heard one of the men who entered the store with him say. She recognized that they had similarities in their skin tones, their styles, and in general, they looked similar. Amionette wondered if they were related.

Doing her best to remain hidden behind the taller displays of dresses, her desire was to be close enough that she could still hear everything he was saying. His voice sounded as smooth as Cognac being poured over double ice. She couldn't help but be drawn to him.

Janelle smiled and led Syncere and his brothers to the back of the store. He felt eyes on him, boring into the back of his head. Syncere looked over his shoulder, his eyes cut to the right to get a look in the direction of where he assumed he would find someone. Briefly, he paused, doing a quick sweep of the area.

"Sir?" Janelle cooed, standing there waiting for him.

"Yes, I'm sorry," Syncere responded and with caution, followed behind Janelle.

"I was thinking—"

"Shit!" Amionette screamed, startled by Zuri, but more so by being caught staring at Syncere walk away. She loved the view of him from the front and the back.

"Mama always says if you jumpin' and lurkin' around, you doin' something you don't have no business doin'," Zuri playfully tapped Amionette on the shoulder.

"If you saw what I saw... I guarantee you'd be lurking around, too."

"Please, inform the class," Sacred said as she walked up. She had selected a dress and was ready to try it on when she saw Amionette and Zuri over in the corner, skulking behind displays like criminals.

Amionette knew that even if she felt comfortable telling Zuri the truth about what happened that night, that she could in no way bring Sacred into this. This was the first time she'd ever been out shopping with other women, and the comradery she felt from being surrounded by women who meant her no harm, was empowering. She didn't want to say a word to push either of them away.

She figured her best bet would be to simply say what she'd seen, rather than what she experienced.

"I just saw three of the finest men I think I've ever seen in my life," she half told a lie. They were three of the most beautiful black specimens she'd ever seen, but she wasn't really checking out Tyrian, nor was she looking at Malicio. Her eyes were dead set on Syncere. His attention was the only person's attention she wanted.

"Why didn't you say something? You're staring so hard, I thought you might have seen someone you knew," Zuri laughed with relief. She was honestly afraid that Amionette might have come across Fletcher. She was bound to run into him at some point. Though she had hoped Amionette would be further along in her healing journey before she did. Zuri had been handling the business for almost a week. She didn't mind, but she also knew that if she was responsible for the business, Amionette still needed time, and she couldn't blame her.

Whatever Amionette had gone through with Fletcher, she knew it was groundbreaking, and she also knew that she didn't have the full story. With time, though, Zuri hoped she would et the full truth of what took place.

"Say somethingggggg?" Amionette craned her neck back in shock. Even if she hadn't just broken up with Fletcher, or escaped with her life, she wasn't the type to say a word to a man if he didn't say something to her first. She thought he was handsome, but she knew one thing about him that made him especially different from her—he drank blood, and what would an actual conversation between them come to?

She shook the thought of exchanging words from her mind. Even if they did find themselves in conversation, Amionette felt she didn't have one thing to get or hold his interest. She believed that her past would be a hindrance, and what would she say to him that would be different than everything else he'd ever heard?

"Hello?" Sacred snapped her fingers. She noticed the light in Amionette's eyes were going out, transported elsewhere.

"Sorry. I wouldn't dare approach a man, considering what I've been through. I think I need to take a long beat when it comes to men," she spoke honestly. Even though she was aching for a chance to converse with her vampire hero, she didn't feel it would be worth it to strain herself to even try.

Zuri shrugged her shoulders. She couldn't say that she

would speak to a man first either. She was beautiful and knew it. She deserved to be approached, and stepping outside of herself for a man's number was the furthest thing from her mind.

Sacred, on the other hand, was in the right position to try such a thing. All her life, Zuri incessantly worried about her because of her frequent panic attacks and social anxiety. With Zuri's help, and her therapist's, she'd gotten better at having conversations and challenging herself to do so. Zuri didn't think her sister would make a move. She'd always been perpetually shy, and at times, became invisible in a room on purpose.

"No, Sacred, please, don't—" Amionette reached out to her, but her hand fell short of getting a hold of her. Sacred playfully jogged away from them, rushing over to the men's side to find the handsome men.

Zuri's hand flew to her mouth—she'd never seen that side of her sister before, and she couldn't say she didn't love it.

Amionette pressed forward, nearly throwing herself onto Sacred's back to keep her from getting any closer, but Zuri wouldn't let her. She thought this playful activity would be good for all of them. Equally for Amionette and Sacred.

Sacred entered the men's side, and it was simple enough to find the men Amionette claimed to have scene. They smelled of Givenchy, Dior, and Giorgio Armani. Sacred's nostrils opened wide, leading her to them like a bloodhound searching for food. Her nose did the walking for her, and when she found them, her eyes grew as big as saucers.

"Damn," she whispered under her breath. Syncere, Tyrian, and Malicio all turned her way. Her hand shot to cover her mouth in disbelief. She hadn't thought she would be heard, but there was a possibility that she'd spoken louder than she thought.

"Can we help you?" Malicio was the first to ask, stepping down from the platform. The boys were standing in a three-panel mirror, being poked and stuck with pins and needles to be fitted for their tuxedos.

Tyrian and Malicio facilitated a house purchase for the governor's son. The deal was extremely beneficial for them and for the governor's son. It landed them an invitation to the governor's Christmas celebration, where the opportunity to rub and shake hands with billionaires would be endless. Now that their brother was home, the money was going to triple. Syncere had a natural knack for drawing attention to himself, healthy and otherwise. But in business, there was no such thing as bad press.

Sacred's heart pounded. Malicio was indeed the most handsome man she had ever seen. Suave, debonair, young-looking like her, but he possessed a swag about him that made her chest tighten.

"Oh, uhm, funny you ask," Sacred began rambling. She bit at her bottom lip to reground herself. She worried she might have bitten off more than she could chew. Her therapist had advised her in moments like this, not to allow herself to be overtaken by the feeling of defeat. Ground herself, and try again.

Which, that's what she would have done, had Malicio not closed the space between them. Malicio glared at Sacred's ruby-stained lips. They reminded him of the color of blood. She nervously chewed into her lip, and it reminded him of himself. When he felt nervous, he too, had a tell. He paced, or he picked at his fingers.

Malicio placed his hand underneath Sacred's chin to refocus her attention. He smiled, and the grin was a wicked reminder that Sacred had no clue what she was doing.

"My.... Uhm. My friend saw you guys over here, and I challenged myself to come and speak. Now I have, so... I'ma head back over that way—"

"Don't leave so soon. What's your name, Beauty?"

Zuri almost puked in her mouth from the corny pick up line, but when Sacred inhaled sharply and started snoring, she realized her sister was extremely into it, and it wasn't for her to judge, or question her sister's feelings.

"N-no, it's Sacred," she kindly corrected. Hearing such an interesting name, Tyrian turned to look over his shoulder. Zuri had boldly approached Sacred. The last she knew, Sacred had never had a boyfriend, and she didn't know anything about interacting with men in this manner. She didn't want to leave her sister hanging out to dry if she could help it.

The moment Tyrian laid eyes on Zuri, he would have thought his brother made time stand still. He had seen many women who were beautiful. He'd been with many women, physically, who had the ability to turn him into a beast. Tyrian had never, in his several centuries of life, met a woman who could command his attention from just being in the room.

Tyrian stretched his hand out to Zuri. She smiled and took his hand. "Hi, I'm Zuri, and you are?" He seductively smiled at her. One thing Tyrian was used to, was being able to turn a woman on, and Zuri would be no exception. "My name is Tyrian. This," Tyrian clapped his brother on the back, "is my baby brother, Malicio."

"It's nice to meet you. Amionette, why don't you come over and introduce yourself?" Zuri called over her shoulder. She stood frozen in place, her shoulders suspended in the air from the shock of her name being called. Amionette had been facing the opposite way on purpose, hoping to blend in with the tile somehow and become a member of the floor, so that no one would mention her. She knew she should have stayed out of sight, but then she wouldn't have been able to get a look at her vampire hero up close. If she thought he was fine before, when he was covered in dirt and grime, the cleaned up version of him made him look like a celebrity.

He had a fresh edge up, and his locs were neatly retwisted. The black tuxedo pants he wore carved out every inch of his body to perfection. Amionette feared she might come off as thirsty, so she'd kept her back turned so she wouldn't reveal just how bad she was at interacting with men. Even with Fletcher, he'd approached her. Amionette knew she was a beautiful woman, and she was a catch, but she also knew that men liked to waste women's' time, and she didn't want hers wasted. She'd spent her life avoiding companionship, and the one time she gave in to it, she'd come to truly regret it.

Yet, here she was, standing before Syncere, wishing that he would notice her. That he would give her a look so she wouldn't have to make the first move. Slowly, she spun around, hoping that Syncere would see that she was just as beautiful as Zuri and Sacred, and he, too, would be compelled from his place.

"This is Amionette. Amionette, this is Tyrian and his brother Malicio," Zuri introduced them. She shook their hands, but she could care less. Her eye contact shifted between them and Syncere, who she was most eager for him to come over.

Tyrian could pick up on the vibe she was putting down and looked to Syncere, who was standing straight in the mirror, looking at how much style and suits had changed. He knew he would enjoy the future, but he hadn't thought he would this much.

From his peripheral vision, he could see Amionette. The way her shirt tied just below her bust, showcasing her belly button and a clear view of her curvy hips. Syncere would never forget a face like hers. She was the perfect caramel gold complexion, with tiny freckles tossed about her face like flickers of paint. He'd noticed her beauty when she was bleeding to death.

Now, she was downright beguiling. Though he'd given her a quick once over, he could not afford to look for long. He promised himself after the massacre in 1918, that he would never get involved with humans again. He hadn't even had an intimate relationship with Emilee. He'd considered her a friend, and to watch her nearly bleed to death on the floor before him was such an intense and overwhelming feeling, he knew he could never put himself back through that.

If his brothers wanted to involve themselves in human relations, whether intimate or otherwise, he would let them make their own choices. He could no longer speak for them. For a century, they had gotten along without him just fine—he wouldn't impose his feelings on them. But, if they did take up with the human factions, creating personal bonds with them, he would have to step away from them. With all the love in his heart, he did not believe he could survive another hurt as bad as what happened to Emilee.

Tyrian and Malicio had told Syncere over the last few days the fate that Emilee met. Even though she was able to physically heal, her mind was forever broken from that night. Tyrian tried to erase the memories in her mind, to make her forget what she'd seen, but something in her shattered when she'd been caught in the crossfire of vampire relations.

Emilee spent the rest of her life in a psyche ward, and in the year 1918, that was just as dangerous, if not more, than being in a jail cell. Emilee was a good person, who had a family to love her. Syncere would never forgive himself, and he would never allow himself to go back.

"Syn, come say hey to these beautiful women," Tyrian teased. He knew his brother's stance on humans, but his brother, if nothing else, was typically polite.

Syncere inhaled, sighing with frustration. He pulled the

jacket of his tuxedo closed, buttoning the ivory button in the center, and stepped down from the platform. Amionette's palms clammed with sweat. She had not expected him to actually come down there. Behind Zuri's back, she felt a slight pinch. Amionette reached over and grabbed ahold of her cardigan. Zuri wobbled in her spot and shot a glare over at Amionette, wondering why she had such a death grip on her crisp cardigan, but her senses had never failed her. Amionette wanted this man to speak to her. She wanted his attention.

Zuri reached over to Amionette and slowly stroked her back. She could tell from the intense heat Amionette's body radiated that she needed some comforting, perhaps a bit of encouragement.

Syncere, along with his brothers, heard the loud gulp Amionette swallowed. She'd just wanted to wet her mouth a bit, but it sounded like horse had just swallowed a gob of spit. When he approached her, rather than stick his hand out to her, he smiled, a smile that came across as polite, and nothing else.

"I believe we've met," he said, finally, acknowledging Amionette. She had wondered if he would remember her. If she was just another face in his centuries of life that had become a blur.

A fast smile appeared on Amionette's face. She could only assume she looked goofy, standing there with a smile as wide as the Joker spread across her lips. Because Syncere had not stuck his hand out to her, she figured she shouldn't. Perhaps he wasn't as friendly as she'd remembered.

"Yes, we have. I didn't get to thank you—"

"There's no need, and please, don't mention it again."

Amionette was confused by his cold nature. He had been so kind to her before, that she had expected, if they were ever to meet again, a much friendlier experience. Amionette released her grip on Zuri, who was nearly star struck by the encounter between Zuri and Amionette.

"The two of you know each other? How?" Zuri's forehead creased as she squinted in Amionette's direction. It wasn't strange for her to know such a fine man. Of course not. People ran in and out of Amionette's office all day. What was surprising was the way Amionette was acting in front of this man.

Zuri had always known her to be confident, assured, very poised. Yet, the last week, Zuri felt she'd been introduced to a totally different person than that of her boss.

"We do," Amionette gritted her teeth to say. The longer she stood before Syncere, the worse she felt. Had she embarrassed herself by thinking he would be kind to her? That he would, somehow show some interest in her well-being?

"We had a very brief encounter—"

"Brief, but memorable," Tyrian mentioned under his breath. His hand shot to his lips, covering it as though a cough had slipped out.

Syncere elbowed him with the force of Mighty Joe Young. He'd told his brothers about the woman's life he saved, and Tyrian knew better than anyone how his brother truly felt about humans. He didn't typically carry the same sentiment—now so detached from what he used to be, but he knew how Syncere felt about it. It was why he'd made one of their biggest rules. They did not kill, at least they weren't supposed to.

While Malicio and Tyrian had maintained the multitude of their souls, they still were darkened the most by their vampirism, the bad choices they'd made, and by how often they'd used their powers for their own personal gain. Without Syncere around to guide them, the Brown brothers made decisions, that while they would be set up for greatness, might ruffle feathers, darken their very hearts, and at times, that meant someone's life would be taken.

Syncere wasn't just the best of them—he was the light for them. Their way back home.

Sacred and Zuri's eyes shot over to Tyrian, who was bent over catching his breath. Only his brother could partially impale him for being so forthcoming with information.

"I meant, yes, brief," Tyrian said through coughs. Malicio laughed and patted his brother on the back.

"Walk it off," Malicio joked and took a step forward. Sacred inhaled deeply as Malicio invaded her personal space. He smelled so good, she wanted to take him behind the building and show him what she thought she could do. At the risk of total embarrassment, Sacred had remained a virgin. But it had not been easy. Peer pressure from friends made her feel she was disastrously behind on the spectrum of sexuality, but she was in no rush, necessarily, to become that vulnerable with someone and end up in tears due to her anxiety. But Malicio caught her off guard—he took her breath away in his tuxedo.

Previously when she saw an attractive man she thought she might just be broken downstairs. Or a lesbian, since none of the lights were going off for her the way they did for her friends or other women. But Malicio had introduced her to a new understanding without even saying a word. His body and handsome face did the talking.

"If you don't mind me asking, what are you ladies doing in a formalwear store? A wedding, perhaps?" Malicio asked aloud, though his eyes were glaring directly into Sacred's.

"We're buying gowns for the governor's Christmas celebration. We're attending the ball with my parents," Zuri spoke up for the group.

"And you'll be wearing this?" Tyrian took the gown for her, holding it into the air. He looked at the dress and compared it to her skin, to her slim frame. It would be beautiful and curve just underneath her breasts. He licked his lips envisioning her putting on the dress, slowly. Him zipping her into it. His hands placed just underneath her bust. Her lips parted…

"I will. Do you like it?" Zuri boldly asked, watching her dress dangle in the air. Tyrian shifted his sights back to her and lowered the dress down directly to her.

"I'm positive it won't be nearly as beautiful as the woman wearing it, but it will do," Tyrian crooned, handing Zuri her dress. She slowly took it, a grin on her face. She liked how bold Tyrian was with his flirtation, but this was just one encounter. She wouldn't allow herself to become too interested.

"Thank you."

Tyrian bowed his head and then looked to Syncere, who seemed to be completely disinterested in the conversation, and he knew the reason, though, from the look on Amionette's eyes, he could tell she'd hoped for more.

"Well, perhaps we will see the three of you there. We, too, have been invited to the celebration."

"We sold the governor's son a home, and he invited us despite the steep ticket," Malicio cut in, and Zuri and Sacred chimed in with a laugh, but the energy between Syncere and Amionette had completely gone stale.

"And these are your outfits? Do the three of you always match?" Zuri questioned, looking between the brothers, noticing their similar looks.

"Not always, but for special occasions, and this occasion is especially special. Our brother has been gone for quite a while. He's just come back home."

"Yes, and how long have you been gone, Syncere, is it?" Amionette tilted her head to one side, curiously waiting for him to answer. When she first saw him, he had graveyard dirt on him, and she couldn't help but wonder if he had either crawled out of a grave, or dug into one.

He had such a... regal air to him, and knowing he was a vampire, along with his brothers, made her wonder just how long he'd been gone.

"Long enough. Tyrian, Malicio, let's not waste Francisco's time. He's taken a day off just to service us. And I for one, would love a bite to eat." Syncere's milky way-colored eyes bore into Amionette's, coyly reminding her that he was a vampire, and not to play games with him.

Amionette, though, felt she could not back down from his silent ultimatum. Move on, or she might become his meal. She advanced toward him, accidentally drinking in his scent. Her nipples stiffened with erection, pressing against her bra.

"What did you have in mind for a meal?" Amionette challenged, her chest poked out. Syncere closed the space between them, hovering over her like a walking billboard of warning.

"I wouldn't be so cute, if I were you," Syncere's voice deepened as he leaned into her ear. He pressed her curls away from her face, his lips teasing her earlobe as they brushed past. Syncere gripped Amionette around the waist, her body jolted from his touch. "Respect what I am, little girl."

He released her, and Amionette breathed deeply. She could still feel the coolness of his breath in her ear as he moved away from her. Had he just suggested he would make her his dinner? Zuri and Sacred stood beside Amionette with their mouths wide open, watching the encounter before them, wondering what Syncere had gotten so close to say.

Malicio and Tyrian were the only ones who heard it, and for someone who wanted nothing to do with the human race, they weren't so convinced by their brother's tactics.

Amionette was mesmerized by his blatant warning, but she didn't believe the force he was aiming to put behind it.

She didn't believe the words coming out of him, and as someone who saved her, she could never fear him. What she did fear, was the fact that she'd never met a man who made her feel this way. So... out of control. She'd never been filled with this much anticipation.

"Sirs, if I could have you join me back on the platform," Francisco called over to the Brown brothers, his hands in his pocket and a tape measure as long as a funeral procession hung from his neck. He didn't want to upset them—Francisco knew exactly what they were, something he'd unfortunately come to know when he surprised them by coming to their house to deliver garments. He'd peeked through the window, where he should not have, and saw them drinking, no, sucking the blood from several women.

Tyrian had been the one to catch him, and rather than compel him, he offered to pay him more for his silence and the delivery service. Their arrangement had since been working out.

Syncere was the first to give Francisco his attention. "We'll be right there. Boys," he beckoned, with authority in his tone. Malicio and Tyrian hesitantly walked away, stepping back onto the platform. Before Syncere joined his brothers, he stalled. He slipped his hands in his pockets, his locs tossed over his shoulder as a beautiful shimmery green and red dress caught his attention.

"That one," he titled his head toward the gown, and Amionette followed his gaze. The dress was gorgeous. It was like nothing she had ever seen. She turned back to face him, but when she did, he was gone. He wasn't even on the platform with his brothers.

Amionette hated to admit it, but the dress he'd selected held her attention and drew her to it.

Sacred and Zuri followed along behind her like two love-stricken puppies. Their lives had forever been changed, and none of the Brown brothers would ever be the same.

Syncere sat in the dining room of he and his brothers' seven-bedroom home. The crisp linen tablecloth that draped elegantly over the edges in the days of him returning had occupied his mind with its intricate patters of swirls and doillie cuts. He could stare at it all day, and he would never be able to take in each and every pattern of the velvet, shimmering fabric.

And yet, with so much to look at, his mind kept reverting back to Amionette. She plagued him with thoughts of the past. Of all the people he'd encountered in his life. All the humans he'd selflessly cared for, who he watched die once they reached old age, or worse, of sicknesses that had no cure.

While he knew no one would end up dead, perhaps, from an incurable disease in this time-period, he also knew that death was inevitable, and he was meant to spend his entire life alone, with his brothers. He would never take a vampire as his mate. He'd encountered very few over the course of his life, but the ones he did meet were terrible, had their own agendas, which were usually to oppose the Brown brothers, though they typically did not bother other people.

Amionette and her brazen lack of restraint left him

dumbfounded. Perhaps in this time-period, people were less afraid of vampires than they had been. He'd noticed many things had indeed changed. Like having several black presidents, black government officials, many black-owned businesses. There were very few of those before he was buried underground, but now, in the world he'd woken up to, it was so different, and there was a world of opportunity. It was possible the same could be said for human-vampire relations.

"If you can't stop thinking about her, why push her away?" Malicio innocently asked his brother as he entered the dining room. Blood dripped from his lips after finishing an appetizer to prepare him for dinner.

Syncere cut his eyes toward his brother, watching the blood trickle down his chin. Anger filled his chest. "I thought I said no humans in the house outside of the staff?" Syncere noted, his eyes darting to the blood falling down his brother's lips.

"Relax. It was a blood bag," Malicio said, defeated. He should have known that with his brother being back, they'd have to go back to being stand-up vampire citizens. Now that there were easier ways to get blood, Syncere wanted them to take every chance they could, so that they blended in, and so no one would find out about their existence.

"Good, where's Tyrian?" Syncere changed the subject. The last thing he wanted to do was talk about Amionette and his confused feelings for her. He'd saved her life and hoped like hell he'd never see her again. And now, after running into her, he wanted nothing more than to continue running into her, though he knew what kind of disaster that would bring.

"On his way down the staircase from the sound of it. But don't dismiss me, brother," Malicio asserted himself. He was often taken as a joke because he was the youngest and did his best to stay out of other people's business, but he wanted his brothers to be happy, especially Syncere. He couldn't imagine someone who deserved it more.

"I'm not dismissing you. I'm just not addressing my feelings with you."

Before Malicio could speak again, Tyrian entered the room, dressed in sweatpants and a t-shirt. Syncere's face crinkled up. He missed the days when even relaxed attire were slacks, suspenders, and a shirt. The sweatpants and tshirt look to him, looked very commonly, poor even.

"Boy, boy, boy the tension in here is so thick it can't even be sliced with a cake knife. What's wrong?" Tyrian looked between Syncere and Malicio as he took his seat at the table. He propped his elbows up and looked between his two brothers. Syncere looked like his head was full of team, waiting to blow like a cartoon character, and Malicio's baby face made him look like he would scream any moment if he couldn't say what he had on his mind.

Knowing him, though, he wouldn't.

"Nothing is the matter. And get your elbows off the table. I know I was gone a century, but manners don't stand up in this time?"

"Yeah, manners stand up, the same way your ass stood up in that formalwear shop and acted a fool today," Tyrian accurately accused his brother and placed his hands in his lap. As he did so, footsteps approached the table.

"Tonight, we have your favorite, Master Syncere, chicken Alfredo, garlic toast, with a side of blood, as the beverage," Ayleene Hudges, the chief of staff at the Brown residence, said as she led the food workers out and into the dining room. She'd been with the Brown brothers since she was a little girl. The Hudges and the Brown family had been close for many years. Ayleene, daughter of Anya, started working for the Brown brothers when she was just 20 years old. She'd gotten into a marriage, a terrible one at that, and Tyrian and Malicio saw to it that she was able to get out of it when she showed up on the doorstep of their boarding house one night, too afraid to tell her father or mother what had happened.

Though she knew her parents, Anya and Simpson, would have gladly done anything for her, and her grandparents, Harold and Amelia, Ayleene didn't want to burden any of them. She just wasn't that way, that she wanted anyone to worry about her. At the time, 1958, being a single woman was difficult. Especially after being married for nearly three years. She'd gotten married early —she thought she'd met the love of her life in high school, and her parents urged her to get married so that she wouldn't be single forever, or worse, on the street with a baby, because more and more women were becoming pregnant, and there were no fathers in sight.

Her parents didn't want her to end up the same way, and they scared her into marriage. But just a few months into the marriage, her husband began to change. He was lazy, violent at times, and frustrated they hadn't had a baby yet. Ayleene had been smart—she wasn't ready for a baby at twenty, regardless of what other people encouraged her to do with her body. Not to mention, while being married, she felt less and less attracted to her husband because of his raging attitude, funky demeanor, and his lackadaisical attitude.

Ayleene knew she had to do something, and it started with getting away. She wasn't ready to leave town, so the boarding house was the smartest place to go. She had very few dollars, but the money she did have, she could pay for about a week. She'd need to pick up some extra shifts at the bus station cleaning up the buses, but she could do that. They always needed extra hands.

A week at the boarding house, turned into a job for her. The Brown brothers, knowing her grandmother, and even her mother, watching her grow up over the years, recognized Ayleene's name on their registry. She'd kept her head down for a week and made no fuss, but Tyrian was curious why she was there, when she had a husband.

She'd explained her dilemma to the boys, and they offered her work, so she could live for free, but she'd have to work for it. After several years of hard work and dedication, Malicio and Tyrian hired her on to manage their home. She had a knack for just knowing how things should be in a home. She was in charge of the decorations and all. She'd done a marvelous job.

But, her life had not been lived or spent without regret, without trauma and drama, much like the rest of her family. She had a daughter when she was thirty-five. It was later in life, and a woman had needs, too. She did her best to raise her daughter, who grew up in a home with vampires, though she had no idea about it.

Angel was wild and free, a girl who could have taken the world by storm if she weren't in such a rush to grow up and find love. Unfortunately, her rush to grow up led her away from her mother, who had done everything she could to provide a stable living for her. When Ayleene's parents passed away and left the funeral home behind, she balanced the funeral home and being a house manager for the Brown brothers, with ease. Angel was good at helping around the funeral home. That seemed to be the only time the two got along, but the second she turned eighteen, she cut the relationship with her mother off completely—they wanted different things from Angel's life, and their differences drove them apart.

For many years, Ayleene tried to make things work with her daughter. Especially once she got pregnant with a daughter of her own. But Angel pushed and pushed, and she pushed until Ayleene could no longer stand to be pushed away. Living in the same city, she'd had nothing to do with her own child. And when Angel passed away, Ayleene had attended the funeral, remaining in the back most of the time. Her daughter's funeral was well-planned, well-staged, and she could feel the spirit of her own family surrounding her.

She met her granddaughter, Amionette, though she didn't have the nerve to introduce herself as such. There was no telling what Angel had told Amionette, and too afraid to find out, Ayleene had kept her distance and kept quiet about being Angel's mother, though it was with great sorrow. A regret she would live with until the day she died. And, at almost eighty years old, it didn't seem like Ayleene would have much longer to carry that regret.

"Thank you, Ayleene, but you can just call me Syncere. I think you've more than earned the right to our names," Syncere corrected her, and she smiled as the servers placed covered dinner plates in front of each of the Brown brothers. The three servers fled the dining room the moment they were done. Even though Tyrian had made sure they wouldn't tell anyone about them being vampires, he had not taken their fear from them. Though the Brown brothers had better manners than to eat the help.

Ayleene came to the side of Syncere and placed her hand on her petite hip. "If that was the case, you would tell me your REAL name. Not the name you boys got during slave times." Ayleene patted Syncere on the shoulder and sauntered away. Even as an elderly woman, Ayleene was just as sharp as she had ever been in the mind, body, and soul. She still moved around like a young woman. And her voice still had a youthful playfulness to it.

Since Syncere had returned, she was the only human that he'd let get close to him. She was not long for this world, but the time she did have, he had enjoyed the last week with her. She reminded him of the good days, telling stories about the things he missed with his brothers. Crushes, heartbreaks, business success and failures. Ayleene's stories allowed him to see his brothers in a different light, the kind of light that helped the picture of what he missed seem more well-rounded.

He was of course happy to hear about his brothers' triumphant moments. Knowing that they'd landed on their feet and that they were happy, but he didn't ask for a cookie cutter fairytale. He'd wanted the good, the bad, and the ugly, and Ayleene always kept it real.

"Perhaps we should tell her our real names. It's not like she hasn't earned the right to know," Syncere advised, and Malicio and Tyrian both nodded in agreement.

"Speaking of the right to know something," Tyrian sat up straight in his seat and removed the cover from his dinner plate. "You wanna tell us what was up with you and that girl Amionette today, or?..."

Malicio's eyebrow rose with anticipation. He, too, wanted to know. Syncere's anger began boiling inside of him. His hands felt like they were burning off he was so upset.

"I think you all are thinking too deeply into the interaction. There's no need for me to be buddy-buddy with her. I saved her life, she's alive. That's the end of it." Syncere slammed his fist on the tabletop, and the eight-foot oak table wobbled, nearly breaking from the strength of his hit.

"So, you throw a fit to cover up how you feel? Who's the child now?" Malicio teased. He was the one who was often accused of being a child or immature because of his tantrums, though he was doing his best to get better at it. Being over 200 years old had not helped him a bit when it came to growing up, or attempting to. It had only extended the period in which he clung to his childlike nature. But, with his oldest brother returning, it put things into perspective for him. He'd always wanted to make Syncere proud of him. But, in his absence, it seemed more important—more quintessential, so that he wouldn't have things to repair when he returned.

And so far, he didn't. Except but to repair himself. He was beginning to question his own rule of getting close to humanity, but Amionette… he could not get her out of his mind, no matter what he did.

He smoothed out the tablecloth, restoring it to its original setting, as if he hadn't just shaken everything on the table out of its place and then reached for his glass of blood, that had miraculously not spilled over. Gripping the stem of the glass, he placed the rim to his lips and chugged the blood. And for the first time that day, he was able to drown out the thoughts he had of Amionette. Of her plump lips. Of her curvaceous body. Of her sultry voice that made him want to hear her moan deeply in his ear.

When the contents of his glass were gone, he called out loudly to the kitchen, "Another glass… now!" His tone was guttural, almost like a growl. Neither Malicio nor Tyrian had ever seen their brother in this state before. They wondered how he was able to keep control so well, how he never let himself loose. Yet, in this moment, they saw their brother coming loose at the seams.

"Make that another!"

"And another!" Malicio echoed after his brothers. Tonight seemed as if it were going to be a long night. Syncere had helped carry everyone else's emotions his entire life, but the truth of the matter was, when it came to his own emotions, he'd shove them out of the way if he could.

And right now, the only way to do that was to drown his human emotions with a glass of vampirism... good ole' fashion blood.

CHAPTER 16

Christmas Eve had come, and it felt like just another day. There was no snow on the ground, the weather was at a record high of 65 degrees, and other than the humongous Christmas decorations and a backed up morgue, there were no real signs of the Christmas spirit. Except for in Zuri's parents' home.

There were two, white Christmas trees; one in the living room, and another upstairs in the bonus room. The house's exterior was decorated with a black Santa on the roof, reindeer, and little black elves in the yard to welcome you to their home. Amionette grinned. She found it cute that other people were still able to enjoy themselves and have a good time and still imbued by the Christmas holiday.

Three men, dressed in suits came to get their things and carried their bags upstairs. Amionette hadn't even had the chance to ask where they were going or where they were taking her things.

"Don't mind Charles and his team. We bring them in when guests are going to stay over. It's so nice to meet you," Christina, Zuri's mother, said as she pulled Amionette into a hug.

"Oh," she yelped as Christina wrapped her arms around

her. She hadn't been enveloped in such a motherly hug since the last time she hugged her mother, which had been many years ago, even years before her mother's passing.

"Mama, don't scare her away," Zuri whispered through a clenched jaw. Amionette was the first friend she felt she had made, and if she hadn't managed to run her away in the time they'd spent together, she didn't want to let anyone else do it either.

"I'm sorry, we're just so happy our Zuri met someone to love on her who isn't us. Isn't that right, Timothy?" Christina stepped to the side to allow her husband the space to enter the room. Her eyes gleamed when she saw Timothy enter. Zuri couldn't help but notice that her parents' love after all these years still felt very real. She could only hope to find a love like that.

"That's right, how you doin', baby girl?" Timothy cooed seeing Zuri. He loved both of his children equally, but with Zuri, it was easy. Their relationship had always been so simple to navigate. She'd always trusted him, gave him her attention, and she had him wrapped around his strong finger.

With Sacred, it was different—difficult. He didn't know how to relate to her, and most of the time, he didn't know how to help her. But, he loved Sacred, and he would be as close as she would allow him to.

He pulled Zuri in for a hug. She nestled in her father's neck as they embraced. "Hi, Daddy, you ready for tonight?"

"I think so. I'm so glad you girls are gonna be by my side tonight," he said, and then reached out for Amionette's hand. "It's nice to meet you. Zuri's been talking about you non-stop since she started working for you," he chuckled. His laugh was hearty and warm like soup.

Shocked by his kindness and overall fatherly demeanor, she was reluctant to take his hand, but did anyway. Rather than shake her hand like a stranger, he gave it a loving squeeze. Amionette's eyes began to water. It wasn't like she'd never been treated kindly. She'd been treated well by many people in the past. But the way Zuri came into her life and loved her outside of work. Truly being supportive of her and how she needed to avoid work right now with little to no questions, she would love her forever for that.

And now, as a direct extension through Zuri, she was receiving love from her parents as well? This was an overstimulation she'd never experienced, but was ready to welcome. For the first time ever, she felt safe around someone other than family. And, if she were being honest, Amionette wasn't exactly sure she felt safe around family. She'd run away from her own several times growing up because she couldn't trust her mother's men to keep their hands off of her or not to make inappropriate comments. There were times she wanted to tell her mother what she'd experienced, about how these grown men made her feel uncomfortable. At the time, she thought maybe her mother wouldn't care. Now, as an adult, she realized it was because she didn't feel she had a safe space to discuss or reveal her scariest fears or traumas.

Sacred flew down the staircase, happy to see both her sister and Amionette. She could see the three of them building their own little family together. She was happy to see that Zuri had someone who would be around, someone to be there for her just as much as she was there for other people. Sacred felt, if there were anyone on the planet who deserved a friend, it was her sister.

"Z-Z, Amionette!"

Timothy released both girls, and Sacred flew into their arms. She'd just seen them not even a week ago, but tonight was special. Sacred had avoided going to prom. It didn't seem special or important. And, she was afraid to go alone. No one had asked her. Sacred had been labeled the weird girl at school, the nerdy, comic-book loving, super-hero Cosplaying, anime watching black girl, who no one believed was truly black. They'd called her the "Inside Out" girl, or an "Oreo," a term she despised but learned to live with. But now, with Zuri making a friend, she was able to also, and neither of them would ever let Amionette go.

Tonight would be the do-over for prom. She and her sister and Amionette would all get ready, while listening to good music, doing each other's hair and make up, and they would be beautiful.

Sacred's hug made a loud thud against the girls.

"Come on! Let's go upstairs and get ready! I've got the music set up, snacks, drinks…" Sacred rambled on for what seemed like several minutes, but Amionette and Zuri both let her go on. While Sacred and Zuri both needed a friend, Amionette needed healing. And this family felt like food for her soul. When she was around Zuri, she felt safe and guarded. Seeing Zuri be loved on by her sister solidified what Amionette already thought about Zuri—that she was a good person who was worthy of her love and attention, and with her family, they were all the perfect fit. Amionette didn't feel like she stuck out. They had embraced her, they'd wanted her.

She only wished she had felt that way with her own family.

Sacred grabbed them both by their hands and began dragging them up the staircase. "Two hours, not a second more!" Timothy called out to the girls. Sacred flashed a smile to her father, one like he had never seen, and his heart warmed. He always worried about Sacred because of her anxiety, her typically being left out and lashing out, but for the first time since she was a little girl, he'd seen a change in her. He happily returned her smile.

Christina reached her hand across her husband's chest, patting the space where his heart was. "Come on, handsome, let's get you dressed, and away from anyone who might see you tear up," she giggled.

Timothy swallowed hard and followed his wife. He had a feeling that his girls would be just fine.

"I tell all my hoes, rake it up! Break it down, back it up!" Amionette squatted and began twerking. It had been ages since she allowed herself to be this free, to have this much fun. Zuri had never seen Amionette let loose like this, and she realized then, that whatever Amionette had gone through in her life, that led her to this point, it must have put her in a box, a place where she believed it wasn't safe to leave. Each and every day, like an onion, Zuri saw another layer of Amionette shedding off, and she loved the person blossoming before her.

Zuri turned the music down, slowing Amionette from throwing her ass back, and she grabbed a champagne glass. "A toast before we put on our dresses!" She raised her glass high and into the sky. Amionette, a bit sweaty, grabbed her glass and met Zuri in the center of the room, catching her breath. Sacred joined in as well, standing there, waiting for Zuri to continue.

"Tonight, I say, we just try to have fun, right?" Zuri smiled so hard, she could have broken her teeth from the strength of her jaw. She just happened to be that happy.

"Right."

"Right," Sacred finished, and the three girls clinked glasses and tossed the liquid back like they were drinking shots. When they were finished, they went into Sacred's wardrobe room and began putting on their dresses.

Sacred and Zuri's family came from money—they'd made plenty of it over the years, and Timothy spoiled his family. Amionette wondered what it would be like to not only be spoiled but loved as well. She knew her mother loved her—it was just a complicated relationship. Angel spent most of her life running from her own family, always mentally and emotionally a bit disturbed, which she'd passed down to Amionette. Amionette grew up wondering why she wasn't allowed to meet a grandmother who lived in the same city. Why it seemed that the family business was more important than literally everything else in their lives. Why it always took precedence.

Amionette grew up with money, but she never felt parented. She was allowed a little too much freedom, where she craved stability and discipline. Angel grew up under, what she felt, were too tight reigns, and rather than raise Amionette the same way, she let Amionette practically raise herself.

Because of that, Amionette was still trying to figure out who she was and what she wanted out of life. That was one of the reasons it was so easy for her to cling to Fletcher. He just seemed to know things. He seemed to be able to just tell her what she needed to do, and for the most part, he was right, until he wasn't. He'd always known what Amionette needed, how she should dress, what she should say, what kind of music and attitude she should have. He'd literally made her into the woman she was, and who he wanted her to be. Without him, though, she had a chance to figure out who she was on her own. What she actually wanted out of life, and find her own strength.

In the wardrobe, Amionette sat down and began working on her make up. She wasn't going to go crazy on the makeup. She never did. Her natural beauty was more than enough for such an elegant event, but she still wanted to have her own flare. She painted her lips like the girls from the 90's, with a 2010 vibe to it. Her lip liner was a dark chocolate, but her lips were stained in a flesh-like pink and glossy top coat to finish her lips.

She'd gone with a light coverage foundation, just to give her a more polished look, sprayed her setting spray, and then went to work on her hair. By the end of her getting ready, she felt like a princess, who would have never seen herself going to such an event. But there was something about the night, something that made her feel uneasy. Her mother had always told her to listen to her intuition, and she found that for the most part, she did. Yet, she wasn't sure if she could trust her own intuition because surely, there were signs about Frederick that she should have seen like neon flags, and she'd missed them. Rather, she'd chosen to ignore them.

Zuri approached her, standing behind her, as she remained seated in one of the many vanities Sacred had in her wardrobe. Though Sacred was typically shy, the only place she felt like herself, away from her sister, was in her wardrobe, where she could dress up in a costume and become anyone else. Anyone that she wanted to be.

"You look beautiful already, I can't wait for you to put on that dress!" she squealed, clapping her hands. Amionette hadn't even tried the dress on at the store. She just paid for it, and they left out of the store without a second thought.

"I just hope it fits," Amionette admitted, looking over to the garment bag she had hanging up on one of the singular hanging closet hooks.

"You didn't seem too concerned about it fitting when you just bought it," Sacred chimed in, a suspicious grin on her face. To her, Amionette's interaction with Syncere was unfolding before their eyes like a book. She knew if their meeting was a book, that meant that something terrible was on the horizon, but she hoped for everyone's sake it wasn't. She'd told herself many times that she couldn't live inside the fantasies of book worlds, because life didn't always turn out that way.

She shook the thought from her mind and waited for Amionette to give her a worthy clap back.

"I wasn't concerned then, because at the time, it seemed like a good idea."

"And it's still probably a good idea. Syncere selected a good dress if you ask me," Zuri pointed out as she went over to the garment bag and unzipped it.

"Did he select it, though? Or, did he just mention—"

"He selected it," both Zuri and Sacred said simultaneously, followed by a roar of laughter. Amionette kissed her teeth, and sauntered over to the garment bag. She had to admit, he did have good taste. He'd noticed right away the dress, and they'd been looking for nearly thirty minutes.

"Oh my God!" Amionette said aloud, though she'd only meant to say it to herself. "Maybe he's gay," Amionette laughed, but not like she found anything about what she just said funny, but as though she'd just made a groundbreaking discovery.

"Who's gay?" Zuri asked, wondering how they'd gotten onto this subject and who they could possibly be talking about. But she got the sense, from Amionette's maniacal laughter, that what she was laughing about wasn't funny at all.

"Syncere! I was trying to figure out why he was pushing me away, and then he mentioned how perfect the dress would look on me. That man is a gay man!" she shouted, like it made all the sense in the world.

Sacred and Zuri's faces twisted in confusion. Sacred placed her hand underneath her chin, rubbing it as she walked over to look at the dress that Zuri was now removing from its bag. She analyzed it and thought back to the moment. She didn't get the vibe that he was gay, although she understood gay people came in all shapes and sizes.

"I don't know about that. The way he was pressed up against you, I don't know if he was "pushing" you away."

"Yeah, and you never said how you knew that man either. Sounds like a storytime to me." Zuri sarcastically shrugged her shoulders and looked over to Amionette. Her cheeks were as red as candy apples. She did want to tell them how she knew Syncere, but now wasn't the time. She'd need to gather her thoughts about what she was going to say and say it carefully.

"That is a story for another time, girls."

"Ooh, avoiding. I bet y'all had sex. The chemistry—"

"The fireworks—"

"The stares—"

Zuri and Sacred traded statements back and forth, and Amionette shook her head. "Zuri, you know for yourself I've been with Fletcher for almost five years. When would I have had sex with that man?" Amionette questioned, dispelling her and Sacred's ideas. Shooting them down to hell.

"I guess you don't have a past like everybody else in this

room," Zuri laughed, but Sacred heard the uneven tone of her sister's voice.

"Speak for yourself. Everyone doesn't have a past, but you, sister, most certainly do," Sacred reminded her sister, and Zuri nearly ripped Amionette's dress out the bag, hoping no one saw her beginning to panic.

"Nah, nah, nah, if we callin' shit out, spill the tea, Zuri," Amionette said as she removed Zuri's hands from her dress and took it out of the bag herself.

"Both of y'all need to mind your business. As a matter of fact, I'm about to go over here and get myself ready. Thank you!"

Zuri fled the area so fast, they could see the wind whipping around her as she left the wardrobe.

"What was all of that about?" Amionette questioned Zuri, knowing if anyone knew, it would be her.

"In time, I'm sure she'll tell it," Sacred giggled and went over to her own dress to begin getting ready.

It seemed like the night had taken several turns that Amionette did not expect, but one thing was for certain and two were for sure; if Syncere wasn't gay, why was he pushing her away? And he saved her, but why did it seem like he felt guilt for doing such a thing?

Amionette was done wondering, and tonight, if she did indeed run into him, she planned to get the answers to her questions, even if it meant getting bitten.

CHAPTER 17

Syncere, Tyrion, and Malicio approached the front doors of the governor's mansion. Inside, the ornate foyer was filled to capacity with people, walking around with drinks. Servers held trays of Hors d'oeuvres, offering food and expensive alcohol to the guests. The There were five men at the door—security and bodyguards, checking and taking invitations from each of the guests. The place seemed extremely secure.

Along with their invitations, they had to show proof of ID. Luckily, their identification was covered by a friend they made along the way who worked for the DMV. While the Brown brothers used their gifts, they tried not to use them recklessly. It would have been simple enough to mind control people into believing something different, but Syncere had made it clear when they first became vampires that they would not take control simply because they had the power to do so. They would earn their place, and so far, the trio had.

Once given approval to enter, the Brown brothers graced the foyer with their presence. They commanded attention from women and men alike as they strolled through the party. The flow of traffic was heading to the ballroom, just beyond a grand staircase. On their way in that direction, Tyrion grabbed two glasses of champagne for himself. His blood lust around so many people, at times, had the tendency to get the best of him. But, drinking helped to offset the fluttering in his stomach.

Malicio had been waiting on Sanya to arrive. She was invited, as a member of their team, and she said she'd be arriving shortly. He felt almost guilty for thinking back to Sacred. She was captivating, breath-taking even, but Sanya, there was something special about her also. She was smart and brave. And, she could deal with the craziness of their office. Sanya was always prepared, very organized, and she knew when to mind her business, but also, when to butt in. Malicio had a crush on Sanya, something he'd done his best to keep to himself, but it was true. Not to mention, he'd accidentally touched her hand one day to keep her from stumbling as she got up from her seat, and for just a second, he got a glimpse of their future together. It was on their wedding day.

He forced the image out of his head then, and he had to do it now in order to carry on for the rest of the evening. He'd learned that his premonitions didn't always turn out the way he saw them based on events and things changing, so he often kept his premonitions to himself for that reason. And the fact that Tyrian had made it his mission to make fun of Malicio at every turn of the day. He couldn't stand to be picked with about most things, but about Sanya? Malicio knew he would become easily frustrated and hateful toward his brother.

Syncere nearly stumbled into the party. He was drunk on blood and wine—his only way of coping with his current predicament. He knew it was not his business to know how Amionette had come to find herself in the center of a construction zone, fighting for her life. He also knew, though, that there was no amount of alcohol or blood on the planet that he would be able to consume to keep his mind off of her and that damn night.

Tyrian grabbed Syncere by the arm. He had been afraid of something like this happening. Syncere was the type of man who internalized things. His issues, his achievements, his failures. Whatever he experienced, he locked it up so tightly inside of him that it always had a way of creeping back out, one way or another. This time, it was showing in his reckless drinking.

"Yo, you need to pull yourself together. Do you hear me?" Tyrian tilted his head over, lowly speaking to his brother. Syncere shook him loose. The last thing he wanted to hear was what he needed to do.

"I been takin' care of you all your life. I don't need to be told what to do," he said once he finally got Tyrian off of him. Malicio, who was surprised that he was the most calm in this situation, approached both of his brothers with a formulated plan for the evening.

"We clearly can't leave this muthafucka by himself all night. He's not being himself—"

"Can you blame him? If I saw the woman whose life I saved and she looked like that…" In under a second flat, Syncere had his brother hung up by his throat.

Tyrian grabbed at his brother's hand, Malicio tried laughing to make it look like they were playing, but this wasn't the time or place for rough-housing or jealous physical interactions.

"Don't be mentionin' her, T. I mean it," Syncere growled, his brown orbs began to swirl with a tint of crimson.

"Put me the fuck down," Tyrian chuckled, and Malicio pulled them both apart.

"I don't know what the fuck is going on with you, but if this girl got you hemmed up like this, you need to just talk to her. This is ridiculous, and overall embarrassing," Malicio whispered and fake-smiled at the guests who were passing by, watching in awe of Syncere's strength, but also the disagreement unfolding before them.

Tyrian smoothed out his satin, chili red tuxedo jacket and shook his head. "You right. The last thing we need to do is be carryin' on up in here like a bunch of niggas." Tyrian tossed his arm around Syncere, who was slowly beginning to calm down. He could not put his finger on it, but the mere thought of someone looking at her, mentioning her, made him feel like his blood was on fire. Like he wanted to kill something.

Syncere felt tonight he needed to compartmentalize in order to make it through the evening. He would put Amionette in a box of her own, by herself and worry about his feelings toward her when he could. For now, he needed to enjoy the celebration with his brothers and show them how proud he truly was. They'd made so much of themselves in the last century—his only focus should be them tonight.

An apology would do no good. Syncere wasn't the type to say he was sorry anyway. He knew the best form of an apology was changed behavior, and he planned to put his best foot forward for the rest of the evening.

"Good evening, good evening, ladies and gentlemen. If I could have your attention," Shaylene Upswing, one of Nashville's district leaders, called the room to attention over the microphone. Her curvy figure donned looks from many male admirers, causing the room to thicken in the front with onlooking men.

Though Syncere, Tyrian, nor Malicio were impressed by a beautiful body. The three men had met their fair share of women who used their bodies for their own agendas. None of them would be so easily swayed.

"I just want to thank you all for being here tonight. The Christmas Eve celebration is one of the most important events of the year. It allows new and old business owners alike to come together to meet, greet, and..."

As Shaylene Upswing serenaded the crowd with her welcome, the hairs on Syncere's neck began to prickle. Inconspicuously, he looked over his right shoulder and into the crowd. His eyes immediately landed on her.

She got the dress, he snickered inwardly. It looked exactly the way he'd known it would. It hugged her torso, lifting her supple breasts even more. He wished he would have known her in the 1800's—the balls they would have attended. The way he would have undressed her...

The oxygen around them seemed to have been sucked out of the room when she entered. Behind her tinted glasses, he could see her eyes. Syncere wondered if she'd worn them to hide behind or to add to her ensemble. Either way, it did not matter. He could see her earthy pupils, glaring directly at him. When Amionette saw him staring directly at her, she looked away, her cheeks rushing with heat.

"I can see why he told you to wear that dress now. Y'all are on a date," Zuri whisper-cackled, clapping Amionette against the arm.

Sharply, Amionette turned toward Zuri and shot her daggers with her eyes. She was glad she'd chosen to wear a very swanky pair of sunglasses, otherwise, her eyes would have given her away. She had never met a man so bold as Syncere. He'd chosen her outfit just so they could match, but wouldn't even hold a conversation with her? The confusion between them was overwhelming, but she'd come prepared to question him until he gave her the answers she wanted. No, desperately needed.

"I'm sorry," Zuri said, and she straightened up her act as if she had not said a word. Sacred, whose arm was linked with Zuri's, suddenly felt a sense of nervousness fall over her. She'd so fervently wanted to prove to herself, and literally everyone else, that she could make her own bold decisions and make it through the night. But, surrounded by so many people, in such an elegant, audacious dress, she began to feel the pressure of almost performing throughout the night.

Her powder blue and mauve dress, with feathers at the bottom, made people not only look, but stare. Her ombre braids complimented her look, and rather than blend in, like most others, she stood out beautifully. Something she was not used to.

Timothy glanced ahead of him at his beautiful

daughters. They had both made him proud in their own way, especially Sacred, who he could see from here was beginning to show signs of her nervous ticks. Her foot pedaled against the floor, tapping away at it anxiously. Timothy promised himself he'd be more involved in the calm-down process with Sacred. His daughter was his first and most important priority.

He kissed the back of Christina's hand and nodded his head forward, signaling their daughter. Christina understood his hint and released him, an endearing smile on her face. Timothy came up behind Sacred and placed both hands on her arms. He was close enough that only she could hear the words he whispered in her ear.

"Sacred, I'm so proud of you for stepping outside of your usual color clothing. You look beautiful. I can only imagine how nervous you might be in this room, but I can truly say, there isn't a woman here tonight, who looks nearly as elegant as you." Timothy placed a kiss at the crease of his daughter's jaw, and her foot instantly stopped tapping.

She spun around on her glass, block heels and wrapped her arms around her father. There was something about the validation of a father that felt special, different than that of a man. A father has no other agenda but to simply reassure and validate you as a woman. Her father, in just a brief moment and with just a few words had done that.

"Thank you, Daddy," she whispered as she reached up on her tippy toes and placed a kiss on her father's cheek.

He cleared his throat, sending away the tears forming in his throat, and then turned behind him to reach for

Christina, who was as proud of him as she could be. Sacred was not a bad child. She just struggled with many mental illnesses. For years, Christina and Timothy blamed themselves for their daughter's struggle, until they all went to family counseling and learned that it was nothing they had done wrong. Unfortunately, Sacred was raised in a generation where social media dictated everyone's lives. Cyber-bullying was at an all-time-high, and unlike Zuri, who naturally marched to the beat of her own "Pleasantville" drum, Sacred became paralyzed in her rhythm.

But, she fought every day to kill the discomfort she felt simply by walking into a crowded room. Started conversations with people she otherwise would not have if she didn't, and when her eyes landed on Malicio, she felt the urge to speak to him. To announce her arrival. She'd felt something between them at the formalwear shop. Something she'd never felt before. It was a tingling sensation she hoped would not fade. Before the night was over, she was going to speak to him.

Malicio caught wind of the girls' entrance when he caught Syncere's neck turned so far back he thought it would break. Checking behind him, he saw Sacred, and her powder blue and mauve dress made his knees buckle.

So fuckin' beautiful, he'd said to no one else but himself, but Tyrian had heard him. He cast his gaze behind him as well to see Zuri, and unlike the two of them, he wasn't afraid to go after what he wanted.

Shaylene Upswing's speech had ended, and the ballroom came alive with conversation. Tyrian left his brothers standing in their place on a mission to speak with Zuri. She smiled as he bridged the gap between them and the sea of people, awaiting his presence. With confidence, he strolled across the room, heading directly to her. When he'd seen her open her arms, he wondered if she was requesting a hug, which he would gladly envelop her, though that seemed a bit personal for them having just met. He opened his arms, to greet her, only steps from Zuri, when a man cut directly in front of him and stole the hug he'd planned to give her.

"Damn Zuri, I haven't seen you in ages!" the man swooned as he tightly hugged her. She clearly knew the man because her arms were wrapped around his neck, and he'd lifted her into the air.

Tyrian didn't like that at all. He lifted his foot to have a word with Zuri when Syncere came up behind him and tugged on his arm.

"But I'm the one going crazy, huh?" he laughed and pulled his brother away from almost causing a scene.

"Yes, you're still the crazy one," Tyrian said like it was a no-brainer and reluctantly left with his brother, and as he walked away, he kept looking over his shoulder, hoping that Zuri was looking back at him.

He'd double-checked for her, and she was still talking to the overzealous man in front of her. If it was the last thing he would do that night, he planned to pull Zuri to the side to get to know her better. He figured the man couldn't be her man, because he wouldn't have let her attend a function on her own.

Tyrian made a mental note to find out more about her

potential suitor, because he could feel in his very human soul, that if he let Zuri get away from him, he would come to regret it.

And as the live band began playing music, the room was a bussling crowd of smiling faces.

The night, so far, had been a success. Just an hour into the celebration, connections were being made, and Timothy had shaken hands with all the right people. He was on the fast track to launching his campaign, and all without having to spend a dime of his own money. The girls stayed close to his side the entire evening, though their own agendas prickled their minds. Amionette had been eye-fucking Syncere the entire evening. Each time he moved, she seductively followed him. A glance here, a stare there, she hadn't lost sight of him the entire night. Each time she tried to get away to speak with him, though, she was cornered by another person who Timothy had introduced her to.

Calling her his "pseudo-daughter" made her feel good, but it was becoming a barrier for her to get to Syncere. The ballroom had finally opened up, the live band slowed down their tempo, inviting couples to come to the dance floor.

A ritardando version of Alicia Keys' "Show Me Love" began to play, the melody becoming a call to those who would want to dance.

Amionette's eyes roamed the room, searching for Syncere. She would ask him to dance. Society had made women believe they couldn't make the first move, and while she wasn't planning on being the type to pop down on one knee and propose, asking a man for a dance was harmless. Yet, as she scoped the room out, she did not see him. Somehow, between the conglomerate of people coming up to her, creating an endless bridge between her and Syncere, she'd lost him.

She sighed heavily, preparing to move out of the way as the floor continued to open up, and for a moment, she thought she might be seeing things. The music began to go even slower. The guests took their strides leisurely, as if they weren't in a hurry. Womens' gowns were in mid-swing, suspended in the air. Time had completely slowed down.

Yet, Syncere was the only thing moving at regular pace. The pathway for him to reach her had cleared, and she took it. She, too, could move at regular speed. He'd met her in the center of the dance floor and held his hand out.

"May I have this dance, Amionette?" he formally asked, and in his tuxedo, that perfectly matched her dress, she could not say no.

Shocked and confused, the two emotions she continuously felt around this man, were creeping their way into her once again. Had he been the reason the room seemed to slow? Or, was she so enamored with him that she wanted to see that? Had her mind been playing tricks on her?

Amionette was unsure, but it would not stop her from

having this dance. With a nod of her head, she joined him on the dance floor. He placed one hand firmly against her hip, pulling her body close to him. She felt the force of his grip, possessing her. But she did not mind it. He took her right hand in his, holding onto it tightly, like he had lost it before and didn't want to separate from it ever again.

He intently stared into her rich, brown eyes, unsure of what to say. It had taken him an hour to ask her to dance. Syncere never felt this nervous around others. What was it about her that made him feel… inadequate? That made him question himself.

"Why'd you ask me to dance?" Amionette quipped. He'd been practically avoiding her all night, yet time stood still for them to dance?

"Were you unavailable to dance?"

"Did it look like I was unavailable to dance?" she shot back. Had she known her response would be met with such disdain, she might have asked a different question to start.

"You did not. Did I need a reason to ask?" he questioned, and frustration filled her. Why was he so annoying?

"You know what, this was a bad idea," she said, letting go of his hand, but she could not move. Syncere's hand was still around her waist.

"Why? Because I'm not going to answer every question you ask?"

"But you're going to question my question? My mama always said, 'I asked you a direct question; I want a direct answer,' is that so hard?" Amionette shrugged her shoulders, waiting for a response. Syncere smiled at her tantrum. He was beginning to see what he liked about Amionette. She was feisty, fine as hell, and she smelled delicious. He'd had just a taste of her blood, and it had driven him mad.

Syncere leaned forward, his lips brushed against her cheek, "There's only one thing hard between us," he said, and Amionette's eyebrow furrowed as she looked down. She hadn't wanted to lick her lips, but she found herself doing it anyway.

"You… arouse me," Syncere admitted. It wasn't the answer she was hoping for, but it was certainly a start.

"I can see that," she swallowed hard, blinking back the bulging erection in his pants. She'd never seen a man, who simply from her touch grew hard. Even Fletcher damn near needed her to turn into an acrobat before his dick sprung to life. Amionette had never felt desired with Fletcher, not the way she wanted. "Is that why you asked me to dance?" She made eye contact with him, and he moved her around the room. She hadn't even realized, that though he was not holding her hand, her body was naturally moving with his. They were floating across the dance floor.

"It is not. I asked you to dance because I'm curious about you. What were you doing in that hole the night I found you?"

Amionette had not spoken the full truth of that night to anyway. She'd tried to block it out, simply to move on from it, but that was highly unlikely. It was a night, that no matter how much sleep she got, there would never be a nightmare that could hold a candle to what she experienced.

"Did you slow time?" she challenged his question with another, hoping he would take the lead so that she could find the words to speak.

"Does it bother you that I did?"

"It bothers me that you that you think you're so funny with all of your questions. I guess the time being slowed down is a vampire thing?" She smirked, and Syncere placed her hand in his again, and suddenly dipped her. While hovering over her neck, where he could hear the blood rushing through her, he said, "It's a Syncere thing."

When he pulled her back up, her glasses were caught in her hair. She quickly reached up for them to pull them back down, but Syncere grabbed her wrist. "Leave 'em," he ordered, and Amionette felt she had no choice but to leave them off.

"Must be some vampire shit," she murmured, and he laughed.

"Also... Syncere shit," and together they laughed.

Simultaneously, the dance floor and the band were moving at a regular pace, and everything around them seemed normal again. Syncere had not wanted to admit it, but he hadn't meant to slow time. When he found Amionette, and he'd seen her searching, he hoped she was looking for him. He used his vamp speed to rush to her direct eyeview, just to make sure she was indeed looking for him. When he confirmed that she was, he'd started moving, and everything around him began to slow.

There had been very few times in his life where his gift

had a mind of its own. Around Amionette, though, it seemed... strange. But in such a good way.

"Now, will you answer my question?" Syncere repeated himself, something he hated to do, but there was such a mystery surrounding Amionette. The more he knew, he thought the better he'd feel. Then he could figure out why he was so... infatuated with her.

"I... long story short..."

As Syncere swept her across the dance floor, she gave him the shortest version of the story she could muster up. From the beginning of how she and Fletcher met, to how he was there for her when her mother died, or so she thought. To him literally trying to kill her.

"I actually felt guilty for him getting that woman pregnant. I blamed myself for grieving too long. That's why we were arguing. He was trying to manipulate me into actually believing this was my fault, and I almost fell for the shit," Amionette admitted as tears creased the sides of her eyes. Syncere's throat tightened with anger. He wanted to kill Fletcher, simply off the strength that he'd hurt Amionette. He felt protective over her. He wished now that he would have never let her go off on her own.

"And this Fletcher, where is he now?" Syncere pried. It had been a very long time since he'd killed a human, or anyone for that matter. But Amionette's pain was enough to make him want to break his rule. His most absolute rule of no killing.

"I honestly don't know. I suppose he'd still be living in the house since he designed it and it was his."

Syncere winced. "So, this nigga's off living his best life knowing, or thinking, excuse me, that he killed you?"

Amionette nodded her head, a small smile peeking through. She had not heard Syncere speak often, but she'd definitely never heard him speak like this. Even she was struggling with the truth of it, except there was one thing she knew, that maybe only three other people on the entire planet knew.

"This isn't the first time he's done this," she painfully acknowledged. "It wasn't until he tried to kill me did I know for sure that it was true." Amionette's voice broke, and something inside of Syncere fractured.

He whisked her from the dance floor and away from the views of the party's population. They fled the ballroom and went back into the foyer, where there were hushed conversations and couples canoodling. He'd pulled her behind one of the foyer's pillars, pressing her up against it. He pulled out a handkerchief. Its red nature would hide her tears, but Syncere would never forget this moment. The look in her eyes.

Syncere blotted at her tears, fumes steaming from his ears and nostrils. He'd made up his mind. As soon as he could, he would be going after Fletcher for what he'd done to Amionette. Damn his rules. He'd have to reserve them for people who actually mattered.

When Amionette's tears dissipated, Syncere felt questioning her any further would be silly. He didn't need to know why he was so infatuated with her. He didn't need to know the semantics. What he knew was that he did not want to see her hurting this way. He knew that if Fletcher killed another previously, he would not stop killing. Most killers didn't just stop. There would always be another and another until they were stopped.

He reached for her cheek, stroking it with the back of his hand. Amionette turned her head slightly. It wasn't quite a jump, but there was apprehension in receiving his affection.

"I would never do anything to physically hurt you," Syncere reassured her as he stroked her smooth skin turned red from crying.

"But you would hurt me emotionally?" she sarcastically asked, yet, she couldn't deny the truth in the question she'd asked.

"I would not. Not intentionally."

Amionette was mesmerized by Syncere's eyes. She could not look away from him, even if she tried. Amionette extended her arms around Syncere's neck, marrying her hands behind him. His hair had been styled in two fishtail braids, permitting her access to his long mane. Amionette gently tugged on one of his locs, twirling the end of it with her finger.

Syncere groaned from the stiffening pain of his ever growing erection. This woman, Amionette, drove him crazy with lust. Her shimmering lips brought him discomfort in an indescribable way. In his time, it was inappropriate to just lunge in and kiss a woman, but he ached to claim her. To feel her.

Knowing there was no turning back after he got a taste of her sweet lips, he craned his neck, leaned in, and placed his lips to hers. His mouth graciously enveloped hers.

Giving each lip an ample amount of playful sucking. Their tongues danced, just as the guests did, to their own rhythm. Amionette found herself softly tugging at the ends of his fish braids with both hands. The kiss was so good, she forgot where they were. She'd forgotten who she was for a second. This was the best and sloppiest kiss she'd ever received. Their tongues spun around each other, twirling in circles around one another. If she could have, she would have climbed up and onto Syncere. She wanted to be in his skin the kiss felt so good.

Syncere slid his hand from her waist up to her right breast. He'd begun fondling her nipple through her thin material, and she felt every flick of his finger. He rubbed his thumb across her budding teat. Amionette leaned forward, yearning for more of his touch. She cocked her leg up on the side of him, holding it tightly against his hip bone, where she could feel the strength of his body. Like a mustang, she wanted to ride him into Heaven or Hell. Wherever he would take her.

The clearing of someone's throat stilled them. Almost completely frozen, Amionette's leg dropped. The clack of her shoe brought her back to reality. Syncere, eager to shield Amionette from seeming indecent, charged to the side of her, to cover her up.

"I don't mean to interrupt, but I wanted you to meet the man who's about to take the Brown Brothers to the next level," Tyrian explained. He knew he was right about his brother. Though him liking someone was utterly knew, Tyrian knew that had to be the reason for his brother acting out. He'd never felt that way before, and rather than dealing with it, like a regular person would, he acted out because for the first time, his life was not dominated by needing to be a protector. He could simply be a man.

"I'll be right there." Syncere's tone was edgy. Kissing and touching Amionette was the equivalent of being blood drunk. Perhaps he had been missing out all those years ago. He'd never been that turned on by a woman in his life. Even when he drank blood—that only lasted so long. With Amionette, he believed he could be drunk on her forever.

Tyrian stepped back into the ballroom, only slightly, so that he could wait for his brother and give him a moment to wrap things up. When he was completely away from them, Syncere helped Amionette straighten her dress out, running his hands along the sides, hoping to get one last feel of her.

"Looks like you need to go," Amionette reminded him. The longer he stood there touching her, the more she wanted to engage in another liplock with him.

"I do, but don't leave tonight without letting me see you."

It was not a request, but a demand, one that Amionette would happily fulfill.

"I won't," she answered. Syncere placed his lips to hers one last time, and before the kiss could deepen, he pulled away. All it would take was one more second of kissing that woman, and he would be puddy in her hands.

Amionette watched Syncere as he walked away, and the moment he was gone, she pulled her phone out from the pocket she'd sewn into her dress to text Zuri to tell her to come and find her. They needed to talk ASAP.

Zuri and Sacred noticed Amionette's disappearing act. Their father had been whipping them around the ballroom, introducing them to the state's constituents, and though Amionette had escaped, neither Zuri nor Sacred had been as lucky, until she received the text message from Amionette to meet her in the restroom in the atrium.

"Daddy, give me and Sacred a minute, we need to go to the little girl's room," she whispered from behind her father. He was so into the conversation he was having with one of the senators, that he simply nodded his head, shewing her and her sister away. Zuri reached for Sacred's hand and whisked her away to the bathroom.

"Thank God for that," Sacred all but shouted. Too much conversation made her feel uncomfortable, especially when the topic was out of her scope. "Where are we going?"

"Amionette wants us to meet her in the bathroom," Zuri rushed out as she looked over her shoulder at Sacred. "I bet it's got something—"

Zuri hit something with a thud. She hadn't been paying attention as she was walking through the crowd and ran smack dab into someone.

"I'm so sor..." she stopped for a second, surprise ringing through her at the person before her.

"Yuzuri? What are you doing here?" the man asked, and Zuri was even more confused why he would be in a place like this. Or how…

"Fletcher, I could ask you the same thing." Zuri placed her hands on her hips. She'd been wondering if she'd ever run into Fletcher or catch him somewhere on a humble. Zuri had wondered about the full story of what he and Amionette went through that would have sent her into such a spiral. Here he was, chipper as ever, while Amionette was left to pick up the pieces of her life.

Sacred came forward. When her sister released her hand, from the force of her snatching her hand away, she knew something was wrong. Fletcher's eyes shifted to Sacred, a smile appeared on his face. Sacred was gorgeous —young-looking, but beautiful.

"Well hello to you," he slurred, and Zuri figured he must have been drunk.

"Oh no you don't. You and Amionette haven't been broken up a good two weeks and you're already sniffing out something else?" Zuri's face twisted with confusion and disgust. She knew she was right about the feelings she had toward Fletcher—he was just the man she thought he was.

"Broken up?" Fletcher's voice up ticked with confusion. The last he'd checked, Amionette was dead. He was certain that he'd killed her, though he couldn't and hadn't let anyone else know that.

"Yes, broken up. She told me the two of you were no longer together—"

"Is she here, by chance? Is Netty here?" He looked

around, behind Zuri to see if he could see her. In just two weeks, his life had changed drastically. The night he killed Amionette, or thought he had killed her, had altered more than just his physical state, but his mental well-being. He was losing time, forgetting things. Ending up in places without even remembering how he got there.

"She is, but I doubt she'd want to see you. Come on, Sacred." Zuri pulled her sister away, headed toward their original destination. "That muthafucka got some nerve," Zuri uttered. Sacred's eyebrows shot up in amusement. When Zuri got mad, she turned into a different person, and if it was one thing she knew about her sister, it was that she didn't play and wouldn't let anyone hurt the people she loved and cared about.

When they made it to the foyer, where it was much quieter, Sacred asked, "Is that guy the reason Amionette's been staying with you?"

"Yep, but don't say that to anybody else. I have a feeling this thing is much bigger than I know. Come on," Zuri said, rushing to get to Amionette. She figured it would be better to inform her that she'd seen Fletcher than for her to see him on her own. That would be frightening.

When they made it to the bathroom, it was void of everyone but Amionette, whose cheeks were so red, she could have easily been mistaken for a tomato.

"What's got you in here smiling like a fat Cheshire?" Sacred laughed and reached into her purse to freshen up her lipstick. She'd consumed so much champagne that night, just trying to give herself a fighting chance to mingle, her lipstick was beginning to fade away.

"I have to tell you about Syncere..."

"Synceeeere?" Both Zuri and Sacred emphasized. Amionette shook her head, trying to remove the smile from her face, but even baby shaking syndrome wouldn't take that smile away.

"Yes, Syncere—"

"Okay, wait," Zuri placed her hands in front of her, "before you get into that, I need to tell you about Fletcher."

Amionette's hand flew to her stomach. The mention of his name aloud caused her immense pain. "What-what about him?"

Her hands began to clam up. Her stomach tossed about like boots in a dryer. She had not seen or heard from him—not that she was expecting to since he assumed she was dead, but hearing his name in the present tense brought a fear about inside of her that was indescribable.

Zuri placed her hands onto the sides of Amionette's arms. This was the reaction she always got whenever Fletcher's name was mentioned. It was common for someone who was going through a break up to perhaps tense up when they heard the name or had to come face-to-face with the person they'd detached from, but this was a different reaction. Zuri registered this severe form of a reaction akin to trauma.

"It's okay, Amionette. I was just going to tell you that I saw him. He approached me—"

"Did you speak to him? Did he say anything?" Amionette began rambling off questions. Zuri, very quickly, recapped their interaction, and noticeable fear flooded Amionette's face.

"Amionette, what's wrong? You're scaring me," Sacred said as she put her nude lipstick back into her bag. She came over to try and assist Zuri with Amionette, but Amionette was already detaching from Zuri and headed for the door.

"Amionette," Zuri said to the back of her friend's head. She knew she wasn't about to just walk away from her, like she wasn't just calling her name.

There was a lock on the back of the door, and if Amionette was going to have this conversation, she knew that no one else needed to hear it. What she'd planned to tell Zuri and Sacred would be so unheard of, so strange, that it would be a wonder if they didn't run out of the bathroom from the tea she was about to spill. Amionette turned the lock on the door and then came closer to Zuri and Sacred.

"I need to tell you all about what happened between Fletcher and I, and then about how I know Syncere," she spoke slowly and calmly, though her heart felt like it was going to come through her throat.

"What does Syncere have to do with you and Fletcher?"

Amionette hoisted herself up and onto the sink. She propped herself up against the cool mirror, going back in her mind to the night that started this whole thing. She exhaled deeply, and then began telling her story. A story she hoped that if her friends cared enough about her, they would believe she wasn't telling a lie.

Eager to return to Amionette, Syncere's foot tapped impatiently as he stood off to the side of the dance floor with his brothers, waiting for the man who was supposedly supposed to help them take their business to the next level. There were eyes on him, though he could not tell where they were coming from. He'd sensed that there was someone who had been looking at him the entire night. It made him feel uneasy. He chalked up the extra irritation of waiting for the man his brother had told him he just had to meet, to the fact that there was possibly someone watching him.

"Tyrian, I don't like people who aren't punctual, and I was busy. Come find me when this man's actually ready to talk," Syncere advised, and just as he was about to walk up, a man approached them. He looked a bit disheveled, and Syncere hoped this wasn't the man Tyrian had given such high praise to.

"This is him right here," Tyrian slapped his brother in the stomach and pulled him toward the man so they could converse.

"Syncere, I want you to meet my guy, Fletcher. He's number one right now in the city for real estate development," Tyrian introduced. Fletcher held his hand out for him to shake, but Syncere felt apprehension going in to shake this man's hand. What were the odds that this

Fletcher was the same as Amionette's? If he was the same man, Syncere would not have to go far to handle business for Amionette, for the woman he'd planned to claim as his own.

"Don't be rude," Tyrian gritted out, looking between him and Fletcher.

"Excuse me," Syncere said, readjusting himself. He reached his hand across the space and shook his hand. "It's nice to meet you," Syncere lied. Malicio and Tyrian both heard the insincerity in their brother's voice. It had been uncommon for them to see, since their brother never lied, but it was clear, he did not think it was nice. They could tell from his stiffened body language.

"That's quite the handshake," Fletcher mentioned as he and Syncere looked one another square in the eye.

"Indeed. My brother tells me you have a plan to take us to the next level? I'd love to know more about it." Syncere's words were normal, his attitude behind them, the force and strength behind them, were not.

"Absolutely—"

"Fletcher, I'm ready to go," Shaylene Upswing approached the men. "I'm starting to feel sick again," she said and reached down to rub her stomach.

"Not right now, Shay. I'm talking business," Fletcher told her, completely dismissing his baby mama.

"Please," she begged. All night she'd been working the room, and feeling exhausted was an understatement. She was completely worn out. Being the mayor of Nashville came with many perks, but it also came with many disadvantages and discomforts. Having to come and mingle tonight was one of the many discomforts she'd experienced, and now that she was pregnant, standing on her feet too long had made her miserable.

"Let's set something up. Let this beautiful woman get home and get her rest," Syncere instructed, and Shaylene smiled at him. She eyed him from feet-to-head, wondering who the fine specimen was.

"Thank you, Mr…"

"Brown. Misters Brown. Syncere," he placed his hand on his chest, "and my brothers, Tyrian and Malicio. It's nice to meet you, Mayor," he finished, taking her hand in his. She blushed, and Frederick didn't like how friendly his baby mama and Syncere were being.

He snatched her hand from his, anger taking over. "Didn't you say you was ready to go?" he questioned, and rather than argue, she immediately agreed. Unfortunately, she had been a witness to Fletcher's anger many times, and she believed if she weren't pregnant with his child, she could have easily become a target. Shaylene knew not to tempt him—after all, she needed things between them to work out. She was an unmarried woman, pregnant, black, and the city already wanted her crown. She had to keep things together. Everything had to appear to be on the up-and-up.

Besides, she planned to have Fletcher killed shortly after the baby was born anyway. A tragic construction accident, she mused, not even realizing the irony in her plans.

"I'll get with you sometime this week. It was nice

meeting you," Fletcher told Syncere and carted Shaylene away like a runaway slave.

When Fletcher and Shaylene were out of earshot, Tyrian stepped in front of his brother, along with Malicio, both with disdainful looks on their faces.

"What the hell was that?" Malicio was the first to question. "I've never known you to be a liar. Tonight, you've been acting completely differently—"

Syncere held his hand up to his brother, silencing him. "We need to go home to have this conversation. I'm going to say my goodbyes to Amionette, and then, we will discuss our involvement, or lack thereof, with Fletcher, at home."

"What do you mean? The papers are all but signed," Tyrian pointed out, throwing his hands into the air.

"I knew everything wasn't going to be peachy when I returned, but I didn't know that even after all this time, you still need me to fact check behind muthafuckas. You don't even know who you're getting into bed with!" Syncere roared. It was so loud, several people in their vicinity turned to look at them, and his eyes were heading in the direction of red.

Thinking about what he'd done to Amionette and how he was just walking around the free world like he'd had no involvement, it pissed him off beyond reason.

Malicio placed his hand on his brother's shoulder, realizing that if Syncere was losing his cool, something was definitely wrong.

"Okay, go say your goodbyes. Meet us outside," Malicio suggested, and when Syncere turned to leave, Tyrian and Malicio both worried about the conversation they were about to have. For the last century, they'd been handling things on their own. They thought they'd been doing a good enough job. But in one night, their big brother was going to dispel the "good enough" job they'd been doing with one simple fact.

Fletcher was not the man they thought he was, and while it seemed like they stood to gain a lot of money, the souls they did have left, they would lose if they got into bed with Fletcher Monahan.

Syncere straightened out his tuxedo. He noticed it bunching from getting upset. At times, it seemed like he got bigger the angrier he became. Syncere searched the ballroom for Amionette, and when he couldn't spot her, or Zuri or Sacred, he figured she might not have come back into the room just yet. On his way out of the ballroom, it became abundantly clear that someone was following him. He rounded the corner, passing several pillars on his way. Syncere wanted to be out of the way so the person following him would be caught off guard when he pulled him into the hallway.

Syncere headed toward the men's' bathroom. It was just up ahead, and there was no one else in the hall. He stopped just short of the door and swiftly turned around. His arms out, he gripped his follower around the collar and tossed him into the bathroom.

The man he'd gripped did not fall to the ground. He swept his leg underneath himself and hoisted himself up. His body never completely dropped to the floor. Syncere had never seen this man a day in his life. He might not always remember a name, but he always remembered a face. And this man's face was anything but familiar.

"What do you want?" Syncere sped over to the man, shoving him against the wall. The man smiled, and then there was a wave of familiarity. Not in the way he smiled, but in the feeling he got from the smile.

Syncere squinted; he wasn't quite sure how he could possibly know this man, especially someone from this time. He had caramel skin, looked to be in his forties, wealthy. A mustache and connected beard, peppered in black and gray.

I've been looking for you, but I've had to be careful, the man telepathically communicated his message. His voice shrieked recognition in Syncere's mind.

He didn't dare mention his name aloud. He didn't even have the chance to think it. The man stole his thought right from his head.

That's right, it's me. Jasper. I told you we would cross paths again.

"Indeed. Is this a friendly visit? Why were you following me?"

Friendly news? Yes. Good news? No.

Syncere let him go, allowing him the space to straighten himself out. What business could Jasper Rich have with him? He knew they would meet again at some point. He'd assumed that it would be under different circumstances—this was not what he had expected.

"News of what?" Syncere asked, leaning against the wall, bracing for impact.

I've come to warn you. I wasn't supposed to tell you everything I told you before. Apparently, I altered the course of history, and because of that, the world has been thrown into some sort of… chaos, Jasper admitted. He wasn't supposed to even be mentioning to half of the things he did to Syncere in the past, and because he did, slavery ended much earlier than it was supposed to. People who were supposed to be born were not. State, government, world officials, who were supposed to rise to power never did because of what they'd done.

Jasper was supposed to be a neutral party. He served a higher counsel, a secret society that served the human and supernatural factions. They were to keep balance and restore it when necessary. For the last few years, Jasper was expected to be preparing to take down the Brown brothers, but there was something special about the young men. He liked them—they were young black brothers who hadn't harmed anyone.

Because of Syncere, he'd been able to have a better life. His soul had given him his appearance back. He no longer looked like the scary thing he truly was. Because of his orders, the orders he could not fulfill, he'd been on the run. The Free Garrison would not be happy when they found him. They would kill him, painfully, for his treason.

"Chaos? What kind of chaos? What does that have to do with me?"

Jasper paced the floor, searching for the words to tell Syncere for him to understand the severity of he situation.

Everything and nothing. The world requires a balance, a balance dictated by the powers that be. You and your brothers are in danger. I'm the one who dug you up. In six month's time, they'll be coming for you...

"They who? Who's coming for us?" Syncere questioned, a stern look on his handsome face. None of this made any sense. He and his brothers had been living peacefully, except for when they weren't, and hadn't bothered a soul. How could something like this come to pass?

The same people who were after you in 1918.

"Vampires?"

Vampires, wolves, witches... you name it. In 1918, they attempted to take you down under the guise of you and your brothers taking over too much of the city. They didn't want you to find out about their existence.

"And now?"

And now, Jasper started, placing his hand on Syncere's shoulder, I've chosen to help you. This is the destiny you are meant to fulfill. You have to overthrow the powers that be. If you don't, the world as we know it will disappear.

Jasper's words had never been truer. Because of the Brown brothers and their contribution to the world, it was thrown out of sync. They couldn't stop black people from winning. And, there were traditionalists, those who knew the true timeline of the world, who wanted things to go back to how they were supposed to be all along.

With white people in power.

With black people struggling. In poverty. Raising

bastard children. It was the only way to stop them. To stop the Brown brothers.

Syncere had wondered about the major difference from his time to this one. He'd found it interesting that there was a black president, and that there had been many. There were a large number of black officials, in the government, in the state. There were a multitude of his brothers and sisters on top.

Another thing he had on his to-do list to find out.

"If these 'powers that be' are so powerful, how are we supposed to beat them? How do we take them down?"

Like any other organization. From the inside.

The bathroom door swung open, and Timothy walked in, his hand extended. "Syncere Brown, my name is Timothy. We have a lot to discuss…"

What does Timothy have to do with the balance of the world?

What is Fletcher up to, and who did he kill?

There are so many questions that need to be answered, and they will be in book 2!

To Be Continued…

Please leave a review <3

It's Time to Get Nastee

Hey! Thanks so much for reading this book. I hope you enjoyed reading it the way I enjoyed writing it. I'm a country girl who enjoys reading, writing, spending time with my family, and stealing snacks from my nieces and nephews.

If you enjoyed this book and would like to keep up with my releases, please join my reading group on Facebook

Help me reach 1,000 followers on TikTok